"Logan? I'm very sorry. Are you okay?"

Melissa asked.

He turned away. "I'm fine." He ached, but it couldn't be helped by one of her little pills. The only cure would be to bury himself deep within her waiting softness and carry them both to a place beyond pain.

Melissa touched her hand to her kiss-swollen lips. She felt like a fool . . . or worse. An incident like this could cost her her job, or at the very least, her self-respect.

She'd heard about patients coming on to their nurses, and she recognized the symptoms. A caring woman helping a man in need, isolated together in a world of their own making.

It was a volatile situation. . . .

Dear Reader,

Happy New Year! May this year bring you happiness, good health and all you wish for. And hopefully, helping you along the way, is Silhouette **Special Edition**. Each month, Silhouette **Special Edition** publishes six novels with you in mind—stories of love and life, tales that you can identify with—romance with that little "something special" added in.

In January, don't miss love stories from Barbara Faith, Christine Rimmer, Nikki Benjamin, newcomer Susan Mallery and veteran Silhouette **Special Edition**-er, Lisa Jackson. To round out this month, you are invited to a *Wedding Party* by Patricia McLinn—the conclusion to her heartwarming *Wedding Duet*! It's a winter wonderland for all this month at Silhouette **Special Edition**!

In each Silhouette **Special Edition** novel, we're dedicated to bringing you the romances that you dream about—the type of stories that delight as well as bring a tear to the eye. And that's what Silhouette **Special Edition** is all about—special books by special authors for special readers!

I hope you enjoy this book and all of the stories to come.

Sincerely,

Tara Gavin
Senior Editor

SUSAN MALLERY
Tender
Loving Care

Silhouette Special Edition

Published by Silhouette Books New York

America's Publisher of Contemporary Romance

To Jolie, Terry, Denise and Carolyn. You are my
partners in the dream, my sisters in the victory. From
conception to birth, you have molded this work.
Without you, there would be no Melissa, no Logan;
a cow would be simply a cow and my life would lack
that special spark that keeps me striving to achieve.
My love and my thanks. Here's to the future.

 SILHOUETTE BOOKS
300 East 42nd St., New York, N.Y. 10017

TENDER LOVING CARE

ISBN: 0-373-09717-4

First Silhouette Books printing January 1992

SUSAN MALLERY

has always been an incurable romantic. Growing up, she spent long hours weaving complicated fantasies about dashing heroes and witty heroines. She was shocked to discover not everyone carried around this sort of magical world. Taking a chance, she gave up a promising career in accounting to devote herself to writing full-time. She lives in Southern California with her husband, "the most wonderful man in the world. You can ask my critique group." Susan also writes historical romances under the name Susan Macias.

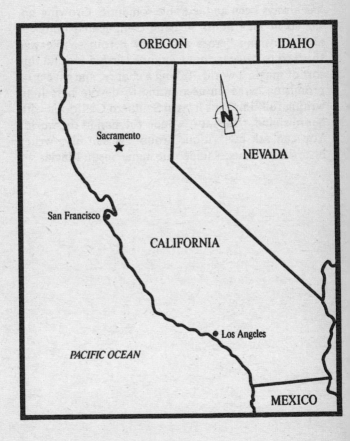

Chapter One

"If you don't cooperate and put this thermometer under your tongue, I'll be forced to take your temperature the old-fashioned way."

Logan Phillips obligingly opened his mouth, then clamped his lips around the offending plastic-covered device. Frustration mingled with irritation when he realized the bandages around his eyes prevented the graduate from the Attila the Hun School of Nursing from seeing his glare. He didn't belong in the hospital—he had a business to run and a daughter to take care of. They couldn't keep him here....

The electronic thermometer beeped, indicating it had taken his temperature. "There. Was that so bad?" The instrument was pulled from his mouth. "In a little while, I'll send someone in to give you a nice sponge bath, Mr. Phillips."

Sponge bath? He rose up on one elbow and addressed the general direction from which he'd last heard her voice. "Just wait a minute, Nurse whatever-your-name-is. You can't expect me to...hell, I'm a grown man, and there isn't any way that...are you listening to me?"

Murmured conversations from the hall and the overloud ticking of a wall clock were the only responses. Perfect, Logan thought as he settled back on the pillow. First the accident, then an eye infection. He'd thought he'd reached bottom when his doctor had forced him into the hospital, but he'd been wrong. They'd poked and probed his sore eyes and ignored his very reasonable demands. Now they were sending in a strange nurse to wash his body. With his luck, they'd probably assign some green first-year student and the poor girl would get a lesson that hadn't been covered in Anatomy 101. Where the hell was his doctor? He had to get out of here.

Under his eyelids, the insistent throbbing began again, like miniature jackhammers at work. He didn't know what time the night nurse had given him his last dose of painkiller, but it was starting to wear off.

Logan reached a hand over to the small table beside his bed. His fingers brushed against something that felt like the call switch, then the plastic square slipped out of his grasp and fell. He couldn't find the cord to pull it back up, and his attempts sent the water jug flying off the stand, as well. It crashed to the floor and bounced twice. There was the sound of ice settling, then silence. He swore under his breath.

Just as he found the thick ribbon of tape that connected to the call button, he heard the click of feminine footsteps on the linoleum.

"Where were you when I needed you?" he asked as he retrieved the small box. "And if you're here about the sponge bath, you can just forget it."

There was only silence. Logan located the switch to raise the bed so that he was in a sitting position. There were two more footsteps and then more silence.

"How very disappointing," the woman said finally. "I hadn't hoped for more than a handshake on our first meeting, Mr. Phillips, but then I've been out of town for quite some time. Are sponge baths now a popular form of introduction?"

Logan felt heat creep up his face. "You're not here to bathe me?" He wasn't really asking a question, it was more a form of self-torture to verify how big a fool he'd just made of himself.

"I can be, if it's that important to you."

Despite his lack of vision, he could almost see her smiling. "I think I'll pass."

"Only if you're sure." The woman's voice was low. Not at all masculine, it was more of a combination of smoky sounds, with long slow vowels. Not Southern, exactly, but definitely intriguing. The way his day was going, she was about eighty... and bald.

He shifted on the bed. "If you're not here to bathe me or draw blood, then what can I do for you, Ms...?"

"Melissa VanFleet, Mr. Phillips. But please call me Melissa."

She moved again. Her voice was right beside him and he instinctively looked up. There was only darkness. The subtle scent of her perfume drifted by his face. The fragrance was unfamiliar, floral but with a hint of spice, almost like magnolias. His eyes had only been bandaged two days, but already his other senses seemed heightened.

"You keep saying my name, so I guess you know I'm Logan Phillips?"

"I did assume that, yes."

"What can I do for you, Melissa?"

"I'm here about the job."

Melissa stared at the man in the hospital bed. She'd been working with the ill and injured since she was eighteen, and Logan had to be one of the healthiest specimens she'd seen since a pro football player had come into emergency with a broken leg.

Even with the bandages covering his eyes, he was handsome. His tanned skin and dark hair contrasted with the white gauze wrappings. Angry red streaks across the lower half of his face highlighted the strong lines of his jaw. The hospital gown stretched tight across his shoulders; the thin cotton clung to the broad expanse of his chest.

His large, powerful hands toyed with the light blanket; the restless movements were the only indication of unease. No doubt Logan Phillips was as comfortable in the bedroom as the boardroom.

She looked back at his face. His mouth was curving into a half smile.

"I don't know what my office told you, but I'm not really prepared to conduct interviews, Melissa, let alone look at a building design. Perhaps you could contact my secretary and set up an appointment."

Was he kidding? "I'm a practical nurse, Mr. Phillips, not an architect. Your boss wants to hire me to look after you for the next three weeks."

"I don't need a nurse," he said flatly.

Melissa pulled the plastic chair in the corner closer to the bed and sat down. "Really? How are you going to get home?"

"Call a cab."

"Who's going to change your bandages?"

"I'll do it myself."

"I believe that's what landed you in the hospital in the first place. Untreated corneal abrasions can easily get infected."

"Maybe I learned my lesson."

She shook her head. The man was completely pigheaded. "What about cooking dinner, going to the grocery store, driving to the doctor's office...."

"Enough," he growled.

"Your boss and my boss are in-laws, Mr. Phillips. I need a break from my usual assignments and you need a nurse/housekeeper/personal slave." His mouth quirked up at the corner, but she decided not to let her hopes go too high. "This seemed a way to solve both our problems."

Logan's jaw tightened in what she could only assume was his tycoon-in-action expression. "Very well, Ms. VanFleet, you've made your point. What are your qualifications? You said you were a practical nurse. I assume that means you have some knowledge of..."

He was impressive, she thought as he went on with questions about her schooling and years of experience. A far cry from her last patient. Bobby had been only six years old. His idea of an interview had been to ask what her favorite flavor of ice cream was and if she'd mind if he watched cartoons in the afternoon.

"Mr. Phillips," she interrupted.

"Logan."

"Logan, I don't think you understand the process going on here."

He sighed. "But you're about to fill me in on the details?"

"Yes." Melissa cleared her throat and glanced away, before she remembered he couldn't see her amusement. "I didn't explain myself before. Your boss is hiring me, but I'm the one who makes the decision about whether or not I want to take the job. I guess, in a way, I'm interviewing you."

"I see."

If the grim set of his lips was anything to go by, he did indeed see and was very much less than pleased. Even sitting in a hospital bed, Logan Phillips looked like the kind of man who got things done in a hurry and his way. Melissa knew that without the bandages, his eyes would be holding her captive. No doubt they were dark and formidable and could have intimidated her into retreat, but today they were safely hidden.

She'd always heard wild animals were most dangerous when injured. The barely controlled specimen in front of her did nothing to disprove the theory. He made her want to bolt for cover.

"I don't think..." He rubbed his temple.

She recognized the involuntary sign of discomfort and sprang up to move to the edge of the bed. "When was your last painkiller?"

"I'm not sure. I haven't been issued my braille watch yet."

"I'll be right back."

She walked into the hall and saw the nurse carrying the medicine tray. After identifying herself, she collected Logan's medication and returned to his side.

"I've got your pills right here. Let me get you water and..." Her foot hit something and she glanced down. A plastic jug rested next to the table. "What were you doing? There's water all over the floor."

"I was looking for the call button, but I couldn't find it."

Melissa went into the bathroom and came back with several towels. After tossing them onto the spill, she filled up his glass and pressed it into his hand. "Here." The pills were next. "Open."

"I'm perfectly capable of..."

"I'm strong and burly, Logan. I could take you out with one punch. Now open." She grabbed his jaw and placed the pills on his tongue. "Drink," she ordered.

He sipped the water. "Do they send you all to boot camp before giving you the starched hats?"

"No. I've just had a lot of practice dealing with difficult patients."

"A mental hospital?"

"I usually work with children."

"Are you trying to tell me I'm being childish, Ms. VanFleet?" One side of his mouth quirked up, then the other.

That grin should be declared a lethal weapon, she thought as she looked at him. He finished the water and handed her the glass. For a moment, their fingers brushed. Now that she wasn't trying to get him to do something he didn't want to do, she had a chance to notice small things. Like the way his touch sent her heart flying up into her throat and then down into her stomach. Must have been the breakfast she'd eaten downstairs in the cafeteria. Hospitals were notorious for questionable cuisine.

"I'm just trying to decide if I can work for you, Mr. Phillips."

One eyebrow raised above the bandage. "I'm sure my boss told you I was very charming."

"Something like that." Melissa remembered Mr. Anderson's promise that Logan Phillips could be stubborn and difficult. The sum he was paying was large enough to let her take the rest of the summer off, so she'd told the senior partner at Logan's architectural firm that she was sure she'd be able to deal with him. It was herself she was worried about. Why were her palms suddenly damp? Maybe she needed to get out more.

"Have I passed inspection?" he asked.

"Almost. I understand you have a daughter."

"Yes." He smiled at her. Obvious pride and warmth at the mention of his child made her like him even more. The flash of white teeth and the single dimple that appeared on his right cheek caused her to catch her breath. "Wendi's twelve. In fact, the mother of one of her friends should be dropping her off here soon."

"Good. I need to meet her before I make my final decision. It's important that all the family members accept my presence in the house."

She didn't mention that she knew he was divorced, and he didn't volunteer any information about there being a girlfriend to contend with. That bridge could be crossed, if and when she came to it. After all, the job was only for three weeks. Changing bandages once a day and helping Logan stay quiet until he healed was a cushy assignment.

"The ward nurse will point Wendi out to me when she arrives," Melissa said. She saw one of the licensed vocational nurses pushing in a cart. "I see Mrs. Roberts is here for your sponge bath, so I'll just leave you two alone."

She patted Logan's arm, but he grabbed at her hand. His grip was like steel. Instinctively she stepped closer and leaned down. "What is it?"

"What does she look like?" he whispered.

Melissa glanced at the pretty young woman unashamedly listening to their conversation and winked. "She's fifty-five years old and about two hundred pounds. Oh, and there's a wart on her chin."

Logan sighed with relief. "Thanks, Melissa."

"Anytime. I'll be back when I've spoken with your daughter."

Melissa automatically waved goodbye as she left the room, then laughed when she realized he couldn't see her. Just as well. If he could, he'd find out what Mrs. Roberts really looked like and they'd probably have a full-scale riot on their hands. A straightforward man like Logan Phillips wouldn't take kindly to deception, however well-intentioned, or confinement, however necessary.

She walked over to the nurses' station and chatted with the two women sitting there. In about fifteen minutes, the elevator doors opened and a young girl stepped out. She was slim and pretty, with none of the gawkiness usually associated with preteen girls.

"Wendi?" she asked.

The girl stopped in the hall. Green eyes met Melissa's and she wondered if Logan's were the same color. "Yes."

At twelve, Wendi was already as tall as Melissa. Her hair was the same color as Logan's, a rich dark brown that reflected the light. Whereas his had curled around his ears and would have barely brushed a shirt collar, hers tumbled down her back in an artfully arranged display.

"Hi, I'm Melissa VanFleet. I'm a nurse and I may be taking care of your dad for a few weeks."

Wendi smiled. The impish grin was pure Logan. "Great. I was afraid I'd have to look after him and it would be totally like gross. I mean, what if there was blood? Yuk."

Melissa laughed. "No blood, I promise. You won't mind then?"

"Nah." She glanced at Melissa's tailored pants and plain cotton blouse. "You won't wear a uniform, will you?"

"Never."

"Good." Wendi glanced down the hall to see if they were alone, then leaned forward and whispered, "I mean they're totally uncool. And the shoes."

"I know, they're like combat boots." She remembered Logan's boot-camp remark.

"So when's my dad coming home?"

Despite her trendy clothes and air of sophistication, Wendi suddenly looked like a scared little girl. The fear in her eyes convinced Melissa to take the job. She knew kids, and this one needed reassurance that her father would be fine. "He'll be home later today. I'm going to find the doctor and make the arrangements, then I'll need to go to the house and check on food and that sort of thing. Can you show me where you live?"

"No problem. I'll just say hi, then we can get going."

Wendi went down the hall, and Melissa turned back to the nurses' station.

After speaking with Logan's physician, she headed toward his room to pick up Wendi. As she walked through the doorway, Logan was speaking.

"So this Melissa person is okay?" he asked.

Wendi looked up and saw her, then smiled. "Yeah. She seems nice."

Melissa bit back a chuckle. Not a bad endorsement from a twelve-year-old.

"What does she look like?"

Logan's question seemed casual enough, but Melissa felt her humor fade. Here it comes, she thought.

Wendi studied her thoughtfully. "I don't know, Dad. Nothing like Mom. She's at least thirty."

Melissa put her hands on her hips and raised her eyebrows.

"Or younger," Wendi hastily amended.

"And?" he prompted.

"Blondish. Not very tall." Wendi shrugged and looked away. "Jeez, Dad, this is embarrassing."

Logan laughed. "I should know better than to ask a girl whose idea of high fashion is anything from MTV."

Melissa forced a smile. She knew why Wendi was uncomfortable. What was the girl supposed to say? It wasn't as though she didn't know she was...plain. She saw the proof every day in the mirror. Wasn't her mother always telling her that beauty came from within? Just once, though, she'd like to be pretty enough that no one had to look deeply to notice.

She listened a few more minutes, but the conversation had moved on to another topic. Taking a deep breath, she walked closer to the bed.

"Hi."

Logan wasn't sure if he recognized the voice first or the scent. "Melissa?"

"Very good. I'll tell the staff that you won't be needing that guide dog after all."

"Thanks. I just want to go home. What's the verdict? Did I pass inspection?"

"Was that a note of pleading I heard in your voice?"

He laughed. "At this point, I'll do anything to get out of here."

There was a rustling noise and the sound of her heels on the floor. When she next spoke, he could feel her soft breath tickling his ear. "How was the sponge bath?"

"I got by." With her help, he thought. Knowing the nurse was old and unattractive combined with him mentally reciting all the states and their capitals had kept him relaxed.

"Here's the deal. I'll work for you for three weeks. While your eyes are bandaged, I'll help with day-to-day living. After the dressings come off, I'll be around to make sure you follow the doctor's orders. Can you live with that?"

He nodded. "I'm yours to command."

"Yeah, right. And pigs fly. You're the type of patient that gives nurses nightmares, Logan."

He tapped his chest in an expression of innocence. "Me?"

"Yes, you. I've cleared your discharge with the doctor. He'll be by in an hour to check your eyes one last time, then you can leave. Wendi's going to take me to the house, now. I'll make sure there aren't any hazards waiting to trip you, and stock up on groceries."

She sounded cool and competent. Wendi's description was clear in his mind, but he still didn't have a clue as to what Melissa looked like. Blondish and not very tall from a twelve-year-old could mean anything. He hadn't realized how much he depended on his eyes to tell him about a person. For now, he had no choice but to trust his instincts. And his gut said Melissa was okay. He had to like someone who could match him quip for quip and even come out on top.

"I'll be waiting for you to rescue me," he said. "Wendi, come give your old man a kiss."

He heard Melissa step back and Wendi move forward. "Bye, Dad. I'm going to spend the afternoon at Kelly's house and have dinner there. The number's on the counter in the kitchen."

"Fine. But be home by eight, kitten."

"Yes, Dad." She sighed with bored resignation and planted a kiss on his cheek. He was still smiling when Nurse Attila walked in, her rubber soles squeaking on the linoleum. "Do we need to use the bedpan, Mr. Phillips?"

Melissa pulled the red Volvo station wagon up to the curb by the hospital entrance. She'd wanted to bring her own small car, but Wendi had told her that Logan's long legs would never have fit. Watching him being wheeled out the door, she had to concede that his daughter might have been right.

Even in the wheelchair, with the white bandages covering his eyes, Logan exuded an air of power. He was a man on the move. The fact that he was wearing jeans and a cotton long-sleeved blue shirt didn't lessen the impact of his presence. If anything, the casual attire clinging to his masculine body emphasized the strength. After six years of dealing with children, a virile, adult male was going to take some getting used to. But she'd better keep her misgivings to herself. Once he sensed her fear, he'd pounce and show no mercy.

Melissa shook her head and grinned. Get a life, girl, she told herself. He's just a guy, like a million others. The fact that her heart was racing and her palms felt sweaty was a problem she'd deal with another time—like the year 2000.

She stepped out and moved to the sidewalk. "Ready to go home, Logan?"

He smiled gratefully. There were lines of tension and pain bracketing his mouth. "Yeah. The doctor gave me a very thorough exam before I left. If you were looking for a way to keep me in line, it worked." The red marks on his face had been treated with a clear ointment that made them seem more raw.

Melissa patted his arm sympathetically. Logan's corneal abrasion was quite severe. He'd ignored his physician's orders and now had an infection to deal with, as well. Just the thought of someone probing his already painful eyes and lids was enough to make her shudder.

"Let's get you home and in bed."

"Not tonight, dear, I have a headache," he joked as she helped him to his feet. He towered above her—six feet of injured, frustrated male. "But it's a hell of a generous offer. I..." He clenched his teeth and drew in a slow breath. "When did the earth start spinning so fast?"

"Hold on to me." She nodded for the orderly to take Logan's other side and then turned him toward the car. "You've been flat on your back for two days. It takes a second to get your balance. Put your hand out in front of you and feel for the car. There. I'm going to put my hand on the top of your head, so you don't bump yourself while you get in. Slowly."

He lowered himself onto the seat and sighed. "Is this the Volvo?"

Melissa closed the door and walked around to the driver's side. "Yes. How did you know?"

"I recognized the smell."

She reached across him and grabbed the shoulder belt. His skin had paled to an unhealthy shade of gray, and his lips were pulled into a tight line of pain. After snapping the buckle, she gave his forearm a reassuring squeeze. "Wendi said my car wasn't big enough for you. Besides, it's a cheap model and I don't think she wanted the neighbors watching it pull in and out of the driveway."

Her attempt at humor was rewarded with a slight smile. "That's my girl, always worrying about what the neighbors will think. She gets it from her mother." He fumbled on the far side of the seat, then lowered the back down. "Home, James."

"Yes, sir."

Melissa started the engine and carefully put the car into drive. After easing out of the hospital parking lot, she turned onto the canyon road that would take them to Logan's place.

The house wasn't that far from the bustling west side of Los Angeles, but once in the hills the only hints of the large city were the occasional glimpses of high rises that flashed through the trees. Houses were set back from the street, with heavy gates and thick, tall trees standing guard.

She watched for the correct turn. Logan lived on a long cul-de-sac, third house from the corner. Although slightly more modest than its neighbors, his house was still impressive. The used-brick facade was elegant. A circular driveway curved in front, then veered off toward a three-car garage.

He probably paid more in property taxes than she'd earned all last year, she thought as she slowed the car to a stop. Maybe she should have gone into a different line of work.

"We're here, Logan."

He sat up slowly and opened the car door. She half expected him to go barreling off toward the house, but he seemed to have learned his lesson at the hospital. He swung his legs out, then waited impatiently on the seat.

Logan inhaled and smelled the roses in the front yard. He remembered fighting Fiona about the color so many years before, but he'd never noticed the scent. Once the yard was finished, it had ceased to demand his attention. Today the heavy perfume filled the air. There was the sound of a car going down the street and a dog barking in the distance. His world had been reduced to blackness, intruded upon only by sound and touch and smell. He felt alone and isolated.

"It's about fifteen feet to the front door and there's one step. I'll tell you before we get there. Now stand up slowly and lean on the car. When you've got your balance, put your arm around my shoulders."

Logan thought about arguing. He disliked being told what to do, by anyone. But the dizziness he'd experienced before, combined with the pain in his eyes, was enough to dull his natural charge-ahead instinct. Most of all, he hated the helplessness.

He rose and gripped the top of the car. The world lurched a couple of times and settled into still blackness.

"Ready?" she asked.

He nodded. As she slipped his arm around her shoulder, he recalled Wendi's description. Melissa *was* short; he had to lean down to let her help him. Her hand held on to his side, providing him with a surprising amount of support for a small person. The gentle round flesh pressing against his ribs could only be her breast. He grinned. His daughter had neglected to mention that Melissa was curvy. Something inside rumbled as if to remind him he'd been alone for too long.

Soft strands of hair brushed against his bare forearm, swaying back and forth with each step. It was like being tickled with silky feathers. He would have teased her about the sensation or wondered about the tingling in his groin if he hadn't tripped on an uneven flagstone.

The sense of falling into nothing jerked him back to reality. He felt Melissa throw both of her arms around him, in an effort to steady him. Her petite body pressed next to his. From chest to knee, flesh warmed flesh.

"Who the hell designed this walkway?" she asked.

He could feel her heart pounding in her chest, and the indignation in her voice made him smile. Heaven forbid that anything should threaten her patient. He moved his hands over her back, then up to her face. She was warm and soft and ready to go to battle for him. He hadn't known he liked that in a woman.

Tilting her chin so that she was looking at him, he spoke. "I did."

"Figures. Concentrate on your footing, Logan. There will be plenty of time for woolgathering when I get you in bed."

She moved back to his side and they began to walk again.

"Step now."

He raised his foot and felt the higher level. "The door should be right in front of us."

"It is. Stay still. I'll go open it."

He heard the sound of metal against metal, then the lock turning. Melissa stepped back and placed her arm at his waist. "Let's try and get through the house without breaking anything."

By the time they reached his bedroom, Logan was covered with sweat. The pain in his head made every inch of the journey painful, and negotiating the furniture and turns had stretched his nerves tight.

He sat on the bed. "Just let me lie down for a couple of minutes. I'll be fine."

"Don't move a muscle until I get back." Melissa ran into the bathroom and dampened a couple of cloths. When she returned, he was sitting exactly where she'd left him. "Come on, Logan. Let's get you out of these clothes and then you can sleep the rest of the day."

"You seem awfully anxious to get me into bed. Is that all you nurses think about?"

Not until today. Just the thought of undressing his powerful body was enough to send sparks skittering through her, but he was her patient and he was in pain. There'd be time to remember the look and feel of his body when she was at her next assignment.

"No. We also think about ways to torture innocent people. I need you to cooperate."

He nodded wearily.

Biting her lower lip, Melissa leaned forward and started unfastening his shirt. As she worked the small buttons, she could feel his breath on her face. Each puff of air made her fingers stumble slightly before resuming their task. The fabric parted obligingly and exposed a well-muscled chest covered with rich dark hair. The pattern continued down his flat stomach, only to disappear into the waistband of his jeans.

When she finished with the buttons, he shrugged out of the shirt, then untied his athletic shoes, pulled them off and afterward, the socks.

"Can you stand?" she asked.

"I think so." He pushed up from the bed. She put out a hand to steady him and he grabbed the support. "Thanks. Maybe I should do the jeans myself."

She eyed the button fly. "Good idea."

Don't stare, she told herself. He mustn't know you're at all interested. But then she remembered that Logan couldn't see her.

Her gaze was drawn to his well-formed hands. Long fingers quickly popped the buttons through the denim. He pushed the jeans past his hips, then sat on the bed. Melissa tried not to look at the tight-fitting white briefs.

"Lie down," she said softly. She took one of the damp cloths and brushed it across his face and chest. He shivered as the compress cooled his skin and washed away the film of perspiration.

On her tour of the house, she'd left several bottles of pills on the nightstand. She opened one container and shook out two painkillers. After he'd swallowed the medication, she pulled the sheet and blanket up to his shoulders and brushed the hair away from his forehead. The welts on his face could wait for treatment.

"Try to sleep now, Logan. I'll check in at regular intervals. Wendi said I could take the room next door. Is that all right with you?"

"That's fine."

She pulled her hand away, but he caught her wrist. His thumb brushed back and forth against the sensitive inner flesh.

"I could get used to this kind of treatment, Melissa."

She tried to laugh, but the only sound that came out was a slight croak. She cleared her throat. "That's what they all say, the first day. I'll be a holy terror by the end of the week."

The medicine was beginning to work, and she saw the muscles in his face relax. "Yeah, sure. I'm really scared," he murmured, then released her hand.

Long after she'd left the room, the inside of her wrist tingled from his touch.

Chapter Two

Three hours later, Melissa crept back into Logan's room. The past few times she'd checked on him he'd been sleeping soundly, but now it seemed as though he were starting to get restless.

The bedroom was large, with stark white walls and a deep blue carpet. Massive pieces of furniture, from the four-poster bed to the two matching armoires, proclaimed the territory as belonging to a man. A chair rail, in the same rich mahogany as the rest of the furniture, bisected the walls. Opposite the door was a white brick fireplace, flanked by two leather wing chairs. The only incongruous note was the French Impressionist paintings hanging on the walls.

The armoire to the left of the bed contained stereo equipment. She glanced at the CDs scattered on the table and picked up the sound track to *The Phantom of the Opera.* When the opening bars of music began to softly fill the room, Melissa moved to the bed.

Logan stirred, then rolled onto his back.

"Hi," she said, stepping closer to him. "How do you feel?"

"You don't want to know." He touched his fingers to the bandage around his eyes. His color was no longer gray.

She perched on the edge of the mattress and pulled his hand into her lap. The literature she'd been reading about the newly blind had said that they need a lot of physical contact with the world around them. Feelings of panic and disorientation weren't uncommon. Even though Logan's eyesight would be fine once the bandages were off, it was her job to deal with his emotional well-being. She clasped the strong fingers within her own.

The contact felt nice... too nice. It's just a job, she reminded herself.

"Are you in pain?"

"Not if you don't count anything above the shoulders." Logan pulled his hand away and raised himself to a sitting position. The sheet fell to his waist, exposing the expanse of his chest. Dark hair, curling across well-formed muscles cried out to be touched, or at the very least, admired. His fingers returned, tentatively searching for hers.

Melissa swallowed and tried to think of something to say. "Are you hungry?" The staff nurse had told her he hadn't eaten any lunch and very little breakfast.

"I think so, but I'd like to wash up. I can still smell the hospital."

"No problem. Only it's too soon for a bath or shower. You mustn't get the bandages wet."

"You are bossy, aren't you?"

"I prefer to think of myself as having well-developed leadership qualities."

He grinned. The overhead light cast shadows on the hollows of his cheeks. "Like I said. Bossy."

She pulled back the sheets, then waited until he swung his legs over the side of the bed and stood up. He was very masculine...and virtually naked. Long legs stretched on forever; the lean muscles were covered by hair as dark as that clinging to his chest. The tight briefs around his middle only outlined the...uh...maleness below. Why did he have to be so damned good-looking?

"I think I might be able to find my way," Logan said, turning toward the hall. "I occasionally make this journey in the dark."

"Suit yourself." She let him walk two steps and bang his shin on the end of the bed.

"Ow. Why didn't you warn me?"

"Would you have listened?" she asked, filling her voice with as much sweetness as possible.

He bent down and rubbed his leg. "I will from now on. Lead the way."

Melissa put his hand on her arm and counted out the steps to the bathroom. When they reached the door, she flipped on the light.

"Why did you do that?" he asked.

"What?"

"Turn on the light. Are you planning to watch?"

The outrage in his voice started her lips twitching. "It's just this weird thing I do. When I walk into a dark room I reach for the light. Call me crazy. And as for watching...honey, you haven't got anything I ain't seen."

"We'll discuss that another time. Just give me a shove in the general direction and leave me in peace."

"Two steps forward. The sink is to the right. I've left out your toothbrush, with toothpaste, and there's a towel next to it."

He turned to her. "Is there anything you haven't thought of?"

The subtle praise of her efficiency caused her stomach to flip-flop a couple of times. "Just call me Florence," she said, and pulled the door shut.

What was wrong with her? she wondered. Had she spent too much time working with kids and not enough time dating? If she wasn't so sure she was really twenty-eight, she'd swear she was back in high school with a major hormonal crush on the football captain.

Later, when he was asleep, she was going to have to give herself a stern talking-to. She'd always prided herself on being competent, disciplined and, above all, professional. Logan was making her feel like a new recruit. None of her other patients had made her think about touching and kissing and . . . not even once.

Maybe it was just the position of the moon or something, and these feelings would go away by themselves. Until then, she'd have to keep a tight rein on her reactions and be the soul of propriety.

By the time Logan stepped out of the bathroom, she had most of herself under control. She led him back to the bed and plumped up the pillows on the headboard. "I'll be right back with your dinner. Don't try anything foolish while I'm gone."

"I wouldn't even think of it."

His expression was shameless. She was sure that if his eyes hadn't been bandaged, he would have been batting his eyelashes at her, like a Southern belle.

Melissa walked down the hall and across the large living room. Once in the kitchen, she poured the soup she'd been simmering into a cup and set the china onto the tray. She hesitated over coffee and decided against it. The caffeine would only interfere with his sleep, and that was the last thing he *or* she needed. She'd be up checking on him most of the night, anyway.

When she entered the bedroom, she paused. Logan was resting, with his head leaning against the pillow. The lines of his face were clenched tight, and his hands were balled into fists.

"Melissa?"

His voice startled her. "Yes. How did you know I was here?"

"I thought I smelled food. What's for dinner?"

She set the tray across his lap. "Spaghetti."

His mouth dropped open. "You've got to be kidding. I can't eat..."

"Yes."

"Yes, what?" He lifted his head toward her voice.

"Yes, I'm kidding. Here's a cup of soup. Careful, it's still hot. Then we have broiled chicken, sliced and chilled, and steamed vegetables, also sliced and chilled." She moved his hand to the small dish on the side of the plate. "A light honey-mustard dressing you can use for dipping. And for dessert ... strawberries."

Logan felt the bumpy texture of the fruit as Melissa touched his fingers to the plate. The nurse at the hospital had brought him a regular meal and had then spent fifteen minutes telling him that his plate was like a clock. In theory the idea worked, but as soon as she'd left, he'd forgotten if his peas were at nine or noon. In the end, it had been easier to go hungry.

"I'm going to put a napkin on you, Logan." Melissa's voice was quickly followed by the pressure of her hands smoothing a linen square across his chest. "Eat up, or I'm going to make good on my threat to serve you spaghetti."

He chuckled. "Are you going to join me? Or don't nurses eat?"

He sensed her hesitation. "Sure. I'll be right back."

After she'd left, Logan searched for and found a chunk of chicken. He took a bite and chewed slowly. The taste of the food seemed exaggerated, yet he wasn't sure he would have known what it was if he hadn't been told. He wanted to throw the tray across the room and shout his frustration.

He'd been alone before; he'd even been scared before. But nothing compared with the black void that was now his world. The simplest task, like brushing his teeth, took on herculean proportions, now that he couldn't see. And he would only be blind for a week.

"You're not eating, Logan. Don't you like my cooking?"

"It's great." He grabbed one of the vegetables and took a bite. "Yum, thanks."

"Okay. You've made your point."

Her voice got farther away, then he heard several grunts. "What *are* you doing?"

"I'm trying to move this...chair. What's it made of? Lead?"

"Just wood. I thought you were big and burly, Melissa."

"I lied."

"Come on." He patted the bed invitingly. "It's a king-size mattress. I'm willing to share."

"I...I shouldn't. It wouldn't be right. I'm your nurse."

He moved his head as if looking for intruders. "I don't see anyone here but us chickens."

"Well, they're here just the same. My professor from nursing school is right there in the corner, glaring at me."

"Come on. I could use the company."

"I don't think..."

He could feel her weakening and grinned. "Are you trying to tell me that you're...*chicken?*"

"Give me a break." There was a slight dipping as she took a seat. Then he felt her lean forward and place something on his tray. "Your water. Don't spill it."

"Yes, Mom." He found the glass and took a sip. "Do you always cook for your patients?"

"No. I work with children, and their parents usually take care of that. Sometimes, I'll be alone with the kids for the day and then I'll fix lunch, or we'll go out for hamburgers."

She kept her tone light, but he could hear traces of pain behind the words. "You sound sad."

"I'm fine, really."

He didn't believe her for a minute. "Do you miss the kids when they get better and don't need you?"

"They don't get better. I work with terminally ill children." She made the statement casually.

"You sound very calm. Doesn't it ever get to you?"

"It's my job to be calm, Logan. And of course it gets to me."

He heard the catch in her voice and knew that if he could see her, there'd be tears in her eyes. Cursing his lack of sight, he picked up the cup of soup.

"Tell me what you look like."

Melissa glanced at the man watching her with his covered eyes. If his daughter was anything to go by, his ex-wife was stunning. What should she say? That *she* wasn't even pretty? Not that her looks really mattered. Even if she did find him handsome and sexy and interesting and very male, he'd only see her as an employee.

"I'm kind of medium," she said finally.

"Medium?"

"Yes. Medium height, medium-brown eyes, medium-blond hair. I wear it short, just past my ears, with bangs. I'm the middle child and I got average grades in school." Boring.

"You don't sound medium. You have a lovely voice."

"Thanks." His compliment pleased her. In a social situation, he wouldn't have looked at her twice, but here, in the safety of his bedroom, she allowed herself a brief moment of fantasy. When the bandages came off and he returned to his regular life, he'd forget all about his nurse. But she'd remember him.

Logan pushed the tray away. "I can't eat another bite."

She finished her last strawberry, then moved the dirty dishes to the table by the fireplace. "I need to change your bandages. Just let me go wash my hands first."

He nodded. The tension returned to his jaw.

Melissa quickly washed her hands, then hurried back to his room. She picked up the scissors from the nightstand and carefully cut through the gauze.

"Did I ever tell you about the first time I saw a naked man?"

Logan felt his mouth drop open. "Excuse me?"

"When I was about sixteen, I had this crush on a guy named Steve. He was on the swim team. We had a social studies class together. I'd spend the entire hour staring worshipfully at the back of his head and wishing that just once, he'd notice me."

Logan smiled as he pictured the scene. Melissa knelt beside him on the bed and he moved over to give her room.

"One day, the teacher had us debate an issue. I don't even remember what it was. Anyway, he and I really got into it. We were arguing back and forth."

The pads were gently removed from his lids. He saw light and tried to open his eyes.

"Keep them shut, Logan. I'm going to put in the cream, then patch you up again. After class, we continued our argument. About halfway down the hall, he put his arm around me. I thought I was going to die. Hold these against your lids."

He held the circles in place while she started wrapping the gauze around his head.

"The next thing I knew, we'd stopped walking. I looked around and realized I was in the boys' locker room. I don't know who was more embarrassed, me, Steve, or the naked guys milling around and ducking for cover. I ran out of there as fast as I could and never spoke to him again. Actually, that was the first time I thought about going into nursing."

Logan laughed. "You made that story up, didn't you?"

"Yes, but it worked."

"What do you mean?"

"It took your mind off the pain when I changed the bandages."

She began to smooth salve over the wounds on his face. He grabbed her wrist and held her still. Search as he might, there was no way to penetrate the thick coverings and study her face. She'd said she was medium, but he didn't know what that meant.

Her breath fanned his face. He could smell the strawberries she'd eaten and the scent of her subtle perfume. He was still holding one hand, and her other pressed against his shoulder for balance. Her fingers felt small yet sure, as if the power to heal and comfort was captured within her delicate touch.

She was very close. Her breasts must be a scant inch from his chest. He remembered the curves pressing into his ribs when she'd helped him into the house. But there was no way to know the exact weight and contour of the feminine flesh.

A hunger started deep within him. He'd been without a woman for far too long, and this sweet creature catering to his every need was a temptation hard to resist. If it wasn't for the lessons in his past, he would have pulled her next to him and shown her that a man without eyes was still a man in every other sense of the word.

He let her go.

"Tell me about the accident." The husky sound of her speech rubbed against his skin.

"I had it out with a sandblasting machine. The machine won."

She continued to smooth the ointment onto his injured flesh. "I guess that's how you got these burns."

He nodded. "The hose ripped and the guy holding it got pinned down. Like a fool, I raced in and pulled him free."

"Sounds brave to me."

He drew his lips together. "Maybe. But the construction worker was wearing goggles and a protective jacket. I was in a business suit. The hose shot me right in the face."

"And then you didn't follow the doctor's orders and landed in the hospital." She finished her work and moved away.

"Something like that."

He heard her walking around the room. Was she going to leave him? Being alone with the blackness wasn't something he wanted to think about.

"You must be pretty tired," he said.

Melissa looked up. Logan was sitting against the headboard, but there wasn't anything relaxed about his pose. He'd suffered her changing his dressings without a fuss, but she knew he'd felt discomfort. The best thing for him would be to sleep through the night. Yet she didn't want to leave him, and if her hunch was right, he didn't want her to go.

"Let me take the dishes to the kitchen, then I can come back and read to you."

The phone rang before he could respond.

She picked up the receiver. "Phillips residence."

"Oh, totally cool, Melissa. I love the way you answer the phone. If a boy calls for me, could you call me Miss Wendi?"

Melissa laughed. "I'll see what I can do. You want to speak to your father?"

"Yeah. Is he...okay?"

"He's fine. Here."

She handed Logan the phone and picked up the tray.

"Hi, Wendi. I'm feeling great...."

Melissa was still smiling when she returned to his room. "Everything all right?"

"Wendi's spending the night at her friend's house. I think she's scared I'm going to die in my sleep or something and she'd rather not be the one to find the body."

Melissa looked over the books resting on the floor by the nightstand. "I'll reassure her in the morning. Don't you have anything fun to read?"

Logan turned toward her. "I read lots of fun books. Maybe you have no taste."

She read a title. "*Architectural Morés in Ancient Byzantium?* I don't think so."

"Maybe you'd prefer one of Wendi's rock star magazines."

Melissa plopped down on the floor and glared at him. A useless gesture but satisfying all the same. "Aren't you just filled with wit and charm. Give a man a little food for his belly and suddenly he rules the world. Got any romances?"

"Nope. Maybe there's a science fiction."

"Ray guns and slimy monsters? Thanks, but no thanks. Here we go. *The Macbeth Murders.* I love a good mystery. That way if my patients really bug me, I can learn new and creative ways to bump them off."

"I like you, Melissa VanFleet." He grinned at her. "You're good at your job without making me feel like an invalid."

"What had you imagined a nurse to be? Someone in a starched uniform with a no-nonsense attitude?"

"I never thought you'd have a sense of humor."

She tossed the book onto the bed and began measuring out his evening medicine. "They tried beating it out of me, unsuccessfully I might add. Here. These should help you sleep."

Logan took the pills without comment and downed them with a single gulp of water. "You could be poisoning me and I wouldn't know."

"You're perfectly safe." Melissa walked around the bed and sat down on the far side of the mattress.

"Why?"

"I haven't been paid yet."

"If I weren't blind right now, I'd..."

She pushed up a pillow behind her back and smiled at him. "Yes? What would you do."

He sighed. "I give. Just read, woman."

She opened the book. "Chapter one. It was a dark and stormy night...."

Logan turned with a swiftness she hadn't anticipated. She didn't know if it was the perfume she wore or her voice or the fact that she was a woman and he had an unerring sense of direction, but even without the benefit of sight he managed to roll onto his side and pull the book from her fingers.

"You're pushing it, Melissa," he growled playfully.

The sheet had become twisted in his legs, leaving his chest bare. He didn't move back. She was close enough to see the individual whiskers forming the darkness shading his jaw. After making a mental note that he'd need to be shaved in the morning, she stared at his mouth. Firm lips, curving in a slight smile, called out to be touched. Thank God, he couldn't see what she was looking at. How could she have ever thought of his bedroom as safe?

"Ah, is this your way of saying you want to do the reading?" she asked, struggling to keep her voice level.

"No, it's my way of saying you're less in control than you think."

Logan was close to her. Even without seeing her, he could feel the warmth of her body next to his. They were alone in the house... stretched out on *his* bed. Now he knew why she'd resisted joining him there. It would be easy to...

He shifted back to rest on his pillow. What was he thinking of? He didn't know the first thing about Melissa. She might be uninterested or attached or...

"Are you married?" he asked.

"What?" She sounded startled by the question.

"Are you married?"

"No. Why?" The mattress dipped as she slid away.

He shrugged, ignoring the unusual sensation of relief. It didn't matter to him one way or the other, he told himself. He knew her type and she didn't belong in his life, or—however tempting the prospect—his bed. "I was just thinking that if you were, your husband must hate you being gone so much."

"Well, I'm not, so it isn't a problem. Now do you want me to read or is it time for a credit check?"

"Temper, temper." He handed her the book. "You may begin now."

She laughed. "Someone left you in charge for too long. It's gone to your head."

"Read," he commanded.

She read.

Melissa broke two more eggs into the bowl and began to beat the mixture. The big bay window overlooking the circular driveway let the morning light into the large rectangular kitchen. Blue-and-white French tiles blended with the white appliances and pine cabinets to create an elegant yet calming work area. If she added the eating nook and laundry room off to the side, she was pretty sure it was bigger than her whole apartment. Melissa shook her head in disgust and continued to hum along with the rock station playing in the background.

She set the bowl on the counter and headed down the hall. "How many strips of bacon do you want?" she asked as she entered Logan's bedroom.

Sitting in one of the wing chairs, staring sightlessly at the television, Logan wore a dark blue robe she'd found in his closet.

"Damn fool economists," he muttered. "Thinking that we're heading into a recession. Three, please. Extra crisp."

"Coming right up." Melissa returned to the kitchen. But before she could begin working, she heard the sound of a key in the front door. She glanced at the clock; it was barely past eight. Logan had said that Wendi wouldn't be home until noon. Did he give keys to the women in his life? She looked out the window. Hers was the only car in the driveway. Why hadn't she bothered to get dressed? She moved into the foyer. It was too late now.

"Hi." Wendi walked in and shut the door behind her. She was wearing shorts and a T-shirt. Smudges under her bright green eyes told of a restless night. Her expression was troubled, and traces of tears clung to her smooth cheeks. "Is my dad..." Her voice broke.

Melissa stepped forward and smiled. "He's fine, Wendi. He was up a couple of times in the night, but he's doing great."

"Really?" She sniffed, fresh tears ran down her face. "I was so worried. I should have stayed home, but I was scared."

"He'll be back to normal before you know it." Melissa gave her an impulsive hug. They were the same height, but Wendi was all long lines and lean limbs. The girl returned her embrace, then stepped back and wiped her cheeks with the back of her hand.

"Can I go see him?"

"Sure. He's drinking coffee and arguing with the morning news show."

Wendi looked at Melissa, her eyebrows raised in outrage. "You went in my dad's bedroom dressed like that?"

Melissa glanced down at the long robe covering her oversize pink T-shirt she'd worn to bed and laughed. "Wendi, he's got bandages over his eyes. He can't see me."

"Oh." Logan's daughter dropped her overnight case onto the floor. "Then I guess it's okay. I'm going to check on him. I'll be right back."

She shot off down the hall and Melissa went back into the kitchen. The girl returned in about five minutes.

Melissa looked up from the oranges she was squeezing and smiled. "I'm making French toast and bacon for breakfast. Do you want some?"

"Yeah." Wendi walked into the kitchen. "I didn't feel like eating any dinner. Wow, you can really cook."

"Most people can. Why are you surprised?"

She shrugged. "My dad barbecues about once a year and we usually have to call the fire department. Mrs. Dupuis does all our cooking. She's the housekeeper."

Melissa peeled off three more strips of bacon. "Where is she now?"

Wendi sat on the stool in the corner and started braiding her long hair. "France. She's got a ton of relatives. I went with her last year, but this summer Dad's sending me to some dumb day camp. Don't you think I'm way too mature for camp?"

Melissa glanced at the preteen; the path of the tears was clearly defined on her face. Despite her height and air of sophistication, she looked like a scared little girl. "Sounds like fun to me. Do you go every day?"

"Nah. Three days a week. It's computers and math and stuff. Dad wants me to be an architect or an engineer."

"And what do you want to be?"

Wendi shrugged. "Maybe a model, or an astronaut. I haven't decided. Wanna see my room?"

The swift shift in conversation caused Melissa to stop squeezing the juice. If Wendi wanted to be friends, who was she to argue? "Ah, sure. I haven't started cooking yet."

Melissa followed the girl out of the kitchen. She hadn't had a chance to explore the rest of the house. Logan's room was to the right of the living room. Wendi moved toward a door on the left side of the kitchen. They passed through the formal dining room, complete with a built-in hutch and buffet and a pair of French doors that looked out onto the patio and pool. A vague sense of unease began to nibble at her confidence. Melissa tugged on the belt of her robe. She suddenly felt dowdy and underdressed.

Wendi pointed down the short hall. "That's Mrs. Dupuis's room. Normally she keeps an eye on me, but this summer I get to play my music really loud."

Her grin eased Melissa's feeling of apprehension. But when Wendi pushed open her bedroom door, the knot returned to Melissa's stomach.

She had a vague impression of delicate furniture and lace draperies, but her attention was caught by a stunning portrait hanging on the opposite wall. The woman in the painting was young, not quite thirty, and dressed in a form-fitting gown. Dark hair fell in a smooth line of satin all the way to the middle of her back. Wide almond-shaped eyes, the exact color of the emeralds clinging to her neck, seemed to stare into Melissa's soul and find her wanting. The high cheekbones and haughty curve of her mouth were familiar... and incredibly beautiful.

"What a lovely picture," Melissa said. "But I can't help thinking I've seen her before. Who is she?"

"She's the spokesperson for Fire perfume and the star of the daytime soap, *The Proud and the Powerful.*" The pride in her voice was evident.

"I don't watch much TV, but I'm sure I've caught her a few times." She moved closer. There was something about the eyes that...

Wendi began to giggle. "Didn't Dad tell you?"

Melissa swallowed, guessing what the girl was going to say. "No."

"Fiona Phillips is my mom."

Chapter Three

Somehow Melissa managed to get back to the kitchen and finish making breakfast. By the time she'd put the two meals on a tray and brought the food into Logan's bedroom, her heartbeat had returned to normal.

Wendi was curled up on the bed, her head on her father's shoulder. It was a perfect domestic scene, the "beautiful people" at home. Bitterness rose in her throat, but she pushed it down. When the job was done, she'd analyze her emotions; today she had work to do.

"Here's breakfast, gang," she said cheerfully. "Logan, I cut your French toast into strips." She set the tray over his lap, then handed Wendi her plate. Taking his fingers in her own, she pointed to the food. "French toast, bacon, more strawberries, juice, coffee."

"I can't eat all that," he said.

"I can," Wendi offered.

"No sneaking food until your dad's done. Promise?"

The girl nodded and nibbled on her bacon.

Melissa measured out his morning medication and placed the pills in his hand. "Drugs first." She was pleased when he swallowed them without complaint.

When he set the empty juice glass down, he sighed. "I can't remember the last time I had fresh squeezed. Thanks, Melissa."

Why did he have to smile at her like that? she thought angrily. Didn't he know it made her feel all weak in the knees? With Wendi watching their every move, she had to guard against any emotion showing on her face.

"You two eat up. I'm going to go shower and change." She started from the room.

Logan called her back. "Aren't you joining us for breakfast?"

Melissa glanced at the bed. There wasn't room for a third person. "No. I'm not hungry."

"Dad, do you know what Melissa's wearing?" Wendi asked. Her mouth curved impishly. "A bathrobe. Good thing Mrs. Dupuis isn't here to see."

Logan looked up. "Mrs. Dupuis is the soul of propriety. She's worked for us for almost five years and I've never even seen her in anything but her uniform."

Melissa smiled self-consciously. "I've got one up on Mrs. Dupuis," she said as she turned to leave. "You've never seen me at all."

Melissa buttoned her cotton blouse and tucked it into her jeans. After giving her hair one more flick with the brush, she stepped out of the bathroom. The mirrored closet doors reflected her image, and she closed her eyes as she remembered the woman in the portrait.

You're a fool, she told herself firmly. Look at who his ex-wife is. So what if he was friendly and teasing? It didn't mean a thing. Patients always came on to nurses; the story was as old as the profession itself. When his eyesight was better, he'd be off living his life, and she'd be off living hers.

But last night, long after he'd drifted to sleep, she'd lain awake and relived the evening. And when she'd gone in to check on him, and he'd rolled over sleepily and called her by name, she'd allowed herself to dream. There were worse things to be than a fool.

She opened her eyes and stared at her reflection. A short, plain woman stared back. Medium, just as she'd told Logan. Her short hair was baby fine and refused to hold a curl. The memory of Fiona's long dark tresses made her want to scream in frustration. Enough, she said silently. *No more feeling sorry for poor little me. I've a job to do and I'm going to do it. He's the patient and I'm the nurse. And that's the end of the story.*

Straightening her shoulders, she walked into Logan's room.

"...and then I'm going back over to Kelly's. I wasn't very good company last night. You don't mind, do you?" Wendi glanced anxiously at her father.

Pulling his daughter closer, he kissed the top of her head. "Of course not, sweetie. I'm just going to lie around all day and torment Melissa." He turned swiftly in her direction and smiled.

"How did you know I was here?"

"Your perfume. What is it anyway?"

She collected the tray of dirty dishes. "Magnolias."

"I thought so." He stretched his arms up and yawned. The fabric of his robe gapped, exposing his chest.

She felt her mouth go dry. "I'll, ah, be in the kitchen, washing up the dishes. When I come back, we'll see about getting you cleaned up."

Logan frowned. "There's no way you're going to give me a sponge bath, Melissa."

"Logan, you can't..."

The phone on the nightstand rang.

"I'll get it." Wendi leaned over her father and picked up the receiver. "Hello." She listened for a moment. "Hi, Mr. Anderson. Yeah, he's right here. No, he looks good. And Melissa's great. Okay, bye. Here, Dad. It's Mr. Anderson."

"I gathered that. Good morning, John."

Wendi followed Melissa down the hall. "I'm going to try and sleep a little this morning, then Kelly and I are going to the movies."

Melissa put the tray on the counter and opened the dishwasher. "Are you going to be home for dinner?"

"Are you cooking?"

Her smile was so much like Logan's that Melissa felt her heart skip a beat. "I could be convinced."

"All right! I'll be back by six." She ran out of the room and skidded around the corner, her long braid flying behind her. Snapping her fingers, she sang, "I'm just too cool for you, boy. Da da, oh yeah. I'm just . . ." The sound was abruptly cut off when her door slammed shut.

The flowers started arriving at nine. By ten-thirty, half a dozen large bouquets filled Logan's room. He's been on and off the phone, fielding calls about various projects he was involved with.

Melissa signed for a spray of perfect peach roses, then carried them into the bedroom. "Here's another one from—"

He jumped and the receiver went flying. She set the arrangement on the floor and picked up the phone, then folded his fingers around the plastic.

"I'll have to get back to you," he growled, and hung up. He turned toward her. "Don't ever do that to me."

The anger in his voice was like a blow. She placed the roses on the fireplace mantel. "I'm sorry I startled you. I didn't know you were on the phone. I won't interrupt again.''

"Melissa."

She stood perfectly still, afraid to move, afraid to even breathe.

"Answer me," he said. "Are you still here?"

"Yes, Logan. I'm right here." She covered the space to the bed in three short steps. "What do you need?"

He reached out his hand, palm up. The invitation could not be denied and she touched her fingers to his.

"I'm sorry I snapped at you," he said. "Would you do me a favor and take the flowers out of the room?"

"Why?"

Logan tugged on Melissa's arm until she was forced to sit next to him. The warm pressure of her thigh against his was comforting . . . and arousing. The desire lapping at his loins was enough to make him feel lazy . . . and hungry . . . and male.

"Because I can't smell your perfume and I don't know when you're in the room."

"Oh."

"That's it? No argument, Nurse VanFleet? Just 'oh'?"

"You're the cranky one, not me."

He heard the smile in her voice. What did she look like? he wondered again. He'd always thought of himself as a visual person, but here he was being turned on by little more than a feminine voice and a gentle touch.

Her hand rested against his, their fingers linked. It had been a long time . . . maybe too long. While his mind told him to resist the urge, his body clamored for more contact. Her perfume enticed him, erasing the last trace of common sense.

Ah, the hell with it, he thought. They were both adults. His palms moved up her arms to rest on her shoulders; her hair was soft, the wispy ends tickled the backs of his hands.

She shifted, but his fingers pressed down as he held her in place. The air around them became charged with an electric current.

Melissa felt the subtle change in the room. What had started out friendly, even comforting, rapidly became erotic. Stand up, she told herself. If she stayed another second, she'd give in to temptation.

She stared at his face, searching for a clue to what he was thinking. The lines of his jaw were taut, his lips pulled straight in a firm line, but neither told her anything.

Then his hands began to move toward her face, tracing random patterns on her neck. He wanted her, she thought with relief and anticipation. She started to lean forward, then stopped. No, that wasn't quite correct. He wanted a woman and she was the only one around.

"Say something," he commanded, pulling her toward him.

"Logan, let me go...."

He silenced her with a kiss. Those lips that she'd been admiring now brushed against hers. The touch wasn't the hungry assault she'd have expected from a man like him, but a tender exploration. Moving from one corner to the other, he made sure every millimeter of her mouth was equally caressed, tasted, savored. Comfort and contact with another person, she told herself. That's all he was interested in. Yet the logical explanation didn't keep her from reacting to his ministration. Her heart pounded in her ears.

Bracing his weight on one arm, he tilted her jaw with his other hand. Now that she was free, she told herself to push away. But instead, her fingers trailed up his arms and shoulders to meet in the middle of his back, then moved to the thick curls at the nape of his neck. He was silk and steel. His skin was hot like fire, his hair was cool like satin.

He pressed his thumb lightly on her chin, urging her to allow him entrance. No, she thought. But the deep moan in his chest was her undoing. She opened her mouth and welcomed his tongue with the touch of hers.

It was like drowning in fire. Flames of sensation ran through her body, pausing only to collect in her breasts and between her thighs. Fighting against his touch became impossible and she gave herself up to the inferno.

Logan's fingers traced the line of her neck, then moved down to her shoulder. He longed to discover the curves he'd earlier wondered about. Even through her clothes, he could feel the roundness of her body; the lush fullness, so different from Fiona's harsh angles and protruding bones, made him ache. He . . .

Logan drew back with a suddenness that caused his head to swim. What the hell was he thinking of? Melissa was his nurse and hired by his boss. He had no business making love with her . . . or any other woman like her, for that matter. Hadn't he learned his lesson? He only wanted sophisticated types who knew the rules of the game: no commitments, no pain. Despite her humor and intelligence, she didn't strike him as the worldly kind.

"Logan, I . . ." Melissa's voice cracked, but it wasn't enough of a clue to tell him what she was thinking. The mattress moved and he knew she'd stood up. He wanted to rip the bandages from his eyes and study her face.

"I'm very sorry," she said, her voice sounding nearby. "I should never have allowed things to get so out of hand. It was very unprofessional of me."

The genuine shock and remorse in her tone filled him with irritation. He swore.

"Logan? Are you hurt?"

He turned away. "I'm fine." He ached, but it couldn't be helped by one of her little pills. The only cure would be to bury that part of him deep within her waiting softness and carry them both to a place beyond pain.

Melissa touched her hand to her kiss-swollen lips. She felt like a fool...or worse. An incident like this could cost her her job, or at the very least, her self-respect.

She'd heard about patients coming on to nurses. It hadn't happened to her before, but she recognized the symptoms. A caring woman helping a man in need. They were isolated together in a world of their own making. It was a volatile situation.

Logan tried to smile. "I'm sorry, too."

She silenced him by pressing her fingers on his arm. "Don't apologize. It happens all the time. Not to me, of course. The only thing Bobby ever did was give me his favorite stuffed animal, but I think the sentiment was the same."

"Thanks."

She stared at his face for a moment longer, memorizing the planes and angles and hollows. If only his feelings had been real, she thought. When he touched her, she burned with a fire she'd never felt before. Who are you, Logan Phillips?

"You're reacting to the blindness," she said quietly, almost afraid to speak the truth. In a way, these words were as much for her as for Logan. "It's very natural to reach out for physical contact. I should have been more prepared. After all, looking after you is my job."

Her matter-of-fact tone doused his desire faster than a cold shower. Part of her job? Did she think he was some weak-kneed mental case who needed to be pampered and coddled? "I see. Thanks for the information. I'll try not to trouble you again. Just get rid of the flowers. I want to know when you walk in the room."

Melissa picked up the nearest arrangement and carried it out. Explaining away his sensual invitation was the hardest thing she'd ever done. But there'd been no other option. She was his nurse.

Besides, Logan had turned to her because he needed a woman...any woman. But she'd turned to him because she was starting to care. It was a combination destined to break her heart. There was no place for her in Logan Phillips's life, now or ever.

When the last bouquet had been placed in another part of the house, Melissa returned to her room. She'd kept the arrangement from John Anderson, Logan's boss, on her dresser. The peach roses had been from Fiona. The card had been signed with just her name. Melissa had stuck them in Wendi's room. She smiled as she remembered the young girl turning over sleepily and calling out good-night. Wendi had just enough of her father's charm to make her hard to resist.

Melissa paced the space between the dresser and the bathroom door. Her room had been decorated in dusty rose. She didn't have a view of the pool, but her window looked out on the side garden. The queen-size mattress was covered with a satin bedspread, and a cherry-wood dresser held all her clothes, with several drawers to spare.

Somewhere in the house, a clock chimed the hour. It was getting close to noon. She couldn't hide from Logan forever; he was her responsibility.

Since her disastrous relationship with Jeff Bernard, she'd avoided entanglements of any kind. Working as a practical nurse protected her from pain. If she didn't date, she couldn't be used or dumped. But at what price? After six years of running from men in general, she was starting to see that she'd given up her chance for love and a family. Not that she expected to be rescued by a handsome prince. They were reserved for the Fiona Phillipses of the world. Still there might be someone—a medium kind of man, who was looking for the love of an honest, giving woman.

If nothing else, her reaction to Logan's kiss proved she wasn't as immune to men as she had thought. It *had* to mean that; she wouldn't let herself think that the only thing she wasn't immune to was Logan.

Maybe when she was done here, she would take some time off and think about her future. She couldn't run forever. However, before she made any grand plans for her life, she still had to face her very attractive patient. The best way to handle the situation would be to pretend nothing had happened between them. She could do it; she'd been hiding her real feelings all her life.

Logan sat in bed, listening to the radio. Maybe he was just getting old, but he didn't understand rap music. The words didn't make sense and the beat hurt his head.

The fragrance of magnolias drifted into the room. Was she angry? Would she leave him now?

"I was wondering where you'd run off to," he said as he held his fists tightly against his sides. He'd suffer whatever was necessary to avoid embarrassing either of them again. Her words still echoed in his ears: reacting to the blindness.

She sat next to him and touched his arm. "I was thinking. We need to talk about a bath."

He wanted to jerk away from the contact but couldn't. By kissing her, he'd broken all his own rules. When she'd explained away the intimacy, he'd reacted with anger and hurt pride. But in his world of blackness, he felt isolated. Her voice and gentle hands provided a guide through this difficult time; she was his anchor. He needed her.

Wiser than he, she'd apparently decided to ignore his outburst. "Am I the biggest jerk you've ever known?" he asked quietly.

She hesitated. "I once knew this guy who was about two inches taller than you."

"Very funny."

She laughed. "Now about cleaning you up..."

"If you mean a sponge bath, you can forget it."

"Isn't this where I came in, Logan?"

"Don't change the subject. I'll take a shower."

She sighed. "You can't get your bandages wet."

"So we'll cover them."

"You know that wouldn't work. I can't very well tape up your face." She touched the gauze around his head.

"Okay. What's the compromise?"

"You take a bath. I saw a huge tub in your bathroom. I bet you've never used it."

Actually he had, about a year ago. If he recalled the night correctly, it had involved a redhead and several bottles of champagne. But he didn't want to remember that now. It was enough that Melissa had returned their relationship to its comfortable footing.

"Okay to the bath," he said.

"I'll go run the water."

He felt the mattress shift. Her fragrance lingered in the room, then faded. Logan swung his legs over the side of the bed, then rose and started toward the bathroom. He was almost at the door when something... or someone ran into him. Putting out his hands to keep them both from falling, he grabbed Melissa's soft arms.

"Yikes! Where did you come from?" she asked.

"Scared you?" He ran his thumb in circles on her skin, then stepped back when he realized what he was doing. No touching... at least no sexual touching. He'd be damned if she was going to acquiesce simply because he was her patient. When he took Melissa to his bed, she'd be burning up as much as he was....

Where had that come from? No relationships, that was his rule. She'd barely been in his house twenty-four hours, and already he was having thoughts he had no business thinking. He leaned against the wall and brushed back his hair.

"The water's ready," she said. Taking his hand, she led him into the bathroom. "The towel's right here, and there's the tub. Do you need any help?"

He could still feel the lingering hardness from their recent encounter. "I'll be fine." He started untying his robe.

"Call me when you're done and I'll shave you."

"I don't think so."

She sighed in exasperation. "Do you have an electric razor?"

"Do I look like the kind of guy to use an electric razor?"

"Logan, you can't shave yourself. End of argument. Get in the tube before I throw you in myself."

"Cheap talk."

"Lo-gan."

He held up his hands. "I'm getting, I'm getting. Shut the door."

He was still laughing when he heard her pull it closed with a bang.

"Hold still." Melissa glared at her patient, but it didn't seem to do any good.

"This isn't my idea of a good time." Logan moved again on the chair.

"I have a very sharp razor in my hand. Now we can complete this operation with or without blood. The choice is yours."

He mumbled something unintelligible and was still. Melissa tilted his jaw toward the left and began to work. The burns from the sandblast were healing nicely, but he flinched as the sharp steel slipped over the welts.

"I know," she said. "I'm being careful."

He was still damp from his bath. Droplets of water clung to his chest hair, individual prisms catching and reflecting

the light. A white towel was wrapped casually at his waist.
The contrast between the soft terry cloth and his tanned skin
made her nervous. Part of her wanted to rip away the barrier and plead with him to take her; the other part wanted to
get into her car and drive until she'd forgotten that Logan
Phillips ever existed.

"Have you ever been married?" he asked.

"Didn't I already answer that?"

"No. You said you weren't married now."

"Fair enough. I've never been married."

"How old are you?"

"Twenty-eight. Why are you so interested in me and my
personal life? I promise, it's not the least bit exciting."

"I feel strange having you know so much about me,
physically I mean, and I don't even know what you look
like."

She finished shaving him and wiped his face with a damp
washcloth. "You'll see me in about five days. I think you
can contain yourself until then. Here." She thrust some
clothes at him. "Get dressed. Then we're having lunch in the
kitchen. Afterwards, if you're very good, I'll let you call the
office again."

He stood up and looked down at her. Even with the
bandages, he was intimidating. What color were his eyes?
she wondered. Green like Wendi's? Or maybe blue or
brown? She had to wait the same five days to find out.

"Who died and left you in charge?" he asked.

"Mr. Anderson. He's signing my check."

Logan turned toward the house when he heard another
burst of laughter. A breeze had sprung up in the late afternoon and was chasing away the heat of the June day. The
French doors leading to the living room and kitchen were
open. He couldn't hear the entire conversation between
Melissa and his daughter, but snatches drifted out to him.

The sentence fragments had to do with clothes and boys and who liked whom.

There was a cry of "Oh, no," followed by silence, then more laughter. He thought about getting up to investigate, but by the time he'd made his tortuous way into the house, whatever crisis existed would have already passed.

"You'd better be hungry, Dad, because there's a ton of food."

Wendi's voice was accompanied by the slap of her sandals on the cement patio. He was seated at the picnic table by the pool. "What were you two having such a good time about?" He smelled Melissa's perfume before he heard her soft chuckle.

"I was having a little trouble with the indoor grill," she said.

"Yeah, you should have seen how high the flames—"

"Wendi!" Melissa said.

"But it was great. Anyway, none of the chicken burned. And I made the salad."

His Wendi had helped in the kitchen? The same daughter who measured every action on a scale of how cool it would make her look? Logan shook his head in disbelief. "I'm impressed."

"You should be. It's so much work. Tearing up all that lettuce, then cutting up everything. Next time, let's go to a salad bar."

He instinctively turned toward Melissa before he remembered that they couldn't share an amused glance over the girl's head. In fact, for all he knew, she wasn't looking at him at all. Frustration knotted up inside him and dampened his enthusiasm for the meal.

"Breast or thigh?" Melissa asked.

"Excuse me?"

Wendi giggled. "She means the chicken, Dad. Jeez."

"I knew that. Thigh, please."

When Melissa had finished serving the meal, she began the now-familiar task of pointing out where his food was located. "Good luck with the salad," she murmured. He could feel her soft breath in his ear. "I wasn't sure you'd want any, but certain people were quite insistent."

"Just tell me if I have dressing on my chin or lettuce in my teeth."

It took most of his concentration to get the food from the plate into his mouth, without any serious mishaps in between, so he simply listened to the talk flowing around him. Wendi was her normal exuberant self. In Melissa's presence, she seemed to have shed some of the hard cynical edge she'd been developing as she grew up. If only he could keep her his little girl forever.

"We're going to have pork chops tomorrow, Dad. Then Mexican the next night."

He carefully wiped his mouth with the napkin and turned his head toward Melissa. "I don't expect you to cook every night. We can have something brought in."

"I don't mind, Logan. Besides, I don't think you're ready to use chopsticks or wrestle with spaghetti."

"You do keep threatening that, don't you?"

He felt her hand on his arm. The brief contact grounded him in space and time; the warm sensation lingered long after she'd pulled her fingers away.

"Mom doesn't cook at all." Wendi uttered the words with all the innocence of youth, but Logan sensed Melissa stiffening in her chair.

"I'm sure she doesn't have time," Melissa said casually.

"Maybe you can meet her when she comes to pick me up," Wendi offered.

Over my dead body, Logan thought with a fierceness that startled him. Fiona had women like Melissa chopped up and served for breakfast.

"Sure. If you'd like."

He wasn't certain, but he could have sworn there was a slight tremor in Melissa's voice. He wanted to reassure her that she'd be safe, that he'd protect her, but it wasn't his place. His reaction was simple gratitude, he told himself. She had been there for him and he owed her. She was just his nurse and he'd better not forget that. If he did, he might do something they'd both regret.

"I'm too cool for you, boy..."

Melissa hummed to herself as she folded the laundry. Except for cooking, domestic chores weren't part of her job description. There were two ladies who came in twice a week to clean the house, but she found the simple tasks of washing and ironing actually quite fun. She couldn't remember the last time she'd ironed a man's shirt. No, that wasn't strictly true. It had been Jeff's shirt... the night of the banquet... when he'd announced he was leaving her for a very successful, very beautiful, pediatrician. Six years was a long time between creasing sleeves, she thought humorously. She'd better get all her fun while she could.

She'd already been with Logan and Wendi for six days and they'd settled into a comfortable routine together. On the days she wasn't at camp, Wendi spent her time with friends or had them over. The kitchen still hadn't recovered from seven twelve-year-olds practicing their baking skills at the same time. The cleaning people would be digging flour out of corners and cracks for weeks yet.

Logan spent his mornings working by phone. Then they'd have lunch together and she'd read to him for an hour or so. After dinner by the pool, the three of them would play games, with Wendi or Melissa taking turns reading the cards or telling him what number he'd rolled with the dice. The temptation to conspire against him was strong, but so far they'd only given in once... well, twice, if she counted the time they'd dug for a really hard question when playing Trivial Pursuit.

After Wendi drifted off to catch up on her MTV, Melissa would spend time with Logan. She'd change his bandages, then they'd stretch out on the big bed in his room and talk, or she'd simply read to him. With the crickets calling outside the windows and soft music playing in the background, she allowed herself to pretend the nights were real. For those few hours, Logan was her handsome prince...and she was as beautiful as Fiona.

All that would change shortly. When she'd driven Logan to the doctor a couple of days ago, he'd been told he was healing nicely. The bandages would come off this morning.

Melissa picked up the pile of T-shirts and headed toward Logan's room. He was pacing restlessly, counting the steps from the wing chair to the doorway.

"Coming through," she called as she ducked past him.

He grabbed her arm. His unerring sense of direction never ceased to amaze her. "Take them off now," he commanded.

She twisted out of his grasp and walked to the armoire. "The doctor is due here any minute. Try and control yourself."

He smiled. "You sound so tough, Melissa, but I won't be blind much longer. Then how will you keep me in line?"

That's what she was dreading most. Part of her felt guilty for wanting to keep his eyes bandaged. She knew it was difficult for him, and he'd handled himself amazingly well. But when he could see, he really wouldn't need her anymore. And all the touching—the gentle brush of her fingers to tell him where she was, the embrace to lead him to the patio— would be unnecessary and inappropriate. She hadn't realized how much she savored those moments, until they were about to be taken from her.

Besides, he'd be able to see what she looked like. She tried to console herself with the thought that it was unlikely he'd run screaming from the room, but still . . . his blindness had been a mask, allowing her to be who she really was. Once he could look at her, she'd become scared and tongue-tied and foolish. Was it so very wrong to want the fantasy to continue just a little longer?

"You'll be here until I go back to the office?" he asked.

"Yes, Logan. You can't do any close work for two weeks. I'll be here to make sure you follow directions." Two weeks until he was out of her life forever.

She shut the drawer and stood up. He was right behind her. For a second, she thought about leaning against him and allowing his arms to comfort her and chase away all her fears. But since that second day, when she'd rationalized their kiss, Logan had been a perfect gentleman. It was driving her crazy.

The sound of the doorbell rescued her from her own fantasies. "That must be Mr. Anderson and the doctor." She scurried away before Logan could detain her.

"How's the patient?" John Anderson asked as he walked into the foyer. The older man was as tall as Logan, but his build was heavier with a round belly hanging over his belt.

"Pacing and cranky, as you can imagine." She turned to greet the doctor. Both men were dressed in bright plaid slacks with matching shirts. They had spent the morning together golfing. Melissa shook her head. The thought of an entire course of men dressed in gaudy attire was enough to keep her inside with the door locked.

"Lead the way, young lady," the gray-haired doctor said, his blue eyes twinkling behind his wire-rimmed glasses. "John is buying lunch when we're through here and I feel an appetite coming on."

"It's just down the hall." She escorted them to the back of the house.

Logan was sitting on the edge of the bed. When he heard them, he stood up and moved forward. "Melissa?"

"Yes. Mr. Anderson and the doctor are here."

"Who won?" Logan asked.

John sighed. "It was that damned sand trap on the thirteenth hole."

The doctor set a small bag on the bed. "Hope you appreciate the house call, Logan. Your boss is a persuasive man."

"Yeah," John said. "It's costing me a bottle of '42 Bordeaux."

The men laughed, but Melissa inched her way closer to the door. She had to get out before the doctor took off the bandages and Logan saw her and . . .

"Nurse?"

She froze, not quite out in the hall. "Yes, Doctor?"

"Would you remove the patient's bandages, please?" He opened his bag and withdrew a small flashlight.

She swallowed, then walked to the nightstand. The scissors were right where she kept them. Slowly she moved around the bed and waited for Logan to sit down.

He smiled confidently. "I've been counting the days, Melissa."

"I bet."

The men watching, combined with her own nervousness, made her fingers tremble. The sound of gauze being cut seemed loud in the still room.

She peeled away the dressings and removed the pads. Logan's lashes were matted from the cream, but they were still long and dark. As he blinked, she resisted the urge to look away or hide her head. At least she'd find out what color his eyes were, she told herself.

But when he looked straight at her, she couldn't breathe. Instead of blue or green, his irises were a rich tawny brown. Flecks of gold radiated out from the black pupil, creating an almost magical glow, as if he had the power to see into her heart. She'd always thought him good-looking, but without the white band around his head, he was...incredible. His nose was perfectly straight and the hollows in his cheeks were more pronounced. The skin and angles and bones blended together into noble, masculine features.

He squinted, as if trying to bring her in focus, but didn't speak. Why didn't he say something, or look away... anything?

"Well, you're a sight for sore eyes," he said finally.

She groaned and ducked her head. "After almost a week, that's the best you can come up with?"

Behind her the doctor chuckled. She spun around, having forgotten the other two men in the room.

"Let's take a look." He clicked on the light and tilted Logan's face up. "Good reactions. Infection seems cleared up. Remember, no close work and wear sunglasses to protect your eyes from the light. Indoors also, for at least a week. Come to the office in about ten or twelve days and I'll see if you're ready to go back to work." He put his equipment away. "Well, John, what about that lunch?"

Mr. Anderson grinned. "Logan, you follow orders. I can't afford any more of these house calls." He winked at Melissa. "Hang in there, Nurse VanFleet. Don't let him get away with anything."

"Me?" Logan asked as he slipped on dark glasses. "I'm the perfect patient."

He turned and gave her that lethal grin. She felt her heart begin to melt. Dear God, she was going down for the third time and there wasn't a lifeboat in sight.

Chapter Four

Melissa shut the front door behind the two men and drew in a steadying breath. She'd barely survived the past five minutes, how on earth would she get through the next two weeks? Between the raging dance her hormones performed every time she and Logan were in the same room and her overactive imagination, she didn't have a prayer of escaping unscathed. She'd probably end up ripping off her clothes, pleading with him to take her and be forced to deal with the ignominy of being thrown out on the street. No job, no references, no money. By the end of the month, she'd be a bag lady on Sunset Boulevard.

A giggle escaped her lips as she pictured herself, dressed in a white nurse's uniform, complete with starched hat, pushing a shopping cart filled with all her earthly possessions. Okay, so that scenario was the tiniest bit extreme. But the possibility of her making a fool of herself over Logan wasn't at all unlikely.

There was only one solution: pretend she didn't care. How hard could that be?

By the time she'd prepared lunch, Melissa had convinced herself that dealing with Logan would be a snap. Then he came out of his room.

The footsteps on the hallway's hardwood floor were the first warning. "When do we eat?" he asked, leaning against the door frame.

His arms were crossed over his broad chest stretching the blue T-shirt indecently. Who was it, she wondered, who designed men's clothing? Couldn't they add an extra inch or two in the shoulders and chest? But no, there he stood, all six feet of tall, lean man. With the dark glasses on his eyes, he looked like a model for a teen magazine. Rock Star At Home would be the photo's caption. Only Logan looked better than any unshaven singer she'd ever seen.

"In about ten minutes. I thought you might be tired of finger food, so I'm making a Chinese chicken salad."

Her gaze lingered on his face. The welts had faded. In another week, they'd be healed, leaving behind faint lines on his cheeks. The scars of battle would only add to his charm. She sighed. Everything was different now. If only...

He grinned suddenly. "You're staring. Do I look that different?"

Oh, no! He could *see!* "Ah, no. I was just..." She spun back to face the counter and started to chop the green pepper she was holding. The staccato sound of the blade against the cutting board didn't block out his low chuckle. Stay calm, she told herself. This is not a crisis. This is a manageable situation. She *was* an adult. Only no one had explained that to her racing heart.

"Melissa?"

"What?" She glanced up at him, but forgot to stop moving the knife. Honed steel nicked her left index finger.

"Ouch!" Jumping back, she turned and stuck her hand under the faucet, then turned on the tap.

Before she could draw a breath, he was at her side and reaching for her wrist. "Let me see."

"No." She tried to pull away from his touch, but he held on tightly. "I know for a fact that your sight hasn't fully returned. Go play doctor somewhere else."

"You might need stitches." Concern furrowed his brow.

"Don't even think about it. You'd probably sew my hand to my knee."

"I meant we could get my doctor back."

"D-don't be silly."

He was so close, she could feel the heat from his body. It didn't matter that the wound continued to drip into the sink; the sensation of his hand holding hers was worth the discomfort.

The front door slammed. Wendi's "Hi, I'm home" seemed louder than any warning bell. Melissa wrenched her arm away and grabbed a paper towel.

"There. The bleeding's already slowing down. I'll go find a bandage and be right back." She ran out of the kitchen before he could stop her.

She heard Wendi's question about what had happened and Logan's low response. As she shut the bathroom door behind her, she wondered how long it would take until she gave herself away.

Logan sat in the shade by the pool. The umbrella overhead kept out most of the sun's strong rays, but he still had to squint as he watched his daughter frolic in the water. Light was painful and his vision was fuzzy at times, but it was a hell of a lot better than being blind.

"Watch, Daddy. I can do a back flip." Wendi climbed out of the water and ran to the diving board. Wet hair clung to her shoulders in a tangled mess. The one-piece bathing suit was more conservative than she had wanted and about half a yard less than the one he'd picked out, but compromise was the first rule of parenting. Or was it discipline? He never got them straight.

She stood proud and tall on the edge of the platform. Shading his eyes, he watched her bounce one, twice, then spring free in a wobbly arc that ended when she entered the water knees first.

"It wasn't supposed to look like that," she said as she broke the surface. "Kelly's a better swimmer than me."

"I," Melissa said as she walked onto the patio.

Wendi swam to the side and rested her chin and forearms on the deck. "I what?"

Melissa planted her hands on her hips. "Kelly's a better swimmer than I."

Wendi rolled her eyes. "Melis-sa!"

"Wen-di. Learn to speak right and I won't have to correct you. *Comprendez?*"

"Oh, great. It's not enough I have to learn English. Now you expect me to understand a foreign language." She slipped under the water.

Logan laughed and gave Melissa a thumbs-up. When their eyes met, her smile faltered and she fled the patio as though hounds were at her heels. She'd been acting strangely ever since lunch. Not unpleasant, but distant, as though she didn't want to be around him. Was it something he'd said or done?

The wind picked up slightly, stirring the fresh flowers in the vase on the table. Plucking out a single rose, he touched his fingers to the leaves. To see the deep red, as well as feel the softness of the petals and the points of the thorns, was glorious. There had been times, mostly at night when the pain had disturbed his sleep, that he'd wondered if he'd ever see again. Those times, when fear and panic threatened to overwhelm him, Melissa had silently appeared beside his bed. Her quiet voice and gentle touch always calmed him enough to allow sleep to claim him once more. They were private moments, never discussed or even acknowledged. Inhaling the fragrance of the rose, he smiled. Life was good.

"I'm going to get a soda," Wendi said as she stepped out of the pool and wrapped a towel around her. "Do you want anything?"

"Tell Melissa to get a bottle of cabernet sauvignon out of the wine rack. Tonight we celebrate my return to the land of the living."

"Do I get a glass?"

Logan held open his arms. His daughter stepped into his embrace and sat on his lap. Her arms curled around his neck as he squeezed her. "You can have a sip of mine."

"Cool. Be right back."

She dropped the towel onto a chair and stepped toward the French doors. The bottom of her swimsuit had crept up and she pulled it down with a quick tug. The movement caught Logan like a kick in the gut. His little girl was growing up. There were curves that hadn't been there last year. Every day she seemed older, more assured. She was turning into a younger version of Fiona right before his eyes, and he didn't know how to make it stop.

"But I will," he said fiercely.

"Excuse me?" Melissa stood in the doorway. "You will what?"

"Talking to myself. Feel free to ignore me."

"Oh."

She walked over to the table and stood across from him, then put down three place mats. Logan waited, but there wasn't any snappy comeback. Maybe she was tired.

"Did Wendi tell you about the wine?" he asked.

"Yes. But I should warn you that you can't have alcohol and then a painkiller." Her hands made quick work of smoothing the napkins and setting up the silverware, but she didn't meet his eyes.

"I'm not in any pain."

"Good."

He tried to study her face, but wisps of blond hair fell forward as she worked and hid her expression from view. Medium, she'd said that first night. There were other words he would have chosen to describe her.

The beginnings of a tan colored her shoulders and arms. His gaze dropped to the pink cotton tank top she wore tucked into denim shorts. As she leaned forward to shoo away a fly, he was treated to a flash of pale, creamy flesh. In the past he'd preferred women who were tall and slender, but there was something to be said for a woman who could fill out a shirt. He clenched his fist against the sudden itch to discover those curves firsthand.

She picked up the flower he'd been examining and placed it back in the vase. "I'll bring out the wine. Where's the corkscrew?"

"In the dining room. Top drawer of the buffet."

Before she could run off, he touched her arm. She jerked away from the contact. "Yes?"

"Melissa, are you feeling all right?"

"I'm fine. Why?"

He shrugged. "No reason. What are we having for dinner?"

She murmured something under her breath.

"What?" He felt a smile tugging at his lips. "Could you please repeat that?"

She glared down at him, her brown eyes flashing fire. "Spaghetti. Okay? We've made such a big deal about it all week that I thought you might have a taste for it."

"I'm not complaining." He raised his hands in mock surrender. "I'd just like to point out *we* haven't made a big deal out of it. You kept threatening me with it. But hey, I'm just the guy who pays the bills."

"If you'd prefer something else, it's not too late to change the menu."

He sighed. As quickly as she'd arrived, the old Melissa was gone and the efficiently subservient automaton was back in place.

"'...and knew the killer had been there not three hours before.'"

Melissa turned the page and continued to read. Logan leaned back against the headboard and studied his companion. In deference to his weak eyes, she'd insisted on sitting across the room and using the reading lamp in the corner. He appreciated the concern, but the ritual of being read to had lost much of its charm.

The king-size mattress was too big without her next to him. Now that he could see, there weren't any whispery noises for him to wonder about. No sudden dips as she shifted her position on the bed, no brief touches to remind him of where she was.

And worst of all, the chair was so far away, he couldn't smell her perfume. He stirred restlessly, thrusting another pillow behind his back.

Melissa looked up from the book. "Are you in pain?"

"No."

"Would you like me to read something else?"

He sighed. "I'm fine." He moved again and waited for some smart remark about his inability to sit still.

She bowed her head and picked up the book. "'Three gray threads were pushed into the corner of the...'"

The light from the incandescent bulb turned her medium blond hair to gold. The shimmering strands moved with each breath, fluttering around her face like soft feathers. Compared to Fiona, she was ordinary to the point of being plain, but he'd been dazzled by beauty enough times to know it was only a temporary spell. There was an honesty in Melissa's face that had been lacking in his ex-wife's. While her features, taken in all at once, wouldn't cause a second glance, her skin was like porcelain. She wore a small amount of makeup, but it didn't conceal the flawless finish and gentle color that naturally stained her cheeks. Brown eyes, so careful to avoid his, allowed brief glimpses of her secret self.

As she read, she licked her bottom lip. The full curve hinted at a passionate nature, something he might not have expected from his efficient nurse—if they hadn't shared that kiss. There were secrets in Melissa VanFleet, and he intended to discover every one.

"You're staring at me."

He grinned. "You've had a week to get sick of looking at me, but today is my first chance to put a face to the person I know. It's interesting."

"Mmm." She slipped off her shoes and tucked one foot under her. "Do you want me to stop reading?"

He shrugged. "I'm perfectly content."

"You look tired." She set the book on the coffee table and walked over to the bed. "It's getting late. You should rest."

"Bossy as usual." But his comment didn't even get a blink in response.

Melissa picked up a bottle from the nightstand. "You need to use eyedrops. Do you want to put them in or shall I?"

He scooted over on the bed and patted the space next to him. "You do it. I'd probably end up pouring half the liquid down my face."

She hesitated as if about to protest, then unscrewed the bottle top and lowered herself next to him. Logan pulled off his glasses.

The only light in the room was in the far corner. Melissa's face was blurred, but he inhaled the familiar fragrance of her perfume. She leaned close and used one hand to tilt his chin up. The touch on his face was gentle and warm. She'd been changing the bandages on his eyes every day for a week, yet, tonight was different. Sight added intimacy. In the past he'd always had to imagine how close her breasts were to his chest, but now he only had to glance down and see.

The round curves were a scant inch from his side. With a deep breath he could force contact.

"Look up," she said.

He complied. Two drops of cool liquid were expertly released into his eyes. She straightened up and recapped the bottle. "How do you feel?"

"Great."

"Any pain?" She took his wrist in her hand and found his pulse.

"No," he said when she released him.

"Your pulse is a little elevated. Do you feel hot?"

A burst of laughter escaped. He coughed, then grinned at her confused look. "I'm sure it's the excitement of finally being able to see again."

"If you're sure. Do you need anything?"

With one hand, he reached out to cup her cheek. She raised her head but didn't pull away. Her skin was smooth beneath his palm, her hair tickled against the backs of his fingers. Soft, so damn soft. Inside and out.

He wanted her. Here, now, in his bed—tumbling together until the heavy throbbing in his groin was buried deep within her...until the pleasure shattered the distance she'd constricted between them.

He wanted her, but there'd be no loving. Not this night, not ever. There was a code to be followed, and it clearly stated that only those who knew the rules played the game.

Melissa wasn't the type for play. When she gave her body, her heart trailed along. And he wasn't interested in hearts anymore. Not after he'd seen what was in Fiona's.

"Go to bed, Melissa." He swallowed against the raspiness in his throat. "Go to bed now."

Her eyes darkened. The tip of her pink tongue swept across her lower lip. Need, stronger than honor, flared and threatened. His fingers moved down her jaw.

"Good night," she whispered, and then was gone.

"Hi."

Melissa looked up and saw Wendi standing in the doorway of her bedroom. "Hi, yourself. What's going on? Aren't you going over to one of your friends later?"

"Yeah, but I thought . . . I mean, if you aren't busy . . ." Wendi shoved her hands into the back pockets of her jeans. With typical disregard for the fact that summer had officially arrived two weeks before, the weather had turned foggy and cool. Wendi's cotton shirt was rolled up at the sleeves and her dark hair flowed loose down her back.

Melissa put her book on the bed. "I'm not doing anything special. What do you need?"

"It's a surprise."

"Now, why don't I trust that evil grin of yours? Does this involve something slimy?"

"No, silly. Just something I want to show you." She moved into the room. "What are you reading?"

"A college catalogue."

"Why? You're old . . . I mean, you're a nurse. You've already been to college, haven't you?"

Melissa patted the bedspread and picked up the book so Wendi could join her. "Yes. But I was thinking of going back and studying something else."

"Like?"

"Maybe psychology."

"Cool. You could be a shrink. And when my dad's driving me crazy, I'd have someone to talk to."

"You can talk to me now."

Wendi grinned. "Yeah, but my friends have warned me that when we get to high school, parents totally lose it. Did that happen to you?"

"Not really. My parents were busy with my two sisters. I was pretty much left alone." A sense of regret for times lost sifted down through her body.

"I wish my parents would leave me alone, but I'm the only one and they're just so intense."

Melissa hugged the girl. "Your dad loves you very much."

"Yeah, yeah, I know. It's just..." She shrugged and stretched out on the bed. "Have you always taken care of people in their homes?"

"For about the last six years."

"Don't you get tired of being in new places all the time? I mean, you don't get to have your own stuff around. I'd die without my stereo."

"You get used to it."

Wendi thumbed through the catalogue. "Would you get another degree?"

She nodded. "My master's."

"School doesn't start till September. What happens when you leave here?"

"There's a nurses registry I'm listed with. The owner tells me about jobs and I pick the ones I might be interested in. Nothing's been lined up yet, but there are always people looking for nurses. Actually, I might even take a couple of weeks off." She hated the thought of leaving Wendi...and Logan. She would never be a member of the family, but that didn't stop her dreaming and wishing. That was the main reason she didn't have another assignment. Rather than admit their time together would end, she'd ignored all thoughts of the future.

"What about work?" Wendi asked. "Can you go to college and still stay in people's homes?"

Melissa laughed. "That's the exact problem I'm wrestling with, my dear. I have some money saved, so I could probably get by with a part-time nursing job. If I could afford *not* to work, I'd be done with school faster. It's a tough call. I'm not sure what I'm going to do. Any suggestions?"

Wendi pulled her long hair into a ponytail, then let it fall across her back. "I'll let you know." She glanced at the clock on the nightstand. "Gosh, we're missing the surprise. Come on."

Melissa allowed herself to be pulled from the bed, then dragged down the hall and into Wendi's room. A space on the floor had been cleared of clothes and shoes. The TV was on one of the daytime soaps. A tall, gorgeous couple was arguing about the appropriateness of telling *his* wife about their affair.

"Have a seat," Wendi said, pointing to a spot in front of the bed. "We've just missed the beginning. Do you want a soda?"

"Sure." As the girl ran out of the room, Melissa lowered herself to the ground. This was the surprise? Despite having spent the past six years inside people's homes all day and night, she'd never developed a fondness for the soaps. Still, if Wendi wanted to share time together, she wasn't about to object.

The scene on the show switched to a bedroom. The camera panned across bodies moving under satin sheets. Covers were thrown back, exposing one long, perfect leg. Melissa glanced down at her own thighs. She could do a hundred leg lifts a day; nothing would make her lower body look like the one on the screen.

"Oh, darling, that was so wonderful. You are the most incredible lover." The woman's voice was husky yet sweet, like rich chocolate rubbing against skin. A man's back came into view. Not bad, Melissa thought. It wasn't Logan but it was acceptable. He turned over and reached for the champagne bottle at the side of the bed. The camera zoomed in on the woman's face. Melissa felt her lunch push back up against her throat. It was Fiona Phillips, Wendi's mother . . . Logan's ex-wife.

"Isn't she great?" Wendi bounced back into the room and handed Melissa an icy can. "I don't get to watch the show much." She lowered her voice. "Dad doesn't approve, but I like to see my mom work."

Melissa shifted her gaze back to the beautiful woman. Hard to imagine anyone calling that creature "Mom." With her wide-set eyes and the sculpted figure flashing through the skimpy lingerie, she seemed more of a Hollywood creation than a flesh-and-blood person.

"What do you think?" Wendi asked.

"You look a lot like her."

"Really?" Wendi sighed with pleasure. "Thanks. I know I have her hair and eyes, but she's so incredible. Whenever I go visit her, there are *tons* of flowers from all these guys. And you should see what she gets for her birthday." Wendi gulped her drink. "Diamonds and furs. One year, the perfume company gave her a car. Wow. I want to be like that when I grow up."

"There's more to life than just being pretty," Melissa said. And she should know. No one had ever fawned over her looks, not even once.

"I know, but wouldn't it be great to be her?" Wendi leaned her head against Melissa's shoulder. "She travels a lot with the show and the perfume ads. I wish . . ."

"What?" Melissa shifted her drink to her other hand and put her arm around the girl. "That she'd take you with her?"

"Oh, I know she can't. At least, not now. She's way too busy with filming and everything. When I'm older, I can go with her . . . she promised." The last words came out wistfully, as though in the past, promises had been made and then broken.

Melissa kissed Wendi's head and turned her attention to the show. Mercifully the scene had shifted again and she was no longer staring at the stunning woman. But just above the armoire holding the TV was the portrait.

What kind of woman are you? she asked silently. Don't you know your daughter needs you? And what about Logan? Why aren't you here with him, at his side, in his bed? But the haughty picture didn't answer. Green eyes stared down as though asking who *she* was to make such judgments. She wasn't part of the family, she was simply the hired help.

"Try keeping your legs straight. Then you won't go in on your shins."

Logan stared out the open French doors of his bedroom and watched Melissa help Wendi with her back flip. He was supposed to be resting, but the laughter and occasional screams had been impossible to resist.

A pink floppy hat settled low on Melissa's ears and protected her nose from the sun. After almost a week of cool and cloudy weather, the temperature had soared into the nineties and showed no sign of relenting until October.

Wendi climbed back onto the diving board and assumed her position: butt to the water, arms out in front.

"You need more push when you lift off," Melissa said.

Wendi scowled over her shoulder. "Excuse me, but have you ever done this before?"

"I'm insulted by your lack of faith."

"That means no, right?"

Melissa laughed. "Well, I've thought about doing it, but you have to stop diving when you turn twenty-five. It's the law in California."

"You think you're so clever." Wendi apparently forgot she was on the board. She turned and started to put her hands on her hips, only there was no ground below her. Her arms windmilled as she tried to regain her balance, but it was a matter of too little, too late. The wave from her crash lapped up against the patio furniture. Logan smiled as Melissa pulled his laughing daughter from the pool.

Patience wasn't a natural trait, but he'd learned it over the years. Now his patience was about at its end. Ten days ago Melissa had taken off his bandages. Since then he'd had ten days of her acting exactly as he would have expected a nurse to act—if he hadn't spent that first week with someone entirely different.

What had happened? Every time he convinced himself he'd only imagined her humor and spontaneity, he saw her with Wendi. There she joked up a storm. Together they teased and giggled until he felt about as necessary as a leper.

Wendi pulled her towel off the chair and wrapped it around herself. She glanced at the window. "Hi, Daddy. Come on and join us."

Melissa turned in his direction, but the floppy hat hid her eyes from view. "Yes, do join us, Logan. I was just about to make a decision about dinner. What would you like?"

"Not chicken again," Wendi said grimacing. "If I have it one more time this week, I'm going to grow feathers."

Melissa laughed and pretended to pluck something from the girl's back. "I see what you mean. Okay, no chicken. What then?"

He'd never spent much time feeling jealous, and certainly not of his daughter, but for a moment too brief to measure he would have gladly traded places with his twelve-year-old little girl. Why was Melissa normal around her and not around him?

He looked at Wendi's laughing face. She was a pain sometimes, but basically a good kid. She was fun and bright and...

The light went on. Wendi was a *kid*. Melissa was used to working with children. That's how she made her living. But he was a different animal altogether. While his eyes had been bandaged, she'd been able to pretend that he was just another patient, but now she was shy.

Not bad figuring for a guy who made his living designing buildings, he told himself. Now all he had to do was charm her into relaxing around him. Easier said than done, unless...

"Chinese," he said, walking onto the patio.

Both women turned to stare at him. "What?" Wendi asked.

"I said Chinese. I know this great restaurant we can—"

"Lo's Garden? Is it Lo's Garden? Oh, Daddy, please, please. Say yes, say yes." She clung to his arm, pressing her wet body against his side.

"If you stop dripping on me, I'll think about it."

She gave him a damp hug. "Great! Can I bring Kelly?"

Over his daughter's head, his eyes sought Melissa's. A half smile curved her lips and she shrugged as if to say "What can you do?"

Her nose was peeling. All her makeup had long since melted. No other woman he knew would have allowed those baggy shorts and shirt into the house, let alone worn them. He wouldn't change a thing about her.

"Yes to Kelly," he said as he pulled out a chair. "Now, why don't you bring Melissa and me a drink? Last time I checked, someone had just squeezed a pitcher of lemonade."

Melissa stood hesitantly by the table. "I really should..."

"You really should sit down and enjoy the afternoon. Come on." He patted the back of the seat coaxingly. "I'm getting tired of my own company."

"If you'd like." She sank down and adjusted the brim of her hat. "There's no need for you to take me with you for dinner. I'd be quite happy to spend the time here by myself and..."

He cut her off with a glance. The plan was to make her comfortable, not give her more chances to avoid him. "And leave me alone with two twelve-year-old girls? Not on your life. What do you think you're being paid for, if not to ease my suffering?"

"I was hired in a medical capacity, Mr. Phillips. Not as a chaperon." She leaned forward as she spoke, lacing her fingers together on the table.

"If you don't join us, I'll have a breakdown and then you'll never be free of me." He touched her arm. "Say yes."

"I..."

"Please."

"Now you sound like Wendi."

"Where do you think she gets it from? There's a lot of Phillips charm running through that girl."

"Oh, really? I hadn't noticed." The sweet smile contradicted her words.

Beneath his hand, he could feel the warmth of her skin. Tiny tremors rippled against his palm. Deep inside her brown eyes he read the concern, the apprehension, the fear. She was scared of *him*. It was a daunting thought. He'd always seen himself as a regular kind of guy, certainly not intimidating, but Melissa wasn't from his jaded circle of acquaintances. Years ago, before Fiona, he'd known how to cajole a woman. Some of the skills had to have survived her betrayal.

It wasn't as if he were interested in Melissa as a lover. A chuckle formed in his throat as he waited for his nose to grow. So he *was* interested in her that way, but he could handle that temptation. He only wanted to make her relaxed enough for them to be friends again.

"What's so funny?" she asked.

He shrugged. "I was just telling myself stories."

"Do you do that sort of thing often? Should I put it in your chart?"

"Here you go." Wendi walked into the backyard, a tray balanced precariously between her hands. "Lemonade all around."

Melissa served the glasses, then set the pitcher in the center of the table. Wendi pulled a chair close to him and sat down. "Dad?"

"Yes."

"Did you know when Melissa's done here, she doesn't have another job lined up?"

"No." He glanced at her. The thought of her leaving caught him off guard. Surely the time wasn't close to being up already. She'd signed on for three weeks and it had only been . . .

He counted. It had already been almost seventeen days. "Do you need time off for interviews? If so, you must take whatever you require." Did the words sound as hollow to her ears? How could she just walk out of their lives like that? And why did her going away sound so bad?

"Logan, stop." She tossed her hat onto the chair next to her and ran her fingers through her hair. The bangs, damp from the afternoon heat, stood up like little spikes. Farmer's daughter goes punk. God, he'd miss her. "I don't have a job lined up because I don't know what I want to do. I'll probably take a few weeks off to regroup, so don't worry. But thanks for the generous offer."

"Daddy." Wendi tugged on his sleeve.

"Hmm?"

"Mrs. Dupuis doesn't come back until September and you haven't hired anyone to look after me yet. Why can't Melissa stay with us for the rest of the summer?"

Chapter Five

"Stay? Here? I... I couldn't." Could she? Melissa took a long drink from her glass. Stay with Logan...in the same house? Watching him, talking with him, t-touching him? It would be a new and impressive form of torture. Only a fool would subject herself to such potential heartbreak. She might not be the smartest girl in the class, but she wasn't a fool.

Logan looked at his daughter and then at her. His dark glasses hid his eyes from view, so she could only guess what he was thinking. If she knew her patient, it was two parts outrage and one part irritation. He was almost completely healed. The only service she provided was to yell at him for reading and put his drops in every night. No doubt he'd been counting the days until she was gone.

"Wendi, it's sweet of you to ask, but I'm not a house-keeper."

"We have the cleaning ladies come in twice a week," he said. "You wouldn't have to do any of that work."

What did he mean? He couldn't . . . there was no way he *wanted* her to stay, was there?

"I have no real child-care training."

"Melissa, you've been working with sick children for six years. I think you could handle one healthy if somewhat bratty twelve-year-old."

Wendi bounced on her seat and nodded. "I'd be an angel."

Her father glanced at her. "Don't make promises you can't keep."

Melissa moved her glass in uneven circles on the table. "Logan, you want me to stay? For the summer?"

"Yes."

She would have been fine if he hadn't smiled. But as soon as he flashed the grin, she felt her insides begin to quiver. Help me, she begged her pride. There was no reply; that part of her brain was tellingly silent.

"Say yes," Wendi pleaded. Her green eyes had that soft, sweet, puppy-dog expression.

"I . . ."

Saying yes would be a mistake. Logan and Wendi were from a different world. There was no place for her with the "pretty people." Staying would only put herself in danger. No, that wasn't true. It would put her heart in danger. If she were to remain with him, he could steal it as easily as a bird stealing a crumb. And like the winged creature, he'd leave nothing in return.

He named a salary that made her almost keel over in a dead faint. That amount, combined with her savings, would let her go to school for two semesters without having to work at all. She could get her degree that much sooner. Temptation began to weaken her resolve.

Logan took off his glasses. The tawny irises glowed with a power she could not resist. She was putty in his hands. She was a fool.

"Yes," she said. "I'll stay."

"Rice, tomatoes, paper towels, laundry detergent, cat food."

"Cat food?" Wendi pulled the shopping list from Melissa's hand. "We don't have a cat."

"Just checking to see if you were paying attention." She put another cantaloupe in the cart. "I think that's everything for the house. Now I need a couple of items and then we'll be off."

"Did Dad tell you I won't be home for dinner tomorrow? I'm staying over at my mom's. She's got a day off from the soap and she wants to see me!"

Melissa smiled at Wendi's excitement. "I was told. I hope you have a good time, sweetie. Does your father, ah, drop you off at her house?" Please, she thought. Let her say yes.

"No. Mom usually comes to get me. But she doesn't come inside much."

Melissa stared upward. Thank you, she mouthed. The last thing she needed right now was a face-to-face encounter with the stunning Fiona Phillips. She turned the cart down another aisle and paused in front of the feminine hygiene section, then counted. Yup, it was almost time. Tossing the pink box on top of the pile, she looked for the shampoo.

"Do you get your period every month?" The girl stared at the box while she asked.

"Like clockwork. My whole family's like that. In high school, my sisters and I would often start the same week. It drove my mom crazy."

"I'm not going to get my period."

"What?"

Wendi pushed her hair over her shoulder and picked up a set of barrettes. "It's silly and I don't want to."

"They don't send out a questionnaire first and ask your opinion. One day, it's just there. It's not so bad. Think of it as a part of growing up, like getting taller."

Wendi glanced around to make sure they were alone in the aisle, then leaned forward. "Or getting breasts?" she whispered. "I like that part. Clothes look better with breasts, don't you think?"

"I bow to your expertise as the resident fashion plate."

Still laughing, she stepped to the rack of cosmetics and searched for her brand of mascara. After locating the familiar dark blue package, she reached for her color.

"Stop!" Wendi commanded. "You can't buy that."

"What is wrong with you? Of course I can buy it. I'm older than you. I can do what I want."

"You can't buy makeup from a grocery store. It's disgusting. You have to get it at the mall."

The rich truly are different, Melissa thought. "It's about three times the price at the mall. I don't need some fancy name on the label to make me happy."

"Melissa, packaging is very important. You wouldn't want people to think..." The preteen floundered. "I mean, what would..."

"Just as I've suspected. You're a snob. But don't worry." She patted the girl's shoulder. "I won't hold it against you."

"I can't stand this. I'm sorry, but I won't be able to wait with you in the checkout line. I mean, what if one of my friends saw me with that package?" She pointed at the offending tube and sighed. "I don't like to do favors, but I won't tell my mother."

"I'm so relieved." Melissa clutched at her chest dramatically and sighed. "Thank you, my child. I'd hate to lose my position over something like this. I prefer to risk my career over powder or deodorant."

"Ha, ha." Wendi turned away. "I'll be in the magazine section when you're finished."

"Good thing," Melissa called after her. "Because I'll be using coupons."

"Whatcha doing, Dad?" Wendi asked as she walked into Logan's study.

He glanced up and smiled. "Reading. I know." He held up his hand. "Don't you yell at me, too. Melissa's already been in here twice to complain I'm not following the doctor's orders."

"I'm going to Mom's tomorrow." Her fingers played with the hem of her T-shirt, the twisting reminding him of when she'd been a little girl.

"Come here." Leaning back in the swivel chair, he held out his arms. When his daughter was settled on his lap, Logan stroked her long hair. "Are you worried about being gone?"

"No."

"I'll miss you."

"Really?"

The raw concern in her eyes pulled at his heart. When she was scared, like now, he knew she'd be his forever. Yet there were times when she seemed all Fiona. The older she got, the more she reminded him of her mother. It wasn't just the green eyes flashing like emerald flames. It was the walk, the smile, the need to possess the newest, most expensive whatever.

"Don't grow up, Wendi," he murmured against her head. "Stay my perfect little girl forever."

"I will, Daddy. I promise."

The grandfather clock in the hall ticked loudly, marking the passage of time. "Want to go for a swim?" he asked.

She jumped off his lap. "Last one in the pool clears the table after dinner."

Wendi ran out of the room, narrowly missing plowing into Melissa, who was standing in the doorway.

"Where does she get her energy?" she asked with awe. "It tires me out just to watch her."

Logan shrugged. "Youth. Vitamins. Who knows? Are you back to check up on me? I wasn't doing anything I shouldn't."

"Don't try and look innocent. It's too late. I know you've been reading."

She tried to look angry, but he saw the smile tugging at the corner of her lips. "Do I get a spanking?"

"Not on your life. I don't cater to any kinky demands by my patients."

"Three days," he said.

"Three days what?"

He leaned closer and leered. "In three days you go from being my nurse to being my employee. Then who will be in charge?"

She laughed. "I'm scared. See." She held out her hand. "I'm shaking."

"Talk is cheap, little one. We'll find out how brave you are when *I'm* the one signing the paychecks."

"Get a life."

He chuckled. At last his irreverent companion had returned. Good thing. He couldn't have endured an entire summer of Melissa kowtowing to his every demand...it would be too boring for words.

"Da-ad." Wendi stood in the hallway, her hands on her hips. "You haven't even put your suit on. I thought we were going swimming."

"Be right there." He smiled at Melissa. "Want to join us?"

"I...me, swimming with you? No. No." She shook her head and backed out of the room. "I couldn't. I mean I have so many things to do that are..."

"Name one."

"Ah...I have some, ah, letters to write that, ah, need writing."

Her face became rosy. He leaned close and inhaled her perfume. "Chicken."

"I'm not afraid."

"Prove it."

"I have no need to participate in your childish games."

"Cluck, cluck, cluck."

The car was a Bentley, dark blue with gleaming chrome. Despite his conservative uniform, the driver stepping out to open the back door looked as if he could have modeled for Mr. July in a male swimsuit calendar.

"Bye."

Melissa turned from the window and smiled at Wendi. "Bye. Have a good time."

"I'll be back tomorrow. Probably after dinner. If you need anything..."

Melissa walked forward and gave the girl a swift hug. "I'll be fine. Really. Your dad has a doctor's appointment in the morning, but other than that, we'll be here."

Wendi's hair was pulled back in a French braid. Her shorts set was preteen chic, but the expression on her face was all little girl. "You won't have a good time without me, will you?"

"Never. Now get out of here."

Wendi picked up her bag and darted out the front door. "Bye, Dad." She ran across the driveway and ducked into the Bentley.

Melissa saw Logan watch his daughter leave. His hands were clenched at his sides. The lean lines of his jaw tightened slightly as he swallowed.

"She'll be back."

"I know." He spoke without looking away from the departing car. "But it's always different. Her time with Fiona changes her and there's nothing I can do to make it stop."

Melissa used the corner of the towel to wipe the steam from the bathroom mirror. After pinning back her wet hair, she began to apply a light coat of makeup. The steaks were ready to throw onto the grill. The salad was made, the potato salad was out of its carton and in a crystal dish. Everything was prepared but her.

Somewhere in the distance, a door slammed. Melissa jumped and spilled base over her fingers. This is stupid, she told herself. After all this time, there was no reason to feel nervous around Logan. She'd seen the man practically naked. And this wasn't the first time they had spent the night alone. The first evening he was out of the hospital, Wendi had stayed over with a friend. Nothing was different now. It was just a case of an active imagination working overtime.

But it *was* different, a little voice whispered. Logan wasn't injured anymore. He was mobile and virile and the best-looking man she'd ever seen. Help!

She took a deep breath. *I am calm. I am in control.* Yeah, right. Then why was her heart pounding like a jackhammer? Hundreds, no thousands of women had dinner with men every evening. They all got through it without making complete fools of themselves. So could she.

The tube of mascara sat on the counter beside the sink. A smile curved her lips as she applied the store-bought product to her lashes. Good thing Wendi wasn't here; she'd probably die from shame-induced heart failure.

She plugged in the curling iron, then flipped on the blow dryer and started on her hair. When the fine strands were dry, she brushed them away from her face and began the tedious process of adding body to limp, uncooperative hair.

In five minutes, half-a-dozen fat sausagelike curls sat on the top of her head. A quick shake sent them tumbling down, leaving the tiniest bit of lift at her crown. Maybe she could puff them up with her comb, then spray with hairspray and...

One hand dropped the metal rod into the sink, the other covered her mouth. What was she doing? This wasn't a date. This was dinner with her soon-to-be boss. He expected a sensible woman who was going to look after his daughter, not some femme fatale in training.

After unplugging everything, Melissa stormed into her room and stood in front of the closet. Shorts? Too casual. A dress? Too suggestive. How about...

"He's not going to even notice, so it doesn't really matter," she said aloud, then closed her eyes and pulled out a shirt.

"When do we eat?"

Logan's voice startled her and the pot lid slipped from her hand. The aluminum crashed to the floor then spun several times before settling in silence.

Without glancing in his direction, she reached down. Their heads cracked. "Ouch!"

"Maybe I'd better let you do the cooking," he said, stepping back and rubbing his temple. "I could watch and offer helpful suggestions."

"Thanks."

He motioned to the table in the kitchen. "Are we eating here or outside?"

"It's still over a hundred. How about in here?"

"Great. I'll do the honors."

His step was silent as he walked into the dining room. She looked down and swallowed... hard. His feet were bare. Her eyes moved back to her own naked toes. It was silly to be rattled, she told herself firmly. But somehow the two of them, like that, seemed so...intimate.

"I thought we'd get wild and have another bottle of wine," he said as he returned. A pale rose tablecloth was tucked under one arm, his other hand held the bottle and napkins.

She stepped back to avoid him brushing too close to her.

He grinned. "You are skittish, aren't you? Always ducking out of the way."

The words were teasing, but his voice caressed each sound as though it were a priceless jewel.

"Skittish? I don't imagine that's supposed to flatter me."

"I like it."

The day before, he'd stopped wearing his dark glasses indoors. His eyes glowed. The flecks of gold reflected the light as though a thousand prisms were contained within the darkening depths. Faint scars marred the perfection of his face. They'd continue to fade, but his cheeks would always carry physical proof of the accident.

Firm lips tilted at the corner. The memory of their taste, their touch, was never far from her conscious mind. If she lowered her lids for just a second, she could relieve the exquisite contact.

One strong masculine hand tossed the cloth on the table, then reached out and traced the line from her ear to her chin. Electric fire seeped from his fingers into her skin, then deeper...into her heart.

"Melissa." He dropped his arm. "The grill's burning."

"What? Oh." She quickly turned down the flames. "I'm ready to put on the steaks. Are you hungry?"

"I guess you could say that."

He was standing so close, she had to look up to meet his eyes. "Logan, I..."

"How tall are you?"

"Five-three."

He tugged on her bangs. "That's pretty short. I didn't realize how much I like that in a woman."

Hope leaped briefly into her heart, then the vision of the tall and beautiful Fiona filled her mind. Who was she kidding? He wasn't interested, he was just passing time. "Five-three isn't short, it's—"

"Medium. Yeah, I remember."

She pushed her way past him. "You just like the fact that you get to look down on me. Now that your eyes are better, you think you're hot stuff."

"And you're determined to keep reminding me I'm not?"

When had it gotten so difficult to lie? "Exactly."

. "So what made you decide to become a nurse?"

Melissa spooned more potato salad onto Logan's plate. "I already told you. When I saw the naked guys in the locker room."

"Give me a break. Was someone in your family ill?"

She jerked her head up to stare at him. "How did you know?"

"Wild guess. I've heard that's how a lot of people get interested in medicine."

She sipped her wine. The crisp taste lingered on her tongue and she savored the sensation. By the time summer was over, she'd have a lifetime of memories stored up—individual moments to be examined through the long winter that would follow her time with Logan.

"My grandmother lived with us the year before she died. I guess I was about Wendi's age." Her brow furrowed as she tried to remember. "My sisters were busy with school projects and both my parents worked, so I took care of her. She was my best friend."

Logan leaned forward and touched her hand. "You must have loved her very much."

The lights in the kitchen had all been turned off, except for a single bulb above the stove. A lamp by the eating area door illuminated the table and three fat, dripping candles provided a flickering glow. She wasn't sure if it was the night or the moment or the man, but for the first time she was comfortable with the past.

"I spent every afternoon with her. We'd talk, or I'd read. Sometimes, we just sat in silence. I'd brush her hair or hold her hand." She blinked to contain the burning moisture.

"You're a very restful person. And I should know. After all, I'm not the easiest guy in the world to get along with."

"No! You think so? I hadn't really noticed." She laughed.

He poured more wine. "So then it was off to nursing school?"

Melissa took a bite of her steak and chewed. "Not exactly. I wanted to be a . . . never mind."

"What? Tell me." He leaned forward and grinned. "A what? A zookeeper?"

"Hardly."

"A test pilot?"

"A doctor, okay? I wanted to be doctor. Pretty stupid, huh?"

"No. Why would you say that?"

"Because I wasn't that bright. I got average grades, but nothing special. My parents told me . . ." Even now she could hear them explaining, oh so calmly, why she couldn't go to medical school. She wasn't smart enough; there were more deserving students; the family needed the money for her sister's wedding. Wouldn't nursing school be more sensible? She looked away from him. "They convinced me that I'd be better off as a nurse."

"And now?"

"And now I suppose they were right."

"So you went to school and met a handsome doctor?"

She smiled. "Handsome, no. As for the doctor part, does podiatry count?"

Logan laughed. "You're kidding?"

"Jeff wouldn't have appreciated your humor."

"Jeff? So what happened?"

She pointed at his plate. "Are you done?" He nodded and she stacked them together. "The usual. We dated, we lived together, I planned on getting married, he planned on getting out."

"What does that mean? He left? For another woman?"

"Silly, isn't it? They tell you at nursing school that young medical students are looking for a meal ticket. But it's hard to remember that when you're innocent and starry-eyed. I did warn you my life was boring."

She carried the plates to the sink and started running water to rinse them off.

"Then you started nursing terminally ill children."

"If you're planning on playing Dr. Freud, don't bother. I've already figured it out for myself."

He put plastic wrap over the bowls of salad, then set them in the refrigerator. "I wasn't going to say a word."

"That would be the first time," she mumbled under her breath.

"What was that?"

"Nothing," she said sweetly.

"I heard you, Ms. VanFleet. You better watch your step. I'm about to be the boss around here."

"Get out of my kitchen, *Mr.* Phillips."

He lingered in the doorway. "Are you reading to me later?"

"As soon as I'm done here."

He smiled and left the room.

After she'd wiped the counters and started the dishwasher, Melissa walked into Wendi's room. She wanted to check that the young girl had turned off all her stereo equipment. A red light indicated that the VCR was still on. She flipped the switch, then stood staring at the portrait.

The woman Jeff had left her for had been a successful and beautiful pediatrician. Only the best, he'd joked as he'd packed. Stunning as the tall blonde had been, she was no match for Fiona.

She remembered reading somewhere that the world was divided into the haves and have-nots. What was true in economics was also true in love, she thought. Fiona and the doctor were the haves. They received the flowers, the diamonds, the Jeffs and the Logans. Where did that leave women like her?

"I believe we left our intrepid detective about to give Belinda a rather thorough questioning."

Logan leaned back on the sofa. The night had finally started cooling off. The living room's French doors were pushed open to allow in any breeze. Melissa sat across from him. The light shone directly over her shoulder, flooding the book and outlining her left breast.

Not a bad way to spend an evening, he thought as he eyed the curve. A good book, a good wine, a good woman. There were worse...

He sat up. Where the hell had that thought come from? Melissa wasn't his woman. She was here to look after his daughter. If he came on to her, which he had absolutely no intention of doing, he'd not only be breaking his own rules, but he'd be acting as badly as the bastard she'd talked about at dinner.

Melissa glanced at him, her eyes wide. "What's wrong? Are you in pain?"

"Stop asking me that. I just thought of something I need to take care of when I call the office on Monday." He settled back down.

"Okay. Chapter seven. 'Julian stared at Belinda. Even as her red lips spoke the lies, he wanted to believe her. There was something about her voice that drew him closer and closer...'"

Logan shifted. Maybe he should have left the air-conditioning on or chosen another book. The detective series had taken a turn for the romantic. He'd been without a woman for a long time. If Melissa continued to speak with her sultry voice embracing each word with innuendo, the direction of his thoughts would soon become graphically apparent.

Maybe it was time to call one of his sophisticated lady friends and spend an evening indulging in uncomplicated sex. He glanced at Melissa. What was she like in bed? Was she silent and passive, waiting for the man to make the moves? Or did she initiate, meeting more than halfway, pushing out the limits of pleasure?

Sweat formed on his brow. He wiped it away with the back of his hand and shifted on the sofa.

Melissa watched Logan out of the corner of her eye. Why had she picked up this book tonight? "'Julian slipped the blouse from Belinda's shoulders. Her bare breasts gleamed like polished globes of golden skin. "Take me," she whispered. "Take me hard."'"

Melissa coughed and set the book down. "I need to get a glass of water."

"Fine."

She walked into the kitchen. Was it her imagination or had Logan's voice sounded slightly strangled. She groaned softly and leaned her head against the refrigerator. He was probably embarrassed, thinking this was her way of trying to entice him. After all she'd told him about her past, he'd feel sorry for her and...

The scenario was too awful to contemplate. She filled a glass with ice, then added water. Maybe she could just skip ahead a couple of pages in the book and hope it returned to the mystery. Another paragraph of Julian and Belinda kissing and touching and she would be tempted to rip her clothes off and beg Logan to take her. Already she could feel the liquid warmth settling against her private places. Taut nipples rubbed exquisitely in her bra. Why couldn't she be more like Fiona and less like herself?

She held the cold glass against her forehead for a second, then turned back into the living room. "Where were we? Oh, dear. I've lost my place." She flipped ahead one page, then two. "This looks like it. 'The body hadn't been dead more than an hour...' "

The air conditioner clicked on, but the cool air wasn't helping. Melissa rolled over on the bed, then flung off the sheet. She was hot and tired and cranky, and sleep was about the furthest thing from her mind.

Erotic pictures, fueled by the book, filled her brain. Only instead of the sensuous Belinda and ever-intelligent Julian, the characters in her X-rated drama were Logan and herself. Half-formed images of embraces mingled with the real memory of their kiss. With each breath, his scent haunted; with each heartbeat, his voice echoed.

Sighing in frustration, she swung her legs over the side of the bed and stood up. Maybe there was still a little wine left. A glass might help her relax enough to sleep. And if that didn't work, there was always the old cliché of a cold shower.

After slipping on a robe, Melissa tiptoed down the hall and into the kitchen. The bottle contained about an inch of ruby liquid. It would have to do.

She sipped delicately, then drank down a long swallow. The tartness made her cough, but a relaxing warmth flared in her belly.

Soft moonlight shone through the kitchen window and highlighted the blooming garden. The temptation to walk into Logan's room and slip into his bed was strong. But it was only a fantasy. The look of horror on his face would be more than she could stand. Besides, she wasn't interested in just one night of pleasure. She wanted a lifetime.

Finishing the glass, she smiled. Although one really incredible night wouldn't be a bad trade. She went through the living room on her way to the hall. A sound outside caught her attention. The French door was open and someone was in the pool.

The swimmer moved with powerful strokes, cutting easily through the water. When he reached the far end, he turned and swam back.

She ducked behind the drapes and continued to watch. Despite the darkness of the night, she recognized those shoulders, the proud shape of the masculine head.

It would be so easy to join him, she thought. To drop her nightgown and robe on the ground and slip into the gently lapping water.

Logan stood up in the shallow end. The moonlight reflected off his naked body. Melissa drew in a breath as she admired the perfectly sculpted back and waist. His buttocks were firm and rounded with an indentation on each side. She took a step toward the patio. He leaned his head back to stare at the moon, then dove into the water and began to swim again.

Back in her room, she lay awake and listened for the sound of his return. Footsteps passed outside her door without ever pausing... not even for a second.

Chapter Six

"The doctor says I'm as good as new," Logan said as he walked out of the examining room.

Melissa looked skeptical. "Uh-huh. You expect me to believe that from you? Mr. I-don't-need-to-follow-the-doctor's-orders-because-I'm-such-a-swell-guy." She set the magazine on the coffee table in front of the couch and stood up. "I want to verify this with him myself, if you don't mind."

He grinned. "I love it when you act tough. Here." He opened the door to the examining room and ushered her inside. "I asked the doctor to speak to you directly."

By the time Melissa had been convinced that he was allowed to resume all normal activities, it was close to lunch. On their way to the elevator, she dug the car keys out of her purse, but he snatched them away.

"My turn to drive. I couldn't bear to listen to you pop the clutch one more time."

She glared up at him. "I warned you I hadn't driven a stick shift more than a couple of times. You were the one who insisted we bring that...that..."

"Yes?"

"Sports car!"

"You're talking about the love of my life. She's fast, responsive, beautiful. What more could a man want...from a car, of course."

Dark lashes fluttered at him. "Of course," she murmured. "Whatever else could you be talking about?" The elevator arrived and the doors swooshed open.

The square space was already half-filled with workers heading for lunch. Logan followed Melissa on, then slipped behind her. They both faced front. Various colognes and perfumes mingled in the air, but he easily identified her spicy-sweet scent.

The top of her head came to his chin. They stood less than three inches apart. When the elevator stopped at the next floor and several more people squeezed on, she was forced to move closer to him. He rested one arm around her waist and pulled her nearer. She was soft. Curves fitted perfectly against the hard planes of his chest and thighs.

"I hate crowded elevators, don't you?" He grinned but was careful to keep his voice serious.

"Y-yes."

He could feel her heart racing, as though she were running a marathon. Her left breast rested a scant inch above his hand, and he fought the urge to move up and search the generous curve. If only...

The doors separated and the crowd flowed out into the foyer of the building. Melissa stepped quickly until a respectable distance was between them.

"Are you hungry? We should probably head back to the house. I guess you have a lot of work ready to get started on.

So you're going back to the office in the morning? Boy, you must be excited." Finally her chattering came to an end.

"Are you done?" he asked as he folded his arms across his chest. "If so, I have a surprise."

She swallowed. "What kind of a surprise?"

Placing his hand on the small of her back, he guided her toward the parking lot. "You're just going to have to trust me on this one."

They collected their sandwiches from the deli and headed across the street. A wide expanse of green lawn marked the entrance to the park.

"One of the founding partners of the firm where I work had a hand in designing the playground," Logan said as they walked along the wooded path.

Melissa laughed. "So we're worshiping at the shrine of the omnipotent?"

"Something like that."

They found a quiet corner behind a hedge of juniper bushes. A weeping willow provided lacy shade and gave the illusion of privacy. Several feet away, children played by the pond, trying to convince the wary ducks to partake of their offerings.

Logan flipped open the blanket he'd stored in the trunk and let it settle on the soft grass. "Madam, we have a wonderful table over here with a view of zee grounds." He bowed elaborately, then plopped down beside her. "I love it here. In college, I used to come all the time and eat lunch or dinner, or just sit by the pond." He shrugged. "It was, as we used to call it, a cheap date."

Melissa unwrapped the food. "Are you trying to tell me you used to be a starving student?"

"Not starving, maybe just hungry. My parents felt working my way through school would help me build character."

"And was the plan successful?"

He returned her smile. "I guess if you have to ask, the answer is no."

She sat crossed-legged on the blanket. Navy slacks clung to her full hips and outlined her thighs. The navy-and-white-patterned T-shirt emphasized the lushness of her breasts. By conventional standards she wasn't model-thin. But he liked the extra ten or so pounds filling out her frame. God knows he'd had enough skinny women to last him a lifetime. Fiona had dieted religiously and then had resorted to surgery to give her the lean, hungry appearance of a third-world refugee. He'd even had one date with a woman who'd proudly explained that she kept herself lean by eating whatever she wanted and then throwing up afterward. It was a disgusting thought that had led to an early end to their evening.

"Look."

He glanced up and saw Melissa pointing to a squirrel. The rodent stood on its back legs about two feet away, sniffing inquiringly in their direction.

"Don't even think of feeding it."

"But, Logan, he looks hungry. How can you resist those eyes?" She tore off a corner of her sandwich. "Come on, sweetie. Here you go."

The animal inched closer.

"It probably has rabies," he said.

"What?" she shrieked.

The squirrel jumped. They both glared at him.

"What did I say?" Logan asked.

She tossed the bit of food to the end of the blanket, and the furry creature grabbed it and ran off. Logan drained his can of soda and reached for another one. "He'll be back with about twenty of his friends."

"Don't worry. I'll protect you." She took a bite of her sandwich.

The sound of a siren roared past, then faded. He stretched out on the blanket. "It's hard to believe we're in the middle of the city. I used to bring Wendi to this park, when she was little. We had a small apartment about three streets away. It was close to the office and the studios."

"Sounds like good times. Do you miss them?"

He glanced at Melissa. Her long lashes swept down to hide her expression, but there was something stilted in her voice. Dappled sunlight filtered through the trees and sparkled on her hair and face.

"You have a speck of mustard right there." He touched the corner of her mouth.

She wiped the area with her fingers. "Is it gone?"

"Yes."

"Thanks."

She leaned back on one elbow. Logan waited, but that appeared to be all she was going to do. Fiona would have run screaming for her mirror and then retired to "repair" her face.

"Sometimes I miss Wendi being little. She's growing up so fast these days. In another couple of years, I'll just be the guy standing between her and a good time with her friends."

"She loves you very much, Logan. Don't lose sight of that."

"I know." He plucked at a blade of grass. "Fiona never wanted to come to the park. She hates places where she can't control the lighting."

"She's very beautiful."

"You've seen the picture in Wendi's room." It was a statement, not a question.

"Yes, and a bit of her show."

He rolled onto his stomach and looked at her. One hand supported her head, the other traced random patterns on the blanket; her eyes were carefully averted. "You don't strike me as the soap type."

"I just happened to catch a glimpse... one day."

"Very diplomatic. I know Wendi watches whenever she can. Did she rope you into joining her?"

"I like Wendi."

He reached out and patted her hand. "You're going to be a great mother someday, Melissa VanFleet. Too bad you can't teach a class, Fiona could use a few lessons."

"I'm sure she's very busy with the show and all."

Why was she defending his ex-wife? he wondered. If the roles were reversed, Fiona wouldn't even waste a breath on a person who couldn't further her career.

"It's not just the soap. Fiona is... different. Something about her beauty draws people to her. Every woman wants to discover her secrets, every man wants to possess her. She's difficult not to love." He pushed up into a sitting position. "Wendi is caught up in the glamour and excitement. She'd rather live with her mother, but..." He shrugged.

"Fiona didn't want her."

"How did you know?"

"I guessed." Melissa looked up at him, her brown eyes filled with compassion. "You're wrong about Wendi. She wants to live with you. Fiona's like having ice cream, fun for a treat or after dinner, but you wouldn't want it as a steady diet. Eventually you'd get sick of all the sweetness. Besides..." Her smile faded. "I'm sorry. I didn't mean to imply... I mean, I didn't want to insult..."

Color flooded her face. The flush of embarrassment crept up until the part in her hair was red.

He laughed. "You're right about Fiona. She is hard to take as a steady diet. I should know. Come on." He stood up and held out his hand. "We should get back before it gets much later. Afternoon traffic in the city is the pits."

Melissa brushed off her slacks, then gathered up the blanket and put the used papers and napkins into the plastic container by the path. Fiona would have left the trash for someone else to deal with, he thought. But then, she would never have agreed to a picnic in the first place, or listened to a man talk about another woman. It had been a hard lesson, but he'd learned it well: Never believe packaging and never, ever trust a woman.

Melissa sat at the foot of Wendi's bed and clicked on the TV. Logan was on the phone with his office, and his daughter wasn't due back for several more hours.

"Don't torture yourself this way," she told herself as the containers of cleanser danced and sang their way across the screen. Yet when the show began, she didn't turn off the set.

"Oh, Roger...whatever will we do?" Fiona's character asked. Her green leather dress, the exact color of her eyes, clung from breast to thigh. Long, lean arms ended with perfectly tapered fingers. Dark hair swayed against her back with each graceful movement. "Tell me you love me."

"I love you," the man whispered, then leaned forward and trailed kisses along Fiona's shoulder.

Had it been like that with Logan? Melissa wondered. What was it he'd said in the park? Fiona was difficult not to love. Did *he* still love her? Had she been the one to leave? Did he long for her return?

She turned her head and caught sight of herself in the mirror over the dresser. Plain, insignificant features stared back. She looked away.

"I'll always love you," Fiona said as she gazed at the camera lens. The shot tightened until only her face filled the screen. "Nothing will change the way I feel."

Melissa glanced from the TV to the mirror. Who was she kidding? What hope did one ordinary woman have against all that? It would take more than surgery...it would take a miracle and right now, she was fresh out.

* * *

The front door slammed. "I'm back," Wendi called. "Did you miss me?"

Melissa started the dishwasher and walked into the foyer. Logan was already gathering his daughter into a hug. An overnight case and a shopping bag slumped together where she'd dropped them.

"Were you gone?" he asked as he pulled her close. "I didn't notice. Did you notice, Melissa?"

"Not me."

Emotions flooded her heart as she watched the father and daughter hold each other tight. The fierceness of their embrace belied the briefness of their separation.

Wendi stepped back and glanced at Melissa. Her French braid was coming loose. Dark tendrils curled around her ears. Hesitation, shyness, and the need for reassurance chased across the young girl's face. Melissa held open her arms.

The preteen smelled like expensive French perfume and chocolate. She was a bizarre combination of grown woman and little girl, still willing to be molded, yet ready to strike out on her own.

"I'm glad you're still here," Wendi murmured.

"Where else would I be?"

She pulled back and shrugged. "Mom said that someone with your skills shouldn't be wasting her time acting as nursemaid. She says I should be kept busy with piano and dance lessons. She says..."

Melissa shook her head. "It's my time, Wendi, and I don't consider it wasted. I want to stay with you."

"Mom says it was wrong of me to ask you to stay." Wendi stared at the ground and rubbed the top of her left tennis shoe against the back of her right leg.

Logan tugged on her braid. "Let's make a deal. Let's not talk about what your mom says. I hired Melissa, not you.

If you want to take dance lessons, we'll talk about it later, but for now, why don't you go unpack.''

"Okay." She picked up her overnight case, then dropped it on the floor and dug into the shopping bag. "Look what I got. It's a remote phone with a built-in answering machine."

"You already have a phone," Logan said stiffly.

"Yeah, but it's boring. This has automatic redial and I can get messages and everything. Mom says I can use it to screen calls. It's important that I only talk to the right people."

The muscle in Logan's jaw twitched ominously. "The 'right' people, Wendi? What does that mean?"

"You know, Dad. The cool kids. It's important to be popular."

He glared down at her. "What about finding friends who are loyal and honest? What about getting good grades and learning something in school?"

She shrugged. "Oh, that."

"Yes, that. Young lady, you'd better—"

Melissa touched his arm. "Logan, why don't I help Wendi unpack? You could discuss this later...when you feel more in control."

"I don't want..." He sighed. "Yes, that's a good idea." He leaned over and kissed Wendi's head. "Get settled. I have some work to do."

Melissa carried the suitcase and Wendi trailed behind her. When they'd reached her room, she flopped on the bed.

"Why is he mad at me?"

"He's not."

Wendi opened the box and pulled out the electronic phone. "He sure acts mad. He hates it when Mom buys me stuff, but I like it. Why does he have to be so mean?"

Melissa unzipped the case. "Your father loves you and he only wants the best for you. Sometimes parents don't agree on what that is. As you get older, your dad worries more."

"He doesn't want me to grow up."

"He'll get over it. All fathers do." She took out the dirty clothes and tossed them into the wicker basket in the corner.

"Did yours?"

Melissa closed her eyes as she remembered her parents' relief when she'd left for college. Even though the school had been close to home, she'd chosen to live on campus. It had been easier for everyone. "I have an older sister. By the time I grew up, he was already used to letting go."

Wendi turned on her stomach and scooted to the edge of the bed. Her long gangly arms hung over and reached to the carpeted floor. "Are both your sisters older?"

"No. I'm the middle one." Not the first born, not the baby. The boring, plain one sandwiched between two beauties.

"Were you the favorite?"

"Parents don't have favorites," she answered automatically, ignoring the stab of pain in her heart as she told the lie.

In less than a heartbeat, she was back in the old family kitchen, watching her mother bake cookies for Judy's ballet recital. Barely seven at the time, she'd asked her mother why she and her father loved the other two girls more. Her mother had protested, claiming that parents loved their children equally. Even then, she'd known it wasn't true. For the longest time, she hadn't realized that her mother had been telling the truth, as she'd seen it. For the longest time, she'd wondered what she'd done to make her parents not love her, and why they'd lied about their feelings.

"I'm glad I'm the only one," Wendi said. "At least I know I'm the favorite."

Melissa blinked away the tears and tweaked the girl's nose. "You'd be the favorite if there were ten kids in the house."

"Maybe." Wendi rolled on her back. "It's hard to know who's right. I love my dad, but he's so straight. Mom knows it's important to have the right friends and wear the perfect clothes. She wants me to be cool and date rad boys and stuff."

Fiona Phillips was still living the life of the prom queen, Melissa thought. And every day on her soap was another crowning ceremony. But it wasn't the real world.

"Your dad wants that, too, but he's interested in who you are on the inside, not just what you look like."

Wendi sat up and rolled her eyes. "That's totally boring. There are tons of girls who are smart and stuff, but nobody wants to hang out with them. What's the point of school if you're not popular?"

Melissa laughed. "Education?"

"Get a life."

"I have one, thank you."

"What did the doctor say about my dad?" Wendi asked.

"He's good as new and will be going back to work tomorrow."

"I'm glad he's okay."

"Me, too." She stood up. "I'll leave you to your remote telephone. There must be a dozen girls waiting anxiously to hear about your evening with a famous star."

Wendi glanced at the electronic device and frowned. "A couple of my friends have asked to meet my mom. You don't think..."

Melissa stepped forward and cupped her chin. The green eyes that met her own were startlingly beautiful...and very young. "I liked you even before I knew who your mom was."

"Thanks." She opened the sheet of directions. "I'm glad you're here," she mumbled without looking up.

"Me, too, Wendi."

After shutting the door behind her, Melissa drew in a deep breath. All this time she'd been worried about losing her heart to Logan, but the real threat might be his special daughter. In previous assignments, she'd gone into the job knowing that her patient was probably going to die. Despite the love she freely offered along with the medical care, a part of herself had been held back, protected from the pain. This time, she hadn't thought to erect the barrier, and her feelings for the girl had found a place for themselves. When the summer was over and she returned to her own life, there'd be two empty places inside.

She walked down the hall and hesitated outside Logan's office. He sat behind his desk, his back to the door as he faced out the window.

Bookshelves lined two walls and a drafting table the third. Between the two sat a small computer. He'd told her he used software to help with his designs. Afraid that the closeness would upset her equilibrium, she'd refused a demonstration. Now, it was all she could do not to pull him into her arms and offer comfort.

"Is she settled in?" he asked without turning around. Dark hair curled over the collar of his cotton shirt. The cream fabric contained flecks of gold that exactly matched his eyes.

"Yes."

"Does she think I'm mad at her?"

"Yes."

He placed his elbow on the armrest and leaned his forehead against his hand. "You don't believe in pulling any punches, do you?"

"I didn't think you'd want me to lie."

He motioned for her to take the seat opposite the desk. She crossed the hardwood floor and sat down. All oak and leather, every inch of the room proclaimed its ownership to be male.

"What do I do with her?"

"I don't think I understand the question."

He glanced up. A deep frown furrowed the area between his eyebrows. "Last time it was a CD player, this time it's a remote telephone. In another year, it's going to be diamonds or furs. How do I make her stop?"

"Have you tried talking to Fiona?"

He laughed harshly. "A hundred times. She smiles ever so sweetly and says nothing is too good for her little girl. It's not the money." Turning the chair back toward the desk, he picked up a pen and tapped it. "I can afford to give Wendi whatever she wants. But how do you compete with a fairy godmother?"

Lines of frustration bracketed the firm set of his lips. She longed to reach out and smooth away the pain, to replace the irritation with pleasure.

"Does it have to be a competition?"

"No. But it is." He shook his head. "I don't know what to say to get through to her. Any suggestions?"

"For Wendi or Fiona?"

"Either, both. Whatever."

"I've never met your ex-wife and I don't have any kids of my own, Logan. I'm sorry."

He leaned forward, the pen clasped tightly in his hands. "You used to be a little girl, Melissa. What does she want from me?"

"She wants you to love her and be there when she needs you. She wants limits and structure, however much she may rebel against both."

"So I'm the bad guy?"

She smiled. "She'll love you for it, I promise."

"When she's thirty. What about today?" He tossed the pen onto the desk and stood up. "You were smart not to get married and have kids. Keep it simple and no one gets hurt." He walked to the door. Shoulders broad enough to carry the weight of the world seemed weighed down by defeat. "I've learned my lesson, believe me. I'm not getting involved again."

The alarm went off at 6:30. Melissa hit the snooze button with enough force to send the plastic box skittering across the nightstand and into the wall.

"Great," she moaned as country music blared in the room. "I really need to hear about lost love and milk cows at this hour in the morning."

Last night Wendi had told her that her father left for work at 7:15. Getting up early to fix his breakfast had seemed like a good idea...at the time. But after a restless night and about three hours of sleep, the thought of facing raw eggs was less than pleasant.

"It's your job," she said aloud, hoping for motivation.

It didn't work. Just ten more minutes and...

The faint sound of Logan's shower drifted through the walls. Melissa sat upright and stared at the clock. Seven o'clock! Oh, God. Now what?

She sprang out of bed and raced into her bathroom. Five minutes later she emerged with a freshly scrubbed face, clean teeth and hair that still looked as if it had lost a fight with a ceiling fan. Her silk robe, an expensive going-away present from a grateful parent, covered her skimpy cotton nightshirt. Not haute couture, but then so few of her things were.

By 7:10 the juice was squeezed and bacon was sizzling in the pan. She cracked two eggs and settled them beside the frying strips. Death by cholesterol, she thought as she popped bread into the toaster. Tomorrow she'd have to serve oatmeal and fruit.

Morning was not her favorite time of the day and certainly not after so little shut-eye. It hadn't been her fault, she reminded herself, as she flipped the eggs over. The memory of her conversation with Logan would have been enough to keep anyone up, let alone the woman who was starting to care about him. News that he wasn't getting involved ever again shouldn't have been a surprise—all the warning signs had been there, no long-term girlfriend, his obsession with Fiona—but she'd been caught off guard all the same. His feelings for his ex-wife were obviously still unresolved.

Smoke from burning bread assaulted her nostrils. "Stop!" she shrieked as she raced across the floor and jerked up on the handle of the toaster. Two smoldering slices popped into the air and landed on the counter before sliding into the wet sink.

Perfect, she thought. What else could go wrong? Maybe the...the eggs! Spinning back, she grabbed the spatula and scrapped the congealed edges from the pan.

"Morning."

She glanced up and saw Logan standing in the kitchen. The dark gray business suit highlighted the strong, lean lines of his masculine body. The white shirt practically glowed against the deep red tie. Tycoon in action; it was a good look. Her heart sighed dramatically, then resumed its slightly elevated beat.

"Sit down," she ordered. "I have your breakfast ready."

He hesitated. "Melissa, I don't usually eat a big breakfast...."

His voice trailed off as she glared at him. "What are you talking about? I've fixed you something every morning."

"I was, ah, staying home. On workdays, I usually just grab a bite at the office."

She pulled the frying pan off the flame and dumped the contents onto a plate. "Perhaps you'd like to rethink your plan."

He looked around the kitchen, taking in the toast in the sink, the smoke still drifting from the toaster, her disheveled appearance and the irritation she could feel flashing in her eyes.

"Excellent idea. A man should start the day with a hearty meal." Setting his briefcase on the floor beside the table, he sank into a chair. "Got any coffee?"

"C-coffee?"

They both glanced at the cold, empty pot. She walked to the front door and unhooked the lock. "You're excused," she said. "Get out of here."

He grinned as he moved toward her. "I appreciate the thought. Maybe next time."

She shook her head. "There won't be a next time. I'll stick to leisurely weekend brunches, thank you very much."

"I'll be home by five-thirty."

"Go build a mall for your daughter to shop in."

By the time Melissa had gotten Wendi off to her camp and then stood under a steaming shower, she felt as if she'd spent forty-eight hours in a war zone.

Coffee went a long way toward improving her outlook. When the beds were made and the house picked up, she felt almost perky.

"Now what?" she asked as she stood in the center of the living room. It was almost nine-thirty. The day stretched endlessly in front of her. The cleaning people did all the heavy work and there wasn't enough laundry to make a load.

She could read. She could go to the grocery store and buy what she needed to make cookies for Wendi. She could get out that aerobic video she'd bought last year but never used.

Behind her, she heard the gate slam shut. The pool man sauntered onto the patio, his bottles and brushes hanging over the edge of the crate he carried.

Melissa walked to the French doors. The blue water sparkled invitingly. For three weeks she had thought about indulging, but hadn't wanted to wear a suit in front of Logan. After seeing Fiona in her teddy on the soap, whatever small measure of self-confidence she'd managed to hang on to had evaporated like a puddle on a sunny day. But now, there'd be no one to see, no one to judge her pale body.

She glanced at the clock. The pool man would be busy for about fifty minutes. That would give her time to run to the market and get chocolate chips. Afterward, an hour or so floating on the water would be just what the doctor—or nurse—ordered.

Chapter Seven

"**Y**ou should know better," Logan said as he shook the spray bottle of aloe vera.

"I do know better."

"You should have used sunscreen."

Melissa moaned as she lay facedown on her bed. "I did, but I couldn't reach my back and I wasn't supposed to fall asleep."

The whiny tone in her voice reminded him of Wendi. He grinned. "Can you pull up your T-shirt?"

"Yes, I'm not..." She started to lift her shoulders off the bedspread. "Ouch. It hurts."

"Let me." Logan knelt beside her and set the bottle on the floor. "I can't believe you'd be so irresponsible. This isn't like you."

"Pointing out my mistake over and over again isn't doing much to make me feel any better. Maybe I should wait and have Wendi spray the lotion."

"Wendi is still at camp and won't be home for a couple more hours. Good thing for you I only put in a half day today."

"How'd I get so lucky?"

"Fate." He grabbed the hem of the cotton top and slid it up her back. She raised up slightly, allowing him to pull it over her breasts and up to her neck. The white straps of her bra contrasted with the bright red of her burned back. "Why the hell are you wearing a bra?"

She turned her head to glare at him over her shoulder. "I don't have to answer that."

"Doesn't it hurt?"

"A little."

"Melissa, this is insane. I'm going to unhook your bra to spray your back and I want you to leave it off for the rest of the evening."

"But I couldn't..." The red flush on her face matched the burn on her back.

"You're acting childish."

"That is my right."

Had she always been this stubborn? "How about if I promise not to look?"

She mumbled something unintelligible.

"Is this how you feel when patients won't cooperate?" he asked as he moved his fingers under the hook.

"No comment."

The band of cloth separated easily. Stretching forward, he pulled the T-shirt off her arms.

"What are you doing now?" she asked, keeping her elbows pressed firmly at her sides.

"Trying to get this damn shirt off! I was going to get you one of my cotton ones. They're soft and button up the front. Any objections?"

"No, but I..."

The top was free and he tossed it across the bed. "To quote someone in this very room, 'You haven't got anything I haven't seen before.'"

Melissa slipped off the bra straps and groaned. "I should have known that remark would come back to haunt me."

Logan picked up the bottle and looked at her back. White skin in the shape of her swimsuit made the burn seem even angrier. "Take a breath," he instructed. "This is going to be cold."

She yelped once, then bore the treatment stoically. The gooey liquid would take several minutes to soak in.

He stretched out beside her and smiled. "Can I get you anything?"

"No."

Wisps of hair drifted across her cheek. Without thinking, he brushed them back, taking the time to trace the shape of her ear as he tucked the locks in place.

"How do you feel?" he asked.

"Stupid."

"I meant about the sunburn."

"So did I." She raised her arms up and shifted until her head rested on the backs of her hands. "Thanks for taking care of me. I promise I'll stay out of trouble from now on."

"This hasn't been your day, has it? First the disaster at breakfast and now this. You were safer when you were practicing medicine."

His gaze slipped from her face to the soft, pale skin at the edge of the burn. Below was the half-hidden curve of her bare breast. The generous bosom that pushed against her shirts was more enticing than he had imagined. He only had to reach down and touch . . .

He swallowed. "I'd better let you rest. I'll come back in a half hour with the shirt."

"Why can't I have it now?"

He laughed. "It's the only way I can be sure you'll stay put."

"I'll get you for this, Logan Phillips."

He could hardly wait.

"I'm not going back there and you can't make me." Wendi's announcement was accompanied by the slamming of the front door, followed by heavy footsteps moving toward her room.

Over the weeks, Melissa had learned that the young girl's greeting when she returned from camp was often a barometer of her emotional state. Apparently this hadn't been one of her better days.

She set down the cookbook she'd been glancing through and walked to the back of the house.

"Can I come in," she asked as she knocked on Wendi's door.

"I guess."

The girl sat on her bed. The dried tracks of what could only have been tears cut through the smudge on her cheek. One knee was pulled up protectively against her chest. "I'm not going back," she repeated.

"So you said, honey. Want to tell me what happened?"

"Nothing." Wendi's lower lip began to quiver. "It's stupid."

"What's stupid? I can't help if I don't know what we're talking about."

"I don't want your help."

Melissa sat down and pulled the girl close to her. At first she resisted, her frame stiff and unyielding, but gradually she relaxed until her head was on Melissa's shoulder and her arms wrapped around her waist.

"Tell me."

"M-Mark said I was ugly." The confession was accompanied by harsh sobs. "I—I thought he liked me, but he doesn't. I don't want to be ugly."

"What a horrid little boy. I can't believe he said that."

"He's not horrid, he's wonderful. But he hates me." Wendi sniffed and raised her head. "Why can't I be like my mom?"

"You are like your mother. Did this Mark person really say you were ugly? Were those his exact words?"

"N-no. He said—" She hiccuped. "He said Sally was prettier." Tears rolled down her cheeks.

"Shh." Melissa drew her close again and held her. Rocking back and forth, she murmured soft words of comfort. "He's just one boy. And if he can't see how lovely you are, then he's blind."

"You think so?"

"Sure."

Wendi leaned back and grabbed a tissue, then blew her nose. "But Sally..."

"I don't care about Sally. I care about you. You have incredible eyes and skin. And that hair." She touched the wavy tresses. "An all-around stunning package."

Wendi turned away. "You're just saying that 'cause you have to."

"I'm saying it because it's true. You're very pretty. And I find it hard to believe this Sally person is prettier than you." She looked at Wendi's red nose and puffy eyes. "Except maybe now, of course."

Logan's daughter giggled. "Yeah. I know. Mom looks awful when she cries, too."

Hard to believe, Melissa told herself, but a cheerful thought all the same.

"Do I have to go back?" Wendi asked as she wiped her eyes.

"I'm afraid so. Just ignore Mark. Are you and Sally friends?"

"Not really. She's kind of wimpy."

"What do you mean?"

"You know. She does *all* her homework and is nice to everybody."

"Gee, she sounds great."

Wendi rolled her eyes. "And you sound like Dad."

"Maybe you should try and get to know Sally. Then boys like Mark won't be able to pit you against each other."

"Maybe." She didn't seem convinced.

Melissa patted her arm. "Wendi, there's more to life than being pretty."

The girl pulled back and glared at her. "How would you know? You've never been pretty."

Melissa felt as if she'd taken a blow to her stomach. All the air rushed from her lungs with an audible sound. Shame, anger and hurt all filled her being, making it difficult to focus on anything but the child in front of her.

Wendi's eyes got wide, and she clamped her hand over her mouth. "Melissa, I'm sorry. I didn't mean . . ." Fear and regret were clearly fighting for expression, but it was too late.

"Don't worry. It's not wrong to speak the truth. You're right, Wendi. I'm not pretty now and I never was. But that doesn't make me less of a person than you or your mother." Stiffly, not quite sure her legs would support her, she rose to her feet and walked out into the hall.

A sense of calm overtook her. She'd handled that well, she thought. And it didn't hurt. Not at all. How could the truth hurt?

At last she reached her bedroom. For the first time in the six weeks she'd been living in the Phillips's house, after closing the door, she turned the lock. Only then did she allow the hot tears to escape from her eyes. All the pain stored up from years of minor hurts and disappointments swelled up and threatened to overwhelm her. It was so unfair, she screamed in her mind. Why?

But there was no answer, just the faint hum of the air conditioner and the carefully muted anguish of her sobs.

"Hey, kitten, what are you doing sitting in the dark?" Logan set his briefcase on the floor and walked over to Wendi. She was crouched on the living room rug, her back to the sofa, her knees pulled up to her chest.

"Daddy..."

Her voice was low and frightened. Adrenaline poured into his system, but he forced himself to speak calmly. "Is something wrong?"

"I...Melissa's..." She looked up at him. In the half-light, her eyes seemed enormous. Guilt stole all the sophistication and left behind a scared little girl.

He squatted beside her, his heart pounding frantically in his chest. "Is Melissa injured? Do I need to call the paramedics?"

"What? Oh, no. Everything's fine that way."

"Then what's wrong?"

"I..." She glanced down and swallowed. "I said something bad."

All this regret over a swear word? It didn't make sense. "Like what?"

"Oh, I can't tell you."

He tried to hide his smile. "Wendi, it's highly unlikely you have come up with an obscene word I haven't heard. I might have even used it."

"You don't understand. I said something that hurt Melissa's feelings." She bit her lip. "Daddy, is she going to go away now?"

"Wendi." He touched her face. "Tell me what you said."

"No. It's too...awful."

"Wendi." Frustration added an edge to his voice. "Tell me."

"I—I can't. I'm sorry."

"Have you said that to Melissa?"

"She hasn't come out of her room all afternoon."

His glance flew down the hall to her closed door. "I'd better check and see if she's okay. And you, young lady, you'd better think about what you've done and how you're going to apologize."

"I will, Daddy. Just don't let Melissa leave, okay?"

He ruffled her bangs as he stood up. "Trust me, kid. It'll be fine. Run on to your room. I'll come get you in a few minutes."

"Thanks, Daddy."

He sighed. How much longer would he be able to make things better for her? She was growing up so fast. He walked to Melissa's door and paused. If only he knew what Wendi had said, he'd have a better idea of how to set things right. Here goes nothing.

He knocked softly. "Melissa? It's Logan." Very smooth, Phillips. How many other men are in the house to knock on her door? "Are you all right?"

He heard the unclicking of the lock, then the door was pulled open. Melissa stood in her robe. One hand rubbed a towel against her wet head, the other clutched the lapels together. "Are you home already? I must have lost track of the time. Don't worry about dinner. I'll be dressed in a few minutes and then . . ."

When he stepped inside, she took a step back. "Logan?"

"Tell me what happened."

"I . . . nothing. Nothing happened."

He wanted to believe her, but she turned away as she spoke. The full curve of her bottom lip was swollen, and there were shadows under her eyes. "You've been crying."

At first he'd thought Wendi had exaggerated the situation. Twelve-year-olds weren't known for their grasp of reality. But now, facing Melissa, he saw pain in the stiff set of her shoulders and back.

"Don't be silly," she said, dropping the towel and picking up a comb. "I'm fine. I just took a little nap."

He grabbed her wrist and tugged until she was in front of him. Fresh from the shower, there was no scent of perfume, just the fragrance of the soap and shampoo and the essence that radiated from her skin. Her face was scrubbed clean; the robe gaped open slightly, allowing him a view of the top of one bare breast. Except for a length of silky fabric, she stood before him naked, raw and exposed. Even the hurt in her eyes could not be concealed.

Years ago, before he'd made the decision not to trust again, had he ever been this open? He'd always thought of Melissa as keeping herself hidden, but tonight he saw into her soul. The gentleness, the vulnerability, shamed him.

"I'm sorry," he whispered.

"You didn't do anything."

"I'm sorry my daughter hurt you."

Melissa closed her eyes. "She didn't say anything bad. You mustn't punish her."

He touched her cheek. "Tell me what she said."

"No."

"Then how can I fix it?"

She pulled back from the contact. "You can't."

But she was lying. He could see the hope flickering in her eyes. She believed he had the answer, but he didn't even know the damn question. "Tell me what to say."

The hope died. "You don't have to say a word. I'm fine. No, I'm better than fine, I'm terrific." She began combing her hair. "If you'll excuse me, I'll get dressed and start on dinner."

"Dammit, I don't want to..."

"Melissa?" Wendi stood just inside the door. "I'm sorry. I didn't mean to hurt your feelings. I—I..." Tears ran down her face.

"I know, sweetie." Melissa stepped forward and Wendi threw herself into her arms. "Hush. I know you didn't. It's all right."

"Don't leave. Please," Wendi cried against her shoulder.

Logan watched Melissa stroke his daughter's hair. Helplessness left him feeling angry and useless. Being sighted was no guarantee of finding the truth, he thought. How could he fix it if he didn't know what was wrong?

"You're stuck with me for the summer," she said. "Wild horses couldn't drag me away."

Logan hadn't known he was worried until relief settled around him. He would have hated to see Melissa go. Wendi depended on her for so much.

"I'm surprised you haven't reported me to the employment development department," Logan said as he dropped the Sunday paper onto the floor.

Melissa adjusted her hat and stared at him. It was about ten in the morning. They'd all eaten brunch and were now lounging by the pool. "Do you expect anyone to have the slightest clue as to what you're talking about?"

He leaned toward her and grinned. "I'm talking about you!"

"Thanks. I appreciate the concern."

"How long have you worked here?"

"Almost seven weeks."

"Exactly."

She sipped her coffee. "Does the hired help get a gold watch after seven weeks?"

"Melissa, I'm serious." And indeed he was. The smile had faded, leaving behind a businesslike expression. "You should have said something."

"Like . . . I want a raise?"

"No. You haven't had a day off. I can't believe I didn't notice. I guess you just fit in so well that I assumed everything was taken care of."

He thought she fit in. Melissa sighed softly. "I don't need time off. Wendi's gone more than she's here and you have the cleaning service. This is hardly the most taxing assignment I've ever had."

"Still, it's not right. You have a life of your own. We've been very selfish."

"Who's been selfish?" Wendi asked as she strolled out of the house. A beach towel hung over one shoulder while her portable radio was tucked under the opposite arm.

"You and me."

"I already told you. I did not eat that last cookie."

"I was talking about Melissa. She's been working without any free time."

"Mrs. Dupuis used to go to the museum and then have tea at one of the department stores."

Melissa grimaced. "Sounds like a fun time to me. I really don't need—"

"Nonsense. I distinctly remember you telling me you kept an apartment. Don't you want to make sure it's still standing?"

Logan pulled off his sunglasses and tossed them onto the table. The pale colors of his print shirt contrasted with the rich brown of his tan. Despite the fact that three feet of wrought iron and glass separated them, she could almost feel the warmth radiating from his body. Tawny eyes framed by impossibly long lashes sought out her secrets.

Sometimes, when the days stretched on endlessly and the mood was right, she allowed herself to pretend that all this was real. That Wendi was her daughter and Logan ... that he came home to her, needed her, ached for her, spending, as she did, each night in restless wanting. Sometimes she prayed for a miracle.

And then there were the days like today, when rude reminders of what was real pushed themselves to the front of her mind.

"I suppose I could go there for a couple of days, if you'd like," she said softly.

"Then it's settled. Let's see. Why don't you take off until Thursday."

"Thursday!" Wendi and Melissa spoke together.

"Daddy, she can't—"

"Logan, I don't—"

Logan glared at his daughter. Wendi spread her towel on one of the lounge chairs, then flung herself down.

Melissa drew in a breath. "I don't need that much time, Logan. Why don't I come back Tuesday?"

"Are you sure? I don't want to take advantage of you."

She almost laughed. "I'm sure. I'll go prepare a couple of things for you two to eat while I'm gone, then I'll be off."

Logan reached out and touched her hand. The contact was electric. After all this time, she should be used to the sensation of fire whenever he was near, but it still surprised her.

"We can eat out, Melissa."

"I know. I'll throw a couple of things together. Just in case."

Melissa exited the freeway and turned left. Her small apartment was across town from Logan's exclusive neighborhood and north and east of the city itself. Resting in the foothills of the San Gabriel Mountains, was the community of Altadena.

The houses on the top of the hill were a haven for the wealthy, but her street was about a mile below. The buildings were mostly old, constructed during the 1920s. The homes were large, some soaring four stories. Many had been converted into multifamily dwellings or duplexes.

She lived in a small apartment behind the garage of one of the more modest homes. Mrs. Graham, the owner, collected her mail while she was on assignment, and Melissa's rent check supplemented the older woman's retirement pension. The arrangement had worked well for almost six years.

After parking on the street, Melissa grabbed her overnight case and walked around to the back door. She'd called ahead to tell her landlord she'd be by, so the box of mail was out and waiting.

"Mrs. Graham," she called as she knocked on the screen.

"Melissa!" The elderly woman pulled open the door and ushered her inside. "How are you, child? It's been ages. Did you see your mail?"

"Yes, thanks. I've been working."

Small dark eyes, like those belonging to a perky robin, peered out of thick bifocals. Mrs. Graham was close to eighty, but she never talked about her age. She was from the old school: Health, politics and religion weren't discussed at her table.

"Can I get you some coffee?"

Melissa shook her head. "I'd like to get settled. Maybe tomorrow we can have lunch."

"I'd like that, dear. How long are you staying?"

"A couple of days, but I'll be back at the end of the summer." She walked to the door.

"Call me if you need anything." The older woman sent her off with a plate of cookies and an admonition to get some sleep. "I see circles under your eyes, young lady."

"Yes, ma'am." She picked up her mail and headed through the backyard.

Fruit trees grew in wild disarray. A grapevine, once trained and decorative, threatened to engulf the garage. Slipping the key into the lock, Melissa turned the metal, then pushed open the door.

She'd always thought the apartment had been built by dolls. Elaborate molding nudged up against the ceiling, and shutters were anchored at every window. But the rooms themselves were tiny. The living room had space for a love seat, lamp and TV. In the bedroom, the walkway between the foot of her double bed and the wall was about eighteen inches. If a mouse ever took up residence in the kitchen, they'd have to take turns using the facilities. Compared to Logan's house, it was a closet—but it was *her* closet.

After unpacking her few items of clothing, she checked the cupboards. Spices, flour and a can of green beans. Not very exciting. She made a list, then went to the market. Tonight there was an old black-and-white movie on one of the local channels. Maybe in the morning, she'd walk around the mall and check out the expensive mascara.

Pulling her car into the grocery store parking lot, she sighed. She should have told Logan she didn't want time off. But then he would have asked why, and that was one question she couldn't answer. What would he have said if she'd admitted she'd rather be working at his house than resting alone at her own?

Logan put down the blueprint and glanced out the window. Long shadows announced the sun had passed its zenith and day was slipping into night. When had an afternoon dragged on so long? he wondered. Wendi had gone to spend the night with a friend and he was home alone. The silence wasn't new. Yet before, he'd always known Melissa was in the house, even if he couldn't hear her.

He stood and stretched, then walked into his bedroom. Her touch was everywhere. A fresh bowl of flowers sat in the center of the coffee table. A matching container would be set in the living room and on the kitchen table. Two casserole dishes were on the bottom shelf of the refrigerator, one for tonight and another for tomorrow. The cookie jar was full, and a cake was waiting on the counter.

But it wasn't just homemade food and fresh-cut flowers. Melissa's presence lingered in the shadows of the house. Her words found their way into his daughter's vocabulary—the memory of her jokes made him smile. A half-read magazine reminded him of her passion for current events. She cared for them and fit in with an ease and graciousness that left him...

He needed a woman. He needed to bury himself into waiting warmth and forget what plagued him. For several weeks he'd lived with a soft, curvy female and not given in to desire. If only Melissa was sophisticated and bound by the rules that didn't let her get involved. Then he could take her and...

He laughed. If she was that kind of woman, he wouldn't be standing here wanting her. Another paradox of the universe. But then wanting what one could not have was a problem as old as man. If he couldn't have the real thing, maybe a substitute would do.

Logan walked purposefully back to his study and found his address book. Flipping the pages as he walked down the hall, he scanned the list. Too tall, too boring, too easy, too...

He hesitated outside Melissa's room. The bed was neatly made, and he'd bet his life that the bathroom was equally tidy. A small crystal bottle on the dresser caught his attention. Moving closer, he glanced over his shoulder as if expecting to be caught. But the hallway was empty.

The cut glass was devoid of designer labels. It was heavy and looked old and expensive. Funny, Melissa didn't strike him as the type to collect antiques. Maybe it had belonged to that grandmother she'd cared so much about.

He pulled off the cap and inhaled the subtle fragrance of her perfume. Memories washed over him—when he'd first come home from the hospital and she'd practically carried him to his bed; the feel of her body under his the night they'd kissed; the way she'd watched the squirrel in the park.

He placed the bottle back on the dresser and swore under his breath. Hadn't he learned his lesson? Did he need to make the same mistake again? Women couldn't be trusted. They chose not to be loyal...or faithful. The last thing he needed was some doe-eyed innocent destroying his carefully constructed world. All he wanted was sex and he knew just where to get it.

He sat on Melissa's bed and dialed the phone.

"Hello?" a soft, feminine voice answered.

"Jackie? It's Logan. How are you?"

"Logan, this is a surprise. Where have you been hiding all summer?"

"I, ah, had an accident and I've only been back at work about a month."

"I'd heard. Didn't you get my flowers?"

Logan reached up to loosen his tie, then realized he wasn't wearing one. He'd received over a dozen bouquets, none of which he'd been able to see. "Ah, sure. They were lovely."

"I'm glad you called, Logan. I'm having a few people over for dinner tonight. I could use a man...to make an eighth." Her voice implied he'd be making more than that.

It was the reason he'd called, he reminded himself. So why was he suddenly so reluctant to say yes? "Jackie, I'd..." His gaze fell on the crystal bottle. Damn Melissa all to hell. "I'd love to, but I promised Wendi we'd spend time together."

"Oh." Jackie sighed. "If you're sure."

"Yes." He was sure. He was sure he was going crazy.

Time for a few laps in the pool, he thought as he hung up the phone. Like about a hundred.

Melissa paused beside the display of blouses. A frilly pink one with lace where the sleeves should have been cried Wendi. Refusing to think how much the designer boutique could charge for a yard and a half of cotton, she set it on the counter and handed the girl her credit card.

Since the day Wendi had come home crying from camp, their relationship had changed. She'd been hurt by the girl's harsh words and Wendi, in turn, had been wounded by the pain she'd inflicted. The realization of vulnerability had exposed a growing affection between them. It had only been twenty-four hours, but she missed the little brat, almost as much as she missed Logan.

Her small apartment, once a refuge, now echoed with loneliness. She glanced at her watch. It was only three. The earliest she could go back was nine in the morning...a whole eighteen hours from now.

After collecting her package, she walked toward the movie theater. There had to be something she wanted to see, some humorous film that would take her mind off the tawny gold eyes of the man who had stolen her heart.

Chapter Eight

"**M**r. Phillips, there's a call for you on line two." His secretary cleared her throat. "It's a woman, sir, and she won't give her name."

Logan grinned. "Thanks, Cathy. I'll take it." Melissa sure was a shy little thing, he thought. He'd have to tell her it was all right to phone him at work if she needed something.

He picked up the phone. "Hi. What's up?"

"That's entirely up to you, darling."

His mind raced to put a name to the voice. A knot formed in his stomach. Jackie. He should never have called her last week. Talk about opening a can of worms. "What can I do for you, Jackie?"

"I was so disappointed you couldn't attend my little party. I was wondering if I could persuade you to make it up to me. Now that you're feeling better and all. I thought…" Her voice trailed off for a moment, then resumed about a half octave lower. "Maybe we could take a long lunch together. Talk about old times, new times. My apartment's not too far from your office."

"Sounds great," he said automatically as lust and logic battled it out. "But I'm afraid I have an appointment in a couple of hours and I won't be taking lunch today."

"What's the matter, Logan? Are you seeing someone?"

"No. Why?" He picked up a pen and started tapping it on the desk.

"I'd heard Fiona was between lovers. I thought maybe..."

He scowled. "I've been divorced for almost five years, Jackie. What Fiona does with her private life is none of my business. And quite frankly, I don't give a damn."

"I see." Jackie sighed. "I won't wait forever. We've been dancing in and out of each other's bedrooms for three years now. Maybe it's time to make a decision."

He closed his eyes and tried to picture Jackie's lithe body. All he could see was Melissa sending him off that morning, her brown eyes still heavy with sleep. She'd stood at the front door, handing him the paper and a bag of homemade cookies. No makeup, no pretense, no demands.

Jackie was right. It *was* time to make a change. He'd start by tying up a few loose ends.

"We've gotten along without each other for almost six months," he said. "And it wasn't difficult for either of us. I take that as an indication there wasn't anything to miss. If you want a decision, then this is goodbye."

He heard a sharp intake of air, then a moment of silence. "Damn you, Logan Phillips," she hissed. There was a click followed by dial tone.

Logan set the receiver down and glanced at the clock. He had to be in the valley by one. If he hurried, he could swing by the house and collect Melissa. He hadn't intended to share the ceremony with anyone, but she might be the one person to understand what it meant to him.

Touching the intercom switch, he spoke to his secretary. "Cathy, I'm leaving a little early. I should be back by three."

He could hear the rock music before he reached the front door. The pulsing beat of the bass vibrated the windows. Wendi! He'd thought she had camp today, but maybe not. How many times had he told the girl that she could damage her hearing with her loud stereo? And where was Melissa? Shouldn't she be keeping his daughter under control?

Between his conversation with Jackie and the steady drumming that was taking up residence inside his head, he was in no mood to put up with this sort of flagrant behavior. He fumbled with his keys and managed to open the front door.

Sound hit him, an almost physical wall of noise that made him clench his fists at his sides before striding purposefully into the living room.

"Wendi," he shouted. "How many times have I warned you..."

"Kick 'em high, now. One, two, three..."

He saw a bouncing Melissa. Clad only in a black-and-hot-pink leotard that did nothing to hide her curvy figure, she stared intently at the exercise video on the television screen.

Her back was to him. A dark patch of moisture stained the fabric between her shoulder blades. Shapely legs stepped up and down in time with the tanned blonde on the tape, only Melissa's flesh-and-blood exertions were much more exciting than any celluloid beauty. Her arms moved side to side, giving him glimpses of her breasts bouncing in time with the music. A sweatband held her short hair off her face.

He could stand here and watch for hours, but there was a group of priests waiting for him. Regretfully he reached down to the coffee table she'd pushed off to the side and picked up the remote control.

The video flickered, then froze in place. Silence filled the room and Melissa whirled to face him. Her face was red and she was breathing heavily. Sweat formed an uneven triangle, broad at her chest and narrowing at her waist. Lips outlined a perfect O and she blinked several times as if hoping to make him disappear.

"L-Logan?" she whispered.

"I guess you weren't expecting me home early?"

"No. I was just..." She waved toward the TV. "You know." She wouldn't meet his eyes as she scuffed her aerobic shoe against the corner of the coffee table.

"Are you almost done?" he asked.

"What? Oh, with the video." She walked to the VCR and ejected the tape. "Yes. Do you need something?"

Did he? Absolutely. He needed to know how her skin would feel when it was hot and wet. He needed to taste the salty perspiration as it trailed between her breasts. He needed to stand with her under the hot water of a shower and savor her clean, then decide which he liked better.

"I have an appointment in..." He glanced at his watch. "An hour and a half. I thought you might want to come with me."

"Me? Where?"

He grinned. "It's a surprise. Do you want to go?"

"Sure. Is it casual?"

"No. You'll need a dress. Nothing fancy, just something you'd wear to church."

"You're kidding?"

"You'll just have to trust me, won't you?"

Her brown eyes grew wide. She glanced down at herself and then up at his navy suit. "Excuse me," she said as she flew past him.

For a heartbeat, he thought about canceling his meeting and staying home with Melissa. When she stepped out of the shower, he could be waiting, naked... in bed. The contrast between her and the other women in his life was intriguing, to say the least. There was a wholesome quality that soothed as much as it aroused. God knows, he'd felt the sparks that flared when they accidentally touched. They couldn't exist only in his imagination. He didn't think Melissa would turn him away. And yet...

It was wrong, he told himself as he paced the length of the living room. Taking a woman like her wasn't the same as playing lover's tag with one of his women friends. She was honest and up-front, leading with her heart and not her fists.

He remembered his father telling him there were girls you played with and girls you married. Melissa was the marrying kind...and he wasn't. There'd never be another woman he'd trust with his feelings. He'd never give anyone a chance to betray him again. He'd never allow someone else to leave. And the only way to insure that was to never get involved.

Melissa leaned back in the passenger seat of Logan's sports car. The smell of his cologne mingled with the fine leather of the interior, and she inhaled the mixture. She'd always remember this, she thought happily. The sounds, the scents, the touches, they were the cornerstone of her memory bank. Years from now, when she was old, she'd think back on these times with Logan. She'd been content before she met him, she would be again. This time in between was like a dream—insubstantial, fleeting, existing only in her mind.

Glancing out of the corner of her eye, she admired the clean lines of his profile. The straight nose, firm lips, hard jaw. He was all man. If only...

She giggled softly. If she had a dollar for every time she'd thought "if only" about Logan, she wouldn't need to work for the rest of her life.

"What are you so happy about?" he asked.

"Just happy in general. Are you going to tell me where we're going?"

He turned left, accelerated up the ramp and onto the San Diego Freeway. "San Fernando."

That was a community at the north end of the valley. "You know that tells me nothing."

"How can you say that? I answered the question."

After glancing out the window, he shifted into fifth gear and moved into the far left lane. Midday traffic was light. As they crested the hill leading into the heavily populated valley, Melissa risked another look in his direction.

Logan had discarded his suit jacket and rolled up the sleeves of his white shirt. His tie was maroon with navy flecks. His tanned hand rested on the gear knob, a scant inch from her thigh. She brushed her fingers down her skirt.

"You look nice," he said without taking his eyes off the road.

His compliment warmed her heart. "Thanks. I hope it's appropriate for this mystery trip."

When he'd said pick something she'd wear to church, she'd thought he was kidding, but now she wasn't so sure. Her wardrobe leaned heavily toward casual clothes; her regular patients were more comfortable with her in jeans and sweatshirts. As her dating life bordered on catatonic, the need for simple elegant attire had never been a problem. She had one fancy silk dress, a suit more for winter than Southern California summer, and the two-piece outfit she'd put on.

The jacket was white, with navy trim and a striped inset at the bodice. The matching skirt was solid navy. Conservative pumps and a small bag completed the look. For once her hair had cooperated. Perhaps it assumed one humiliation per day was sufficient. If she lived to be a million years old, she'd never forget the horror of turning around and finding Logan watching her exercise. All that bouncing and jiggling. What must he have thought?

His hand moved on top of hers and stilled her restless fidgeting. "Calm down. You're going to be fine."

"I have to take your word for that, don't I?"

"Yes. And I'm going to enjoy every moment of keeping you in suspense."

He didn't move his hand. Slowly, inch by inch, she turned her wrist until her palm touched his. She braced herself, waiting for him to pull back or frown, but instead, his fingers laced with hers.

She stopped breathing. This wasn't the act of an injured man reaching out for any available comfort...this was conscious and deliberate. She exhaled a long sigh. The weight of his arm pressing against hers was heaven. Please God, don't let this journey ever end. Let them just drive forever. Let it be real.

"How long have you been doing aerobics?" Logan asked. "I don't remember hearing the video when I was home those weeks."

Melissa closed her eyes as she felt the heated blush climb her cheeks. She tried to pull her hand back, but he tightened his hold. "I've had the tape for a while, but I don't use it as regularly as I should."

"I know what you mean. There's a gym in the building where I work, but I only get there a couple of times a week."

She stared at his broad chest and flat stomach. Obviously they weren't even discussing the same concept. "It seems to be working," she said softly. "At least you don't have chubby thighs."

He raised one dark eyebrow and tapped his fingers on her leg. "Are we talking about these thighs?"

She nodded.

"I wouldn't call them chubby. They're feminine and fit you perfectly."

Great. He thought all of her was chubby. "A rose by any other name," she muttered.

"Is this a family problem?" he asked. "Sort of a curse on the VanFleet women?"

"No. My mother and sisters have perfect legs. I think grandmother had chubby thighs. Maybe that's why we got along so well."

"Women obsess too much about their bodies," he said. "Men don't care what you look like."

"Logan, you go to hell for lying, same as stealing."

"Okay. We care a little, but agonizing over five or ten pounds is crazy. I hope Wendi escapes the whole diet disease."

He untangled his hand and downshifted as the car moved off the freeway. The north end of the valley was old and, in many parts, run-down. Apartment buildings covered with graffiti lined both sides of the streets. Men looking for daily work lingered on corners.

"We're almost there," he said.

She still didn't have a clue as to where "there" was. The neighborhood made her uncomfortable, and the loss of physical contact with Logan didn't ease her apprehension.

He signaled and turned the sleek car into a parking lot next to a small Catholic church.

"You weren't kidding," she said, staring at the white stuccoed building.

"I told you."

"But..."

He stepped out of the car and moved to her side. After helping her out, he locked both doors and set the alarm. "About seven years ago, Father Jeremiah approached the architectural firm and asked if they would donate the design of a church. I volunteered. We raised some money and they got a bank loan for the rest. Today, the mortgage is paid off. There's going to be a ceremony in—" he looked at his watch "—ten minutes and I was invited."

Melissa looked up at the pointed spires reaching toward the heavens. "You did a wonderful job. The building reminds me of an old Spanish mission."

"Really?" He looked pleased as he tucked her hand into the crook of his arm. "That's what we were trying for. The old church had been destroyed by fire. There weren't many pictures, but the foundation gave me an idea of the layout." They moved up the short flight of stairs. "Some modernizing was involved. The wheelchair ramp over there, and of course the living quarters, but other than that, it's pretty much as it was seventy years ago."

The interior was cool and dark. Candles flickered along the center aisle and up at the altar.

"Logan, I'm so pleased you could make it." A middle-aged priest hurried toward them, his right arm outstretched. "Your generosity made this possible."

As the two men shook hands, Melissa tried to crush down her feelings of warmth and admiration. She was having enough trouble dealing with Logan without developing a serious case of hero-worship. Besides, what kind of person would turn down a request to build a church?

The ceremony was brief but meaningful. A handful of clergymen gathered in the back garden. Words were spoken, then the mortgage was burned in a small dish. After the ashes had been scattered, Logan took Melissa's hand and guided her around the juniper hedge.

"The first time I saw this place, it was a pile of rubble," he said.

"You'd never know it."

Around them, lush plants—bird of paradise, roses, marigolds—provided color against the trees heavy with fruit. A stone bench circled a gnarled old olive tree. In the far corner, vegetables ripened in the summer sun.

"When my boss called me in and offered me the project, I was delighted. I hadn't been with the firm more than a couple of years, so I took it as a sign he was pleased with my work."

Logan sat on the bench and pulled her down beside him. His forearms rested on his thighs; his hands were loosely clasped together. A single shaft of sunlight drifted across his head and highlighted the hint of red in his dark hair. When they'd arrived, he'd slipped on his jacket, and now she watched the lightweight wool stretch across his broad shoulders.

"I couldn't wait to get home and tell Fiona," he continued. "She'd worked late that night. I still remember sitting alone in the living room." He glanced at her briefly and tried to smile, but only his lips reflected humor. The expression in his eyes remained remote. "We couldn't afford much furniture yet, and she wanted only the best. There was one couch and a lamp. I don't know how long I waited. Till midnight maybe. But she finally came home. I told her about the assignment. She was outraged."

"Why?"

He shrugged. "She didn't like the idea of me working for free. When I explained how good it would look on my record and all, she acquiesced. After the construction was finished, she wanted to call the media and have them cover the event. You know, for publicity."

Lines of tension stiffened his back. Melissa longed to reach out and soothe away the hurt. She held back. It wasn't her place—he wasn't her man.

"Did you agree?"

"As a matter of fact, we argued about it. She moved out for a couple of weeks and then it blew over."

She'd left? Over that? Melissa frowned. It seemed so trivial. "I'm sorry."

He straightened up and slipped off his jacket. After laying it next to him, he leaned back and braced his elbows on the bench back. "Don't be. Fiona is . . . not like the rest of us mortals. We met in college. She was a sophomore and I was in my last year of school. It was pure chance. One of my buddies tutored to supplement his income. He had the flu and I took the session. Fiona was having trouble with calculus. And the rest, as they say, is history."

Melissa sighed. "It sounds very romantic. She must have been beautiful."

"Have you ever accidentally looked at the sun? For a long time afterward, you're still blinded by the light. That's how it was with me. I was taken in by a winning smile and a pretty face."

A sharp pain spread out from the center of her chest. A pretty face. It always came down to that. The pretty ones in life are the ones who win, she thought. It wasn't fair. It wasn't right. It was simply the way the game was played.

Part of her wanted to stop him from talking. Hearing about the love of his life wasn't doing anything for her ego or her heart. Yet the need to know everything about him, no matter how much it hurt, couldn't be denied.

"Was it a whirlwind courtship?"

"Nothing that romantic. Two months of lust. And then, she got pregnant." He glanced at her. "You look shocked."

"I'm n-not. I thought . . ."

"It was all roses? It was. For me at least. But Fiona had a plan. She knew she'd been born in L.A. for a reason. She was going to make it to the top and no baby was going to stop her."

"With an attitude like that, I'm surprised she decided to have it." She leaned on the seat back, then jerked forward when her shoulder came in contact with his hand. He pulled on her until she rested against the back of the bench.

"The day after she informed me, I got the job with the firm. Then I told her we were getting married. I was young enough or foolish enough to think it would all work out. She was practical enough to know she might not make it right away and could use a little financial support. Her family wasn't enthralled by her career choice."

He toyed with her hair. She could feel the gentle tugging, the occasional brush of his fingers, the soft breeze drifting against her neck. She *should* pull away or ask him to stop touching her. But she didn't. Soon enough he'd realize what he was doing and the sweet connection would be severed.

"Just before Wendi's second birthday, she got the job on the soap. Suddenly she was a star and things began to change."

"Logan, you don't have to tell me this."

He looked at her. The gold in his eyes seemed muted. Lines, deeper than she'd ever noticed, fanned out along his temple. "I want you to know. For Wendi."

"Oh. Of course." Could he hear the disappointment in her voice? For one moment she'd allowed herself to think he might want to tell her for himself, so that she could share his pain, ease his burden. Don't be a fool, she told herself. Don't get hurt any more than necessary. "I know you worry about her."

"She's growing up so fast. I wish . . . I wish I could make it stop, but I can't. You . . . she likes you, Melissa. I was hoping you could try and influence her."

"How?"

He shrugged. "Keep her on this side of sanity. She's all I've got."

"I'll do my best."

"I know."

He moved his hand to her far shoulder and pulled until her head rested in the crook of his neck.

There was more to the story. She felt it in the way tension corded the muscles against her cheek. Not just yet, she pleaded silently. She needed time to absorb the heat radiating from him, time to savor his scent, his breathing, the texture of his shirt.

"Her first affair started six months after she got on the soap. He was her new leading man. There was no warning. One afternoon, she simply didn't come home. She was gone almost a month." His voice reverberated through his chest, but the echo didn't disguise the pain. "It was her way of breaking in newcomers. In six years, there—"

Melissa covered his lips. "Don't," she whispered. If he told her everything, he'd never forgive himself . . . or her.

He kissed her fingers, then pulled them away. For a moment she allowed herself to hope. "I let her come home for Wendi's sake. But after a while, I couldn't stand it. Five years ago, I told her if she moved out again, not to return."

Oh—Wendi. It was still about his child. If only . . . "And Fiona has been gone ever since?"

"Yes." He drew in a breath. "When I was growing up, I thought marriage was forever. Now I know it's just for suckers and fools. I'm never going to be either again."

She sat up. Her chest was tight, as though it were being squeezed from within. "You can't mean that."

Determination lit his tawny eyes. "Every word."

"But, Logan . . ."

"Hush." He pulled her head back on his shoulder. "This isn't about me. It's about Wendi. I needed you to understand exactly what I'm up against."

It wasn't right, she thought as a single tear slipped from behind tightly closed lids. He hadn't deserved Fiona's treatment. Her callous behavior had left him scarred and bitter.

"I wish . . ."

Logan felt her soft sigh whisper across his neck. She probably wished she could make it better. No doubt she still believed the myth of happily ever after. She'd seen patients—children—die, had witnessed suffering he couldn't begin to imagine, yet she faced life with a sureness and innocence that mocked his cynical stand.

Fiona would have called her a do-gooder, or worse. He closed his eyes and waited for the familiar wave of shame and anger to crash over him. Those first months, after he'd found out about his wife's betrayals, he'd wondered if he'd drown in his hate. The feelings had lessened over time but never gone away completely.

Melissa moved her head, and he felt the dampness from her tears. When was the last time someone had cried for him? If he didn't count his mother, the answer would be never.

The watery proof of empathy and concern washed away the bitterness . . . the anger.

"Hush, little one," he murmured into her ear. "It's going to be all right."

"I'm being stupid," she said.

"No. You're being a good friend."

She stared down at the ground. Placing one finger under her chin, he tilted her face toward his. Mascara collected under her lower lids. Her nose was red and her lips were puffy. Brown eyes met his, then skittered away.

"I must look awful."

"I wouldn't change a thing." He bent down and touched his mouth to hers. The contact was fleeting, barely enough to let him register the salty taste. The spark that flew between them wouldn't have started much more than a camp fire. And yet he felt cleansed.

The car pulled into the driveway.

"Will you be all right?" Logan asked.

Melissa climbed out. "I'm fine, Logan. Stop asking. I feel silly enough about my breakdown."

"*You* stop. I appreciated the concern." He smiled slightly. "I need to get back to the office. I'll be home at the usual time."

She shut the door and watched him drive off. It wasn't until the car had disappeared down the street that she moved to the house and unlocked the front door.

What an afternoon, she thought to herself. She felt as if she'd been beaten by two burly henchmen and left for dead in the river. In her room, she stripped out of the dress and pulled on shorts and a T-shirt. The bathroom mirror revealed the extent of the damage. Melted face makeup and raccoon eyes. It was a look all the French designers would be showing in their spring collection. Only the memory of Logan's confession and the brief kiss that followed kept her from packing her bags and running off to Borneo.

Five minutes later, she emerged freshly scrubbed. After she'd hung up her outfit and straightened her room, Wendi had returned from camp.

"And how was your day?" she asked as she poured the lemonade into two glasses.

"Somewhat cool. There was supposed to be a party at Sally's house on Friday, but her baby sister got the mumps."

"Is this the same Sally who Mark said was prettier?"

"Yeah." The preteen avoided Melissa's eyes and began braiding her long hair. "I kinda took your advice and talked to her. She's nice. And she can't help it if she's responsible and all that stuff."

"How generous of you."

"So. What are we going to do this weekend?"

Melissa laughed as she sat down at the kitchen table. "Now that your plans have fallen through, I'm supposed to entertain you?"

Her mouth full of peanut-butter cookie, Wendi nodded.

"There's always the mall."

"There's that movie I've been talking about," the girl mumbled.

"Absolutely not. It's been rated for people over seventeen."

Wendi gulped her drink. "Mel-issa, I can go with a parent or guardian. Come on. All the kids have seen it but me. I'll be an outcast."

"No." The doorbell rang. She rose and crossed the floor.

"Please!"

Melissa glanced back. "I'll talk to your father."

"Oh, thank you, thank you."

"You're a brat."

She pulled open the front door. The young deliveryman looked up. "Melissa VanFleet?"

"Yes."

He handed her a crystal vase filled with pink roses. "Enjoy."

"For me?"

The man smiled and turned back toward his truck. Melissa shut the door and stared at the fragrant bouquet.

"Wow. Who sent those? There must be a hundred flowers." Wendi hopped from foot to foot, trying to count.

"Hold still," Melissa said. "I'll put them down." She set them on the counter in the kitchen. A small white card poked out on one side. Her fingers trembled as she removed the square envelope and opened it.

Thanks for listening, Logan. She recognized the strong masculine scrawl. The fact that he'd written the card himself instead of letting the flowershop clerk write it meant almost as much as the roses themselves.

"So?" Wendi asked. "Who sent them?"

"Your dad. He wanted to thank me for, ah, all my hard work." Was her grin as big as it felt?

Wendi looked at the gift. "He never sent Mrs. Dupuis flowers." Her green eyes were dark and troubled.

Melissa reached out to touch the girl's arm. "Wendi, it's not anything to worry about."

"Really?" The concern faded as she smiled. "I guess you have been working hard. Mrs. Dupuis doesn't make cookies like you do." She ran across the kitchen. "Wait until I tell Sally. Two dozen roses. When I grow up, I want boys to send me flowers every day."

Melissa was still grinning when the phone rang. Her heart fluttered. Logan!

"Phillips residence."

"Good afternoon. Is Logan in?"

Melissa felt as if a blizzard had suddenly formed inside the house. She recognized that voice. She'd heard it several times on TV. Fiona.

"He's still at work. May I t-take a message?"

"Yes. You must be that Melissa person my daughter keeps talking about. I'm Fiona Phillips. Tell Logan I have some free time this weekend and would like to take Wendi Saturday morning. I'll bring her back late that night. If he has a problem with that, he knows how to find me."

The sultry voice made her want to retch. "I'll give him the information. Wendi's here. Do you want to talk to her?"

"I hardly think that's necessary." She hung up without saying goodbye.

Melissa replaced the receiver. How could that woman not want to speak with her own child? When Wendi found her mom had called, she'd be terribly hurt.

After scanning the numbers printed beside the phone, she quickly dialed Logan's office. "Mr. Phillips, please," she said to the answering secretary. "It's his housekeeper calling."

"One moment, Ms. VanFleet, and I'll put you through."

Talk about efficient, she thought, allowing herself a small smile. It was positively frightening.

The soft music was replaced by a click, then a warm masculine "You're welcome."

"What?" She glanced over her shoulder at the flowers. "Oh, thanks. They're lovely. I've never seen roses that shade of pink."

"It's the color you blush when you get embarrassed."

She closed her eyes and groaned. "Terrific. I'll treasure the knowledge always. Logan, I have a little problem."

"What?"

"Fiona just called and wants to see Wendi on Saturday. Is that okay with you?"

"Sure. But why are you asking? After she'd cleared it with Wendi, I would have just said yes."

"She didn't talk to Wendi."

There was a long silence, then he sighed. "I understand. I'll call Wendi on her own line and tell her that Fiona wants to see her. If we're lucky, my ex-wife won't mention she phoned the house and didn't want to talk to her own daughter. I'm sorry to put you through this."

"I'm sorry for Wendi." And you, she amended silently.

"So, are you going to use your exercise video this weekend?"

"Goodbye, Logan."

Chapter Nine

"If Sally calls, tell her where I am and that I'll call her Sunday," Wendi said as she zipped up her jeans.

"One, I am not your personal secretary. Two, don't you have a brand-new answering machine?"

"Yeah, but I gave her the house number just in case. I mean John Green said he might call her. That kind of information can't wait."

Melissa grinned. "John Green. You should have said something before. How foolish of me. Of course I'll take a message."

"Okay. You've made your point. I gotta go. Bye." She leaned over and kissed Melissa's cheek, then walked to the doorway. "I don't think I'll be home in time for dinner."

"I know. I'll save dessert."

"Thanks. You're the best."

The young girl scampered toward the front of the house. Melissa trailed after her and hovered in the kitchen until she heard the soft purr of Fiona's expensive car.

Once again, the uniform-clad driver stepped out to hold open the back door. Who are you, Fiona? she asked silently. What kind of woman would throw away the love of a husband like Logan? Was her life so blessed that she could depend on another loving, giving, handsome man to whisk her away? For most mortals, the magic only occurred once, if at all. Some of her friends from high school were still together, others were on their second or third marriages.

She'd never expected a knight or a prince for herself. A simple man with honor and the need to give of himself was all she required. Perhaps when she had left Logan's house, when the memory of his face was less bright, when the losing had dulled to a bearable ache, she'd search for that man.

Melissa walked into her bedroom and glanced at the vase on her dresser. After three days, the stunning roses continued to bloom. Their fragrance was the last thing she thought of at night, the first scent she inhaled in the morning. Touching the soft petals, she smiled. There were only twenty-three blooms now. One was being pressed flat inside a book. When it dried, she'd store it in her jewelry box, along with the other treasures from her past.

"Morning."

She looked up and saw Logan standing in the hall. His hair, brushed back from his face, was still damp from his shower. Red shorts settled low on his hips. His chest was bare. She took in the crinkled covering of hair, the rippling play of his muscles, the vast expanse of tanned skin, then he slipped a T-shirt over his head and tugged it down.

"Is Wendi already gone?"

"Yes. About ten minutes ago."

He grinned. "I overslept."

"You must have had a late night," she said, not giving away the fact that she'd lain awake until she'd heard his key in the lock. It had been after two.

The day before, he'd called in the afternoon to say he wouldn't be home for dinner. The fact that he didn't say where he was going—or with whom—had left a bitter taste in her mouth. Wendi's speculations about her father's string of women had made for a long and lonely evening.

In all the weeks she had lived in his house and cared for him and his child, he'd never been on a date. That small piece of information had allowed her to dream. Oh sure, when the summer was up, she knew she was leaving. But sometimes it was easy to pretend that all this—the house, the child, the man—was hers. His empty seat at dinner had been a harsh reminder of reality.

"The boss can really talk up a storm," he said casually, leaning against the doorway.

"What?"

"John Anderson? Your former employer? He had all of us back to his house to talk about a new project. We got the go-ahead on the revitalization of the shopping district in Santa Barbara."

He'd been working? How nice. "What does that mean to you?" she asked.

He grimaced. "It means I need about a thirty-hour day for the next six months. I'll be working all weekend. What are your plans?"

"I'm going to study."

"Study what?"

"I've decided to go back to college and get my master's degree in psychology. With my nursing background, I'm eligible to challenge courses. The tests are at the end of October."

Logan reached his arms up and clutched the top of the doorjamb. Stretching from side to side, he yawned. "I don't have a clue as to what you're talking about. And I can't listen to another word without a cup of coffee. Come on.''

He led the way into the kitchen. After pouring them both a mug of the steaming liquid, he motioned for her to sit next to him at the table. ''Start at the beginning.''

''I've been thinking of getting out of nursing for quite a while. The terminally ill children are very draining.''

''I can imagine. You're not the sort of person to hold back. When they finally—'' he hesitated ''—ah, pass on, it must be difficult.''

''Sometimes.'' She stared at her cup. ''With others it's a relief. I used to work in a hospital, but I don't want to go back. I have some money saved so I applied to California University and was accepted.''

''Congratulations.'' He smiled. ''When do you start?''

''The end of September. Thanks to the generous salary I'm earning here, I'll go to school full-time.''

''You're welcome. So what was this about challenging?''

''I know you're busy, Logan. You don't need to listen to all this.''

''Believe me, it's much more exciting than checking the local fire code to figure out how many sprinkler heads we need to design into the stores.''

If only there was a vaccine against his smile. Whenever he flashed that grin, she felt her insides melt. The little resolve she had was washed away, and she was left emotionally naked. One word, she thought. It would only take one word and she'd be his...forever.

''If you qualify, there are certain courses you can challenge. That means you take a comprehensive exam. If you pass, you get credit without actually sitting for the course.''

''What class are you going to do that for?''

''There's one on physiology. I have a lot of practical knowledge and...wipe that smirk off your face. You should be ashamed of yourself.''

"Who? Me?" He put his hand on his chest in a gesture of innocence. "I'm simply listening to you talk about all your practical experience. Gee, Melissa. All this time I thought you were shy and retiring. I'm not sure you're the kind of woman I want raising my daughter. Who knows what practical experience you might be passing on."

She stood up. "I meant with the children and you know it. I don't have to sit here and take your abuse."

"You're not sitting."

"I'm leaving now."

"Does this mean I don't get any breakfast?"

She opened the refrigerator and took out one egg, then tossed it in his general direction. *"Bon appétit."*

"I'll remember this when you come looking for a reference," he called after her.

By eleven-thirty, the wonders of human anatomy had lost their thrill. Melissa placed the book onto the patio table and strolled inside. She could hear Logan typing away on his computer. He'd been busy working on the new project for the past two hours.

There was laundry to do, a grocery list to compile, but neither sounded fun or remotely interesting. Across the living room, on the white mantel, sat several photographs. Most of the silver frames contained pictures of Wendi, from infancy to her current age. She'd always been a beauty. How proud Logan must have been, Melissa thought. He'd been a good father to the little girl.

Responsibility and honor were his code. Fiona's infidelity must have eaten away at his very essence. More than the breaking of vows, the betrayal would have defiled his masculinity. No wonder there was no long-term girlfriend. A man like that wouldn't easily trust again.

The urge to go to him, to tell him that all women weren't like that—that *she* wasn't like that—was overwhelming. Instead she picked up a picture of Wendi and her father. It had been taken several years before. Wendi looked about five. Her chestnut hair was tied into pigtails. Emerald eyes gazed up at her daddy with all the love in the little girl's heart. The affection was returned in Logan's smile.

Melissa closed her eyes. If she concentrated with all her might, she could imagine Logan looking at her with the same expression. The vision crystallized for a second, then faded. Who was she kidding?

"What are you up to now?"

Logan's voice washed over her like a thick velvet cape.

"Spying," she said casually as she replaced the picture. "You can't have secrets from your housekeeper."

"I don't imagine I have any left."

She turned slowly, steeling herself against his lazy grin. "We all have secrets."

"Even you?"

"Especially me."

"What secrets do you have?"

She planted her hands on her hips. "If I tell you, they won't be secrets, now will they?"

"You're right. How about a swim?"

"What?"

"A swim."

She swallowed. "In the pool?"

"It works better there than on dry land."

"I—I don't think that's a great idea."

He took her hand and tugged until she was forced to follow him. "You think too much." When they reached her room, he pushed her inside. "The last one in the water has to cook lunch."

"Since when did you learn to cook?"

He smiled. "It's going to cost you a swim to find out."

With that he shut the door and she heard him run down the hall. Oh no, you don't, she thought, pulling off her blouse. Her shorts and undergarments quickly joined the pile. Within two minutes, she'd pulled on her suit and was sliding her feet into thongs.

But when her hand touched the doorknob, she paused. She couldn't go out to the patio dressed in her bathing suit. Not in front of Logan. What would he think?

The logical half of her brain reminded her he'd already seen her in exercise clothes and that the black yard or two of Lycra clinging to her body wasn't any worse. The romantic half insisted that if he didn't see her in a swimsuit, some illusions might be maintained.

"Oh, the hell with it," she said, and walked into the hall.

After grabbing a beach towel from the linen closet, she walked out to the patio. Logan was already in the pool, doing a lazy backstroke from the shallow to the deep end.

"What took you so long?" he asked without looking up.

"Indecision." She dropped her towel onto the table and quickly moved over to the steps. "You must have tiptoed past my room. I didn't hear you."

He chuckled and pointed at the open French door off his bedroom. "I took the shortcut. I guess we'll never find out if I can cook or not."

She plunged under the water and surfaced, smoothing her hair out of her face. "I know you can't."

"How do you figure?"

"If you could cook, you wouldn't have cheated to win."

"Cheated!" He pushed off the end of the pool and, in four powerful strokes, reached a depth he could stand in. The shimmering water reflected in the gold flecks sparkling in his deep brown eyes. "Nobody calls me a cheater and gets away with it." He continued to move forward.

"Logan, no. I was kidding." She inched back until the rough edge of the pool pressed into her shoulders. "Honest. I know you didn't cheat."

He stopped about a foot in front of her. The water lapped around his waist. Small droplets clung to the curling hair on his chest. He was six feet of ego-injured male. "Can you swim?"

"Yes. Why—"

The rest of her sentence was cut off when he dove under the water and captured her ankle. She tried to cling to the cement lip, but he was too strong. She took a breath just before she went under.

He was pulling her toward the deep end. When she realized his game plan, she let herself go limp. Turning back to make sure she was all right, he was forced to loosen his grip on her foot. She twisted away and kicked to the surface.

They broke through at the same time.

"Very sneaky," he said as he treaded water beside her.

"Bully." But she smiled so he'd know she was teasing.

"Did your family have a pool?"

"No, why?"

"You do all right. For a girl."

"For a girl? You're a chauvinist. I'll have you know I've played pool tag with the best. And won." Her smile faded as she remembered the circumstances.

"With one of your kids?"

"Yes." She kicked over to the side. "One of my patients had three older brothers. She was too weak to go in the pool, but she liked to watch. I filled in for her and sometimes the boys let me win."

"I don't believe in letting people win," he said, wiping the water from his face.

"Who says I'm going to play?"

"Me." He lunged forward and tapped her arm. "You're it."

She reached out to tag him back, but he was gone and she only succeeded in swallowing a mouthful of water. By the time she was done coughing, he was at the far end of the pool.

"Catch me, catch me. *If* you can."

"Go ahead and laugh, Logan Phillips, but I'm going to win this game."

Strategy, she thought. He was bigger and stronger and a better swimmer, but she had the brains. A plan began to form. The first step was to lull him into a sense of false security.

She struck out toward him. When she was about three feet away, he dodged left and dove under her. The chase went on for several minutes. Logan was always one step or stroke ahead. Finally he stood in chest-deep water. She calculated the approximate downward slant and moved forward. He jerked back. She followed, then attempted to stand.

Pretending to lose her footing, she fell backward under the water. Within a heartbeat, he was at her side and pulling her to the surface. To add to the effect, she coughed weakly.

"Honey, are you okay? Did you get hurt?" Strong arms carried her to the steps in the shallow end. He sat on the second stair and settled her onto his lap. "Melissa?"

She grinned and pushed back her hair. "Logan?"

"Yes?"

"You're it."

His jaw dropped. "And you call me a cheater?"

She shrugged. "Whatever it takes to win, sugar. Didn't your mama teach you that?" Her faked Southern accent made them both chuckle.

Hers faded first. Realizing that her arm was draped over his shoulder and around his back, she tried to pull away. He squeezed slightly to keep her still. Underneath her thighs, the dark hair on his legs tickled her skin. They were eye to eye . . . close enough for her to see the spiky length of his lashes, to count the individual slivers of gold staining his irises.

Her free hand raised slightly, like a bird attempting flight, then fell back to the water. The line of his jaw was strong and smooth; it hadn't been that many hours since his morning shave. Firm lips curved in a faint smile.

His arm rested around her waist, his fingers kneaded her hip. Slowly he raised her hand from the water and placed it against his chest . . . just left of center . . . over his heart.

She felt the cool crispness of his hair—rough velvet woven on satin. Felt the steady thud of his heartbeat, a whole lifetime slower than her own.

Her lips parted. More air was needed to keep her alive. Every nerve was on fire . . . quivering with anticipation for his touch. She was not disappointed.

He cupped her face with his free hand, then slid it back through her hair and pulled her closer. The last thing she saw was the satisfaction that filled his eyes, then her lids lowered and the world exploded into a kaleidoscope of colors.

His mouth slanted against hers. The seductive assault stole her breath, then reached further for her heart. Masculine lips pressed, enticed, demanded. He tasted of chlorine and that essence she remembered from so many weeks before.

His other hand joined the first, holding her head still, as though he were afraid she would resist. Her arms wrapped around him as she strained to get closer. Pulling her toward him, he shifted until she straddled him, her feet resting on the step on either side of his hips.

Unintelligible phrases of need and desire were murmured against her lips. When she tried to reply, he plunged his tongue inside, making speech unnecessary and unwanted. She stretched forward to bid him welcome. The tentative touch made him stop his assault. She felt a shudder race through his frame, and it triggered an answering response in her.

Gently, as though the journey had never before been taken, she explored. His teeth were smooth . . . he moaned when she tickled the roof of his mouth. His clean, sweet taste made her want more...made her need more. Like the water itself, the feeling was wet and insubstantial. It supported and released, saved and threatened. What had passed between them before had been a spark; this was a storm.

She moved her hands across his back, tracing the ropes of muscles she'd only seen for so many weeks. She continued the journey around his sides, then ran her fingers through the hair on his chest, losing herself in the sensation, reveling in the way he grew still with pleasure. Hard under soft, rough over smooth. She rocked her hips gently on his legs.

Then he began the dance. His strong hands slipped to her shoulders and then to her elbows. They took with them the straps of her suit. The wet material clung stubbornly to her breasts, even after she'd pulled her arms free.

"I want to look at you." His voice was husky, each word an effort.

"Yes."

With infinite gentleness, he peeled down the Lycra. The warm summer air felt cool at first. She glanced down and watched her rosy nipples harden.

"You're so beautiful," he murmured as he raised his hands to cup the curves.

His fingers investigated each pale inch, making smaller and smaller circles until they hovered over the straining flesh. Feather-light touches. Her head rolled back; she arched forward. The ache was part pleasure, part pain. Please, she thought. It was too much to bear.

Heat pulsed down, settling uncomfortable between her thighs. She shifted, both to alleviate and to urge him on. The movement made her aware of the ridge pressing against the thin swim trunks.

He reached down and touched the tip of his tongue to her right nipple. An audible gasp broke through her lips. Licking, sucking, tasting, he lavished attention upon each breast.

Logan felt her rhythmic rocking. If she kept it up much longer, the debate over whether to consummate the relationship in the pool or his bedroom would be moot.

He raised his head. The contrast between her pale round flesh and the tan above was tantalizingly erotic. Passion had darkened her eyes to black.

"You're a seductress," he teased before trailing bites along her neck. "And all this time I thought you were just shy."

She glanced away. "I—I'm not usually like this." A blush swept up her face.

"I know."

A cold knot formed in his stomach, chasing out the heat that had erupted there. He knew who and what Melissa was. She was the kind of woman a man shouldn't play games with or lie to. She was the kind of woman a man couldn't take lightly. She was the kind of woman who didn't understand the rules . . . his rules.

Melissa placéd a tentative kiss on his lips. Lord, he wanted her. In the pool, in his bed, in her bed, it didn't matter. He wanted her with a fire that threatened to consume him. What was it his father had always told him? If you're going to be a man, then act like a man. He pulled up the top of her suit until it covered her breasts.

"What . . ." Her voice mirrored the confusion in her eyes.

"This isn't right." Did that sound as stupid to her as it did to him? "I mean, I don't want to do something that you'll regret later."

"Oh. I see." She slipped back into the water and stood up. Turning her back, she pulled the straps over her arms. "You've changed your mind. I understand."

The pain in her voice was like a blow to his gut. "No. You *don't* understand. This isn't about you, it's about . . . other things." How could he admit there wasn't enough left inside to give her what she deserved? "Melissa, I—"

She cut him off with a shake of her head. "Please don't explain. It will only make things worse. I understand how easy it is for a... situation to get out of hand." Her chin tilted up as pride straightened her shoulders. "If you want me to continue to work for you, you must promise this will never happen again."

He felt like a snake. "Of course. You have my apology and my word."

What had started out as a morning of promise had turned into an afternoon of strained conversations and avoided eyes. If lunch had been stilted, dinner was a disaster. Neither ate, neither spoke. Melissa washed the last trace of food into the sink and flipped on the garbage disposal.

When was Wendi coming home? she wondered. Things were so bad, she would almost welcome a conversation with Fiona as a relief from the tension. This had been the worst day of her life... and the best.

Why? she asked for the thousandth time. Why had he started something he had no intention of finishing? Why had she allowed him to go so far? Why had he stopped?

Twilight was settling on the balmy evening, changing the hot sultriness of day into the relative coolness of night. The overhead light in the kitchen turned the window into a mirror. The answer to the last question was reflected back. He'd stopped because she wasn't a Fiona or one of the countless stunning women who peppered his life.

Her eyes drifted shut. She could have sworn he'd said something about her being... beautiful. The concept was almost too embarrassing to even think about, let alone discuss. Apparently the compliment existed only in her mind. An overactive imagination could make almost anything seem real.

What now? If the rest of the day had been any indication, going on as before wasn't possible. The playfulness had been lost, drowned in the vortex of passion that had surrounded them.

She could leave. Run away and hide like the mouse she was. Or she could stay the rest of the summer. Five weeks. How difficult could it be?

She heard the soft purr of a car engine, followed by the slamming of a door. Wendi!

Melissa rushed to the front door and pulled it open. "Welcome home, kid. It's been . . . oh, my."

The girl ran into the foyer and spun in a slow circle. "What do you think? Don't I look great?"

The preteen's long hair was a riot of curls around her shoulders. Subtle makeup highlighted her eyes, making them appear bigger, the lashes longer. Red lipstick gave her a pouty, seductive look. But what shocked Melissa the most was the dress. A black sheath skimmed over her budding breasts, then curved gently at her hips. The front dipped low enough to suggest, the back scooped down to her waist. Dark stockings and spiked heels completed the look. The transformation from girl to ingenue was instantaneous.

"Mom had some free time before her party so she gave me a makeover. Do you know where the camera is? I want you to take some pictures. Sally will never believe me when I tell her. Where's my dad?"

Melissa's heart stopped at the last question. If Logan saw his daughter, he'd lose it completely.

"Let's go in your room," she said, starting to lead the way. "I'll find the camera, then you can change."

"But I want to show Dad."

"Show me what? Is that my Wendi?" Logan stepped out of the hall and stared at his daughter. His smile faded as the muscles in his jaw tightened. "What the hell are you doing dressed like that?"

Wendi took a step back. "Dad-dy? Don't you like it? Mom helped me. I thought . . ."

"You're still a little girl. How dare you step outside dressed like that? Get into your room. I don't want to see you again until you've washed your face and changed your clothes. Do you understand?"

Chapter Ten

Wendi fled to her room. Melissa stared after her and, when she disappeared around the corner, turned on the girl's father.

"How could you yell at her like that? She thought you'd be proud of her."

"Proud? That her mother dresses her like a slut?" He shook his head. "As long as she lives in my house, she lives by my rules."

"Listen to yourself. You sound like a general in the army. We're talking about a little girl . . . *your* little girl. She needs understanding and affection right now, not rules."

"What do you know about raising children?"

She stepped back. "I know when not to act like a jerk."

"Melissa," he growled.

"I'm not twelve years old. I don't scare so easily." She brushed past him. "If you'll excuse me, I have to go explain your behavior to your daughter."

She walked away slowly, hoping he'd call her back, but the foyer remained ominously quiet.

After collecting sodas and cookies, she went down the hall and tapped lightly on the closed door. "Wendi?"

"What?"

"Can I come in?"

"I don't care."

Melissa stepped inside. The young girl was standing at the sink of her bathroom. She'd already changed into jeans and a shirt. The mass of curls was pulled back with a ribbon.

As Wendi washed away the makeup, Melissa opened the soft drink cans and settled on the bed. She stretched out on one side, her back to the portrait.

"Are you going to yell at me, too?" Wendi asked as she picked the black dress up off the floor.

"Did your mom give you that?" She pointed at the designer garment.

"Yeah. She said it's not her style anymore and that I'd grow into it." Bunching it up in her hands, she glared at the offending fabric. "I hate it. It's ugly. I wish I'd never seen the stupid dress." With that, it was tossed into her closet and landed in a heap on top of her shoes.

Melissa patted the bed and held out the plate of cookies. "You don't mean that."

"I do."

"Wendi, your dad is afraid you'll grow up to be a stranger. He's concerned that you're not turning out the way he'd imagined." She held up her hand to stop the interruption. "There's nothing wrong with you. You're sweet and honest and you try really hard to please your parents... both of them. When you came in, you looked like a woman and not a little girl. That made him feel uneasy. Instead of telling you what was wrong, he got angry."

Wendi sat cross-legged on the floor and stared at the carpet. "Do I have to choose? Can't I love them both?"

"Of course you can love your mom and your dad. Sometimes adults forget that's the way kids are."

"How do you know this stuff?"

"I've spent six years living in other people's houses, watching the way they handle their children. Some of it rubbed off. Now, tell me about your day."

Wendi smiled and began an hour-by-hour description of her time with Fiona. The sadness and hurt left her eyes, and gradually the humor returned.

The next few years were going to be difficult for Logan and his daughter. He wanted to keep her little and she wanted to grow up. And Wendi had time and Mother Nature on her side.

It wasn't hard to imagine what he must have thought when Wendi walked into the house. All his worst nightmares had come instantly to life.

". . . a party in Beverly Hills," Wendi continued.

"Sounds exciting."

"I wish I could have gone with her, but she has a hot date with a movie star."

Melissa feigned being suitably impressed. As far as she was concerned, not even the number-one box-office draw could hold a candle to the man at the other end of the house.

"Yeah. She's not seeing anyone special right now."

Melissa pulled herself into a sitting position. "What?"

Wendi tugged on a pair of hot-pink-and-lime-green socks. "She said she's between men. You know, playing the field."

"How nice." As long as she didn't plan to play in this backyard. "I'm glad you had a good time today." She stretched out her hand and touched the chestnut tendrils brushing against the girl's neck. "Your hair looks pretty. Is it a perm?"

"No. Mom said I could get one if I want, but we did this with those skinny hot rollers."

"I like it."

"Really? Do you think..." Wendi nibbled on her bottom lip. "I mean if there's a party or something, could you help me with my hair?"

"Of course, kitten."

"Dad calls me 'kitten,' too."

"Do you want me to stop?"

Wendi shook her head. "I like it. It's just..." A myriad of emotions flashed across her young face: confusion, fear, jealousy, acceptance.

Melissa knew what the girl was thinking...what she was afraid of. "Your dad and I are friends," she said, trying to block out the memory of what had occurred in the pool. "I'd never come between you."

"I know." Wendi scrambled to her feet and walked over to the stereo in the corner. "Do you think...I mean, are you staying until school starts?"

"Yes. Mrs. Dupuis returns the seventeenth of September. I'll be here until then."

"That's only five weeks more." She leaned forward and carefully studied her pile of CDs. "I was wondering if we'll still be friends when you're gone."

It was as if a giant fist had reached inside Melissa's chest and squeezed her heart. The day had been a roller coaster of emotions, culminating with the touching question from Logan's daughter.

"I'd like that," she said softly.

"Really?" Wendi faced her, her eyes filled with tears. "I thought you might be glad to get rid of me. I know I can be a pain."

"Not you!" She held out her arms and the girl flung herself into the embrace. "I'll always be there for you, Wendi. Even when I'm gone, you can call me and we'll talk or go shopping."

"Good idea," the twelve-year-old said. "You could use some new clothes."

"What's wrong with my clothes? Everything is very useful."

Wendi pulled back and grinned. "Yeah, for cleaning house. You need something, you know, in."

Her grin was so much like Logan's, Melissa felt a knot form in her stomach. "I've been 'in' before."

Wendi rolled her eyes. "Please."

"Please, what?"

The low male voice sent shivers up Melissa's spine. She didn't know how long Logan had been standing, listening to them talk. The urge to run from him was overwhelming, but to do so would require her to walk past him. She remained on the bed.

Wendi looked up at her father. Pride made her stand her ground, fear made her tremble.

"I was wrong," Logan said quietly. "I didn't like the way you were dressed, but I had no right to yell like that. I know..." He drew in a deep breath. "I know you're growing up. I don't have to like it, but I do have to accept it. I'll do better next time, kitten."

Wendi smiled. "I know, Daddy. And I'll always be your little girl, no matter what."

"But it's red."

"So?"

Melissa glanced at Wendi. It had taken the girl two weeks to talk her into the shopping trip and she already regretted giving in. "I'm not really a red person. I prefer navy, gray, or beige."

"Bor-ing. Lighten up. Red's a great color. Very hip."

Anyone who chose a twelve-year-old as a fashion consultant had to be prepared for the unconventional, Melissa reminded herself as she stared at the armful of clothes Wendi had picked out.

"But it's a jumpsuit. I'm too short to wear a jumpsuit."

Wendi began hanging the garments on the hook in the dressing room. "We are in the petite department. They make things for short people. That's why they're called petites. And you're supposed to be the adult."

"But..."

"Jumpsuits make short people look taller. Trust me... I know." Wendi sat on the stool in the corner and folded her arms across her chest.

Melissa bit back her grin. "Yes, Mom." She pulled off her skirt and blouse, then stepped into the jumpsuit. The silk caressed her skin like an early-morning breeze. Unlike others she'd tried on years ago, this one fit. The crotch didn't hang around her knees and the pant legs were only a couple of inches too long.

"With heels, the tapered hem will bunch around your ankles."

Her eyes met Wendi's in the mirror. "How do you know that? You're only in junior high."

"I can read. If you don't keep up with fashion, how will you know what's cool? I mean, what if I showed up in neon jams and they were out of style?" She shook her head. "I'd be a laughingstock. Daddy would have to put me in boarding school or something."

Melissa finished doing the buttons on the bodice. "What a lot of responsibility. I had no idea. Well..." She turned around for inspection. "What do you think?"

"I like it." Wendi sprang up and adjusted the collar until it was straight. "You need bigger earrings. Jeez, how do you expect anyone to see those? They're smaller than a pinhead. What is that? A bug?"

"It's a shell, thank you very much. And a nurse can't wear gaudy jewelry."

"You said you weren't going to be a nurse anymore."

Being backed into a corner by a precocious child was embarrassing, she thought as she faced the mirror. "Should they be red, too?"

"No. That's overdoing it. Something gold. Or diamond studs are nice."

"I'm fresh out this week. Gold it is. Fake gold."

Wendi cringed. "It's better to have one or two pieces of good jewelry than a box full of trash."

"Snoblet."

Wendi stuck out her tongue.

Melissa stepped out of the jumpsuit and tossed it to her. "Hang this up, please." She pointed to the next item. "Who picked that out, if I even had to ask?"

"What?"

"Don't get all innocent on me. It's a leather miniskirt. Wendi . . . I'm almost thirty."

"Really? That is old."

"Very funny. Do you think I could . . ." She held the supple skirt against her middle. "What would I do for a top?"

"Anything. A sweater. A shirt. A nice silk blouse."

"Oh." Sure. She had what thirty, forty silk blouses just waiting to be teamed up with a red leather miniskirt. "Pass. What's next."

"A dress."

She continued trying on clothes until they were both exhausted. In the end, she purchased the jumpsuit and a cotton skirt and blouse, all in red.

Tossing her shopping bag into the booth of the mall restaurant, Melissa slid in and smiled up at the hovering waiter.

"Coffee, please."

"Soda for me. And a hot-fudge sundae."

The waiter glanced back at her. "For you, ma'am?"

"Nothing else. Except . . . okay, bring another spoon. I'll mooch my share."

Wendi flipped her hair over her shoulders and leaned her elbows on the table. "There's an eighth-grade dance the week school starts. We don't really have dates, but some guys have their parents pick up and drive the girls they like. Sally says that Mark likes me, but I'm not sure. Do I wait for him to invite me, or do I accept the first boy who asks?"

"Tough question. Has anyone asked yet?"

"No. I just want to be prepared."

Had her junior high life been this complicated? Probably not. She didn't remember being taken to any dance but the prom, and that invitation had come a mere week before the event.

"Why don't you wait and see who invites you? If you like the boy, say yes. If you don't, turn him down. Whatever happens with Mark, you'll still be doing the best for you."

"Maybe."

Their drinks arrived. Melissa sipped gratefully on her coffee. Her feet hurt, her back ached and there was a six-inch scratch on her leg from a pin in one of the dresses. Who said shopping was fun?

"Barbara's older sister slept with a *boy* last week."

Melissa choked. "Excuse me?" Her first thought was to wonder what else Barbara's older sister would have slept with. The second was a realization that she needed to ask Logan for a raise. She plain wasn't getting paid enough to handle Wendi.

"How old is..."

"Elsie? She's fourteen. Almost fifteen."

Fourteen years old? It boggled her mind. Now what? She wasn't a mother. How did one discuss sex with an impressionable girl without encouraging her to jump into bed or scaring her for life?

"What do you think about Elsie and this boy?"

The hot-fudge sundae arrived. Wendi licked a scoop of whipped cream off her spoon. "I'm not sure why she did it. I don't think I want to kiss a boy, let alone do...that."

A questioning look fluttered in and out of Wendi's eyes. The expression was so fleeting that Melissa wasn't sure if she was imagining it or not, but she couldn't take the chance.

"Do you know what happens when a man and a woman go to bed together?"

"Of course. They taught us in health last year. It's pretty disgusting if you ask me."

Health class? Unless it had changed considerably since her day, most of the information was technical rather than practical. "Making love with a boy is a difficult decision, Wendi. It's important to make sure it's what you want to do and not just what your friends are doing."

Wendi stared intently at her dessert. "Can we change the subject?"

"I'm almost done. When you decide it's right, you need to practice safe sex."

"Melissa!"

"I'm not kidding. A condom will keep you from getting diseases as well as getting pregnant. What if Elsie and her friend didn't use one? Do you think she's ready to have a baby?"

Wendi smiled smugly. "Elsie can't get pregnant."

"Why?"

"It was her first time. Everybody knows you can't get pregnant your first time."

Melissa felt her jaw drop. Wherever had Wendi heard that idea? It was so wrong it was frightening. Should she say something now or talk to Logan first or...

"Do you think Dad would let me have a slumber party for my birthday?" Wendi asked.

The transformation from teen to little girl was as fast as it was confusing. "I—I don't see why not."

"Good. Okay, let's get going. We haven't touched the second level of the mall."

Later, Melissa thought as she stood up. She'd speak to Wendi later. Better yet, let her father deal with her.

"Logan, I need to talk to you."

He looked up from the computer report and motioned for Melissa to take the seat next to his desk. The smile she offered was tentative, and he wondered how much longer they were going to tiptoe around each other.

For two weeks, her eyes had watched him. The wary expression lurking in the brown irises had been a constant reminder of her pain. Between the way he'd yelled at his daughter and the discord he'd created with Melissa, he thought it might be time to join a monastery in Tibet...one with a vow of silence and chastity.

"You look fierce," she said softly, as she folded her hands on her lap.

The lamp on his desk cast a pool of light far enough to include her. The wisps of hair around her face seemed translucent, giving her the look of a tired, troubled angel. His gaze traced the shadows under her eyes, the creamy smoothness of her skin. Dropping lower, he admired the way the cotton blouse hugged the full curves of her breasts. Now that he knew the exact shape and feel of the hidden lushness, it was harder than ever to keep from reaching out to take her. Only his promise...his word, kept him seated firmly on his side of the desk.

"I'm a little stressed out," he said, rubbing the bridge of his nose. "One of the store owners is giving us trouble. The purpose of the revitalization is to give the area the look of an old Spanish town. This guy—" he looked down at his papers "—wants used brick on the front of his shop. Not Mexican pavers or even tile, but used brick. It could just be me, but I don't think the conquistadores had much call for that. What do you think?''

She laughed. ''I think you'll persuade him to see the error of his ways.''

''I appreciate the vote of confidence. I wish I had your faith. The awful part is I keep having nightmares of the street with everything perfect except one storefront that looks like a colonial haberdashery.'' He leaned back in his chair. ''What can I do for you?''

''I need to talk about Wendi.''

''Wait.'' He held up his hand. ''Before you say another word, I want you to know I've been a perfect father for the last couple of weeks.''

''Oh?''

''It's true. Wendi told me so at breakfast.''

''I'm glad.'' Melissa's smile faded as she twisted her fingers together.

The night was still. His daughter was in her room watching music videos. The air-conditioning had just clicked off. From outside, the sound of crickets drifted through the shut windows, but other than that, there was only his heartbeat pounding in his ears.

''Have you ever...'' She cleared her throat. ''I don't know how to say this.''

''Just spit it out.''

She looked up at him, her mouth pulled into a straight line. ''When we were shopping this afternoon, Wendi was telling me about Elsie. She's the older sister of one of her friends. Elsie is fourteen and made an announcement that she had sex with a boy.''

His heart stopped. ''Fourteen?''

Melissa nodded. ''When I asked Wendi what she thought of all this, she said that she couldn't imagine kissing a boy, let alone doing anything like that.''

His heart started beating again. "That's something to be grateful for. Thanks for telling me, Melissa. I appreciate...what?"

"That's not what I wanted to say. It's about Wendi. When we were talking about Elsie, Wendi made a couple of statements that led me to believe she doesn't really understand about sex and pregnancy. The statistics on teen pregnancy are alarming. Have either you or Fiona talked to her about this? Does she know about birth control? Does she know how to go about making a rational decision at a time when her hormones are surging out of control?"

The anger began slowly. He'd been betrayed before. God knows his wife had caused enough heartache for one lifetime. He even expected women to be less than honorable, but he had never thought that of Melissa.

"How dare you?" he said as he rose to his feet. "Just because Fiona and I made one mistake is no reason to assume our daughter is destined to do the same."

She stood up, as well. "Logan, what are you talking about? This has nothing to do with you and Fiona. I'm worried about Wendi. She's almost thirteen. Don't you think she deserves to have a clear concept about sex and her sexuality? Do you expect the schools to inform her?"

"I expect you to have a few children of your own before you start passing judgment on my parental skills."

Her chin jerked up. "Why are you taking this so personally? For once, look past your male pride and think about your daughter. Wendi told me that Elsie didn't have to worry about having a baby because everybody knows you can't get pregnant the first time."

The flash flood of rage dissipated as quickly as it had arrived. "Oh." He sat down.

"Oh?" she asked. "That's it? How about 'I'm sorry I lost my temper'? Or, 'Gee, Melissa, you're a swell human being and I don't deserve to lick the ground you walk on'?"

He grinned. "The last sounds a little extreme. But I am willing to admit I was wrong to overreact and lucky to have found you. Is that good enough?"

"It'll do," she said grudgingly. "So, are you going to talk to your daughter?"

"About...that? Ah, isn't that more of a woman thing?"

Melissa placed her hands on her hips. "Coward."

"About this? You bet. I don't suppose you have a book or something you could give her?"

"As a matter of fact I know of a great pamphlet on the subject. I'll get a copy this week or next, and pass it on to Wendi. But I expect you to talk with her. She needs to know your feelings on the subject."

His feelings? Right now he was so confused, his child could probably help clear *his* mind. "Let me know when you have your conversation. I'll speak with her after that. Okay?"

"Okay." She walked to the doorway. "Thanks, Logan."

He stood and moved next to her. "I'm the one who's grateful. I know you care about Wendi and I'm sorry I lost my temper. It was just..."

She smiled up at him. Trust, compassion and something he didn't want to identify lurked in her eyes. "I understand," she whispered. "Don't give it another thought."

He watched her walk away, then moved to the window. Darkness and his own reflection stared back at him.

Melissa was one of the few people he knew who would stand up to him when he was angry. Most of the time, Fiona had simply pouted in the bedroom until his temper had faded. But Melissa...if someone she cared about was in trouble, she'd face an army for them...and win.

She'd known, he thought as he jammed his hands into his front pockets. She'd known why he'd gotten angry and she'd understood. In less than three months, she'd tangled herself in the workings of his life. When the time was up, unweaving her was going to be a long and painful process.

They'd keep in touch, he decided. Wendi would like that. And he could keep tabs on Melissa. When she got involved, he could make sure the man was suitable. She needed someone strong yet gentle, responsible yet fun. The kind of guy who would . . .

But the image of Melissa with another man was unthinkable. He wanted things to stay as they were. She would take care of him and Wendi and he would . . .

He would do nothing. When her time was up, she would leave. To hold her with false promises of what could never be was a far greater crime than he was capable of committing. She needed the affection of a good man. While he considered himself a decent person, love between them was impossible. Love required trust. Trust left one open to betrayal.

The irony of the whole situation was that he still wanted her. The flames fanned by their earlier intimacy threatened to consume his soul.

Returning to his chair, he tried to block her from his mind. Echoes of words and laughter broke his concentration. Everything had been simpler before the petite nurse had entered his home and started interrupting his sleep and haunting his dreams.

Melissa flipped on the TV, then turned down the sound. Well-dressed men and women paraded across the screen, their lips moving as they argued, threatened and proclaimed. When a familiar raven-haired beauty appeared, her lithe body draped in a formal gown, Melissa shook her fist.

"This is your fault," she said aloud. "Wendi is *your* daughter. *I* don't know what to say to her. Why aren't you here taking care of your responsibilities instead of playing bedroom tag with every available movie star in the city?"

The figure in the daytime drama continued with her scene, unaffected by the impassioned plea.

"What kind of a person are you?" Melissa asked. "You didn't even care enough to get joint custody of your only child. What am I supposed to do? Stop caring about her? Care more? Damn you, Fiona!"

Melissa picked up one of the floral throw pillows on the sofa and tossed it at the television. It hit the left corner and dropped harmlessly to the floor. "And you hurt Logan, too. He won't let himself trust anybody again. Did you ever think there might be another woman who would want what you so easily threw away?" She pitched another pillow, and another.

"What happens now? If you decide you want to come back to the fold, am I supposed to just walk away?"

There weren't any more pillows, so she picked up one of the seat cushions and hurled it along with a string of curses that questioned everything from Fiona's parentage to her reason for being born.

"How am I supposed to leave Logan and Wendi? How am I supposed to compete with you?"

Hitting the off button on the TV, she gave the stand a kick for good measure.

"Melissa?"

She spun and found Wendi standing in the room. "When did you get home?" she asked.

"Just this second. What..." Wendi looked at the cushions and pillows piled on the floor. "What happened?"

"Nothing. I was, ah, looking for spare change in the sofa."

The girl looked doubtful. "If you say so. Do you feel all right?"

Melissa smiled. There was nothing like throwing things to work through anger, she thought. "Never better."

"You're sure?"

"Positive." She began picking up the cushions and setting them back in place.

"I'll be in my room if you want me to call a doctor or anything."

Melissa remembered the brochure she'd picked up that morning. "No doctors, but I do want to speak with you. Let me clean up the mess and I'll be right there."

Chapter Eleven

"I stopped by a clinic and got you this brochure." Melissa handed the pamphlet to the girl, then set a shopping bag on the bed.

Wendi flipped through the pages. "Sex education? I knew I shouldn't have told you about Elsie."

"I'm glad you did." Melissa smoothed the girl's bangs out of her face. "Sit down."

Wendi plopped down and tossed the booklet onto her desk. "I don't want to do this. I know everything."

"Then I have some news. You *can* get pregnant the first time."

"Really?"

Melissa sat next to her. "Really. Are you ready to listen now?"

"Can't I just read about it?"

"Wendi!"

"Melissa! Come on. This is embarrassing."

Yeah. For both of them. "Do you promise to ask me if you have any questions?"

"Yes." The girl stared at the ground.

"Okay. I'll let you look over the information, then we'll talk at the end of the week." She reached down and opened the grocery bag. "Has anyone explained about getting your period?"

"It's not going to start for ages. I'm still a girl."

"You'll be thirteen in a couple of months. Trust me, your days of being a girl are numbered."

Step by step she went over what would happen and the logistics of handling the monthly cycle.

"Will I get PMS?" Wendi asked.

"Not if you're lucky."

"I kinda like the idea of being cranky once a month. Mom says it keeps men in line."

"Fiona should know," Melissa muttered under her breath.

"What?"

"Nothing." She gathered up the supplies and carried them into Wendi's bathroom. "I've put everything on the bottom shelf. Don't be scared when it starts. If I'm gone, you can call me or talk to Mrs. Dupuis or your dad."

"My dad!" Her cheeks flamed. "Jeez, Melissa. I couldn't tell him."

She hid a smile. "Sure you can. You can tell dads anything."

Wendi flipped on the TV. "Are we done now?"

"Yes. Dinner's at six."

She went out and closed the door behind her. That hadn't been so bad, she thought. A sliver of guilt worked its way down her spine. She should have actually talked about sex. Putting it off wasn't going to make it easier. But the reprieve, however short, seemed like a gift from God.

Would it be easier with her own children? she wondered. Although Wendi and she were very close, it wasn't the same. There was still an element of best behavior on the girl's part. With the exception of her outburst a few weeks ago, they rarely fought.

Don't go looking for trouble, she told herself. There were only two more weeks until her job ended. That was plenty of time for a disaster or two.

When Melissa heard the key in the lock, she glanced up at the clock. It was after ten. She stood and tossed her magazine back onto the sofa, then stretched.

Logan pushed open the door. "Hi." His weary smile was matched by the slump of his shoulders.

"Hi, yourself. You look awful. How do you feel?"

"Don't ask." He dropped his briefcase in the foyer and moved toward her. "I just spent fourteen hours either staring at a computer screen or looking over blueprints. I have a headache, I'm hungry and I just want to sleep for three days."

"Come on, big boy, I've got dinner waiting."

"You saved me something?"

She nodded as she walked into the kitchen.

"When we all get to heaven, I'll put in a good word."

She flipped on the lights and opened the refrigerator. "That's quite an assumption."

"Melissa, I'm sure you'll get to heaven. Don't worry."

"That's not what I meant."

He grinned and slipped out of his jacket. "I know you're not talking about me."

"Take a seat over there." She and Wendi had made homemade pizza for dinner. She adjusted the heat on the oven, then slipped the prepared dough and toppings onto a cookie sheet. Once it was baking, she served the salad and poured a glass of wine for each of them.

Logan undid his tie and pulled off the length of yellow cloth. After unbuttoning the collar, he did the same to the sleeves, then folded them up to his elbows. Long fingers adjusted the cotton and smoothed the cuff flat. As she sat across from him, she tried not to stare. There was an elegance in his movements; fluid masculine gestures tore through her wall of defenses. He might be hungry for dinner, but her wanting was more primal.

"Where's my daughter?" he asked, spearing a bite of salad.

"She had a long day at camp. I checked about fifteen minutes ago and she was already asleep. Tell me about the project."

Logan discussed the details of the revitalization. By the time he'd eaten his pizza, it was almost eleven. Tiredness scored deep lines around his mouth.

"You'd better get to bed or you'll end up spending the night at the table," she said.

"You're right. Thanks for dinner. Did I ever tell you you're a great cook?" He rose and tossed his napkin down.

"I bet you say that to all the girls."

He crossed the room, then paused and glanced at her over his shoulder. "Melissa?"

"Hmm?"

"Would you mind . . ." He cleared his throat.

"What, Logan?"

"My back and shoulders are stiff from being hunched over all day. Could I trouble you for a back rub?"

If it hadn't been for the lazy, sheepish grin tugging at his lips, she would have said no. Two glasses of wine had weakened her resolve enough for her to acknowledge the desire filling her. Despite the pain of his rejection, she wanted him.

"Sure. Go lie down on your bed. I'll be right in."

In record time, the dishes were rinsed and stacked in the dishwasher. She wiped the counter and the table, then folded the dishcloth over the sink. When there was nothing else to detain her, she walked to the back of the house.

Only the lamp in the corner was on. Light spilled out as far as the coffee table, but the bed was in shadow. The bedspread had been pulled back, along with the light blanket and top sheet. Logan lay on his stomach in the center of the mattress, his body bare except for a pair of cotton shorts.

He turned his head toward her. "There's lotion on the nightstand. I really appreciate this, Melissa."

"N-no problem." Had that squeaky voice belonged to her? She swallowed against the lump in her throat.

It was just a back, she told herself. No different from others she'd seen and massaged. So what if it was a little broader, slightly more muscled, and deeply tanned? No one needed to know that her knees were shaking or her core damp with desire.

She approached the bed and slipped out of her thongs. Taking the lotion in one hand, she crawled next to him.

"Go ahead and sit on me," he said.

"What?"

He tensed his shoulders, then released them. "You'll be able to reach more if you sit on me." He offered her a lazy smile. "After all, there's no one here but us chickens."

She couldn't! It would be so... intimate. "I..."

"Move," he commanded, tapping her knee.

He *was* her boss, she told herself. And it would be terribly rude to disobey a direct order. She glanced at the wide expanse of skin and sighed. It was a dirty job, but someone had to do it. "If you insist..."

Heat. The warmth from his body was instantly transmitted to hers. Her thighs cradled his hips. Every fiber inside her screamed at him to turn over and take her. Only her lips were silent. She poured lotion into her hand and reached down to touch his skin.

The muscles around his neck and shoulders were taut. Wide, kneading motions loosened, then relaxed the sinewy ropes. Logan rested his forehead on his hands and groaned softly. The sound was a dagger to her heart. It pierced the last layer of her reserve and left her unprotected.

Rubbing the heels of her hands into his back, she worked her way down his spine. On the return trip, she splayed her fingers and massaged the areas by his sides. Knots disappeared, tension melted.

The muscles in his upper arms were too large for her to span, so she worked on one side and then the other. The scent of his body and the last trace of his after-shave mingled, aroused and enticed. Dark whiskers outlined the shape of his jaw.

"I can't tell you how great this feels," he murmured.

Amen, she thought as she stretched back to his neck. The pressure from his buttocks was enough to tease but not satisfy. If she pressed a little harder, arched her back...

The pleasure built...her breathing quickened. But it was the increased temperature of his skin that sounded the alarm. She froze in midstroke. Her fingers trailed along his spine, then were still.

What was she thinking of? she asked herself. Stupid question, came the answer. This might not be the most embarrassing moment of her life, but it was certainly in the top ten. Easing her weight off him, she slipped onto the mattress and turned to leave.

"Don't go," he said softly. One hand reached out and grabbed hers. "Stay here for a second more."

Sleep made his voice heavy, desire made her willpower weak. She stretched out on her back, next to him. Their fingers entwined. He pulled her hand up to his lips, then kissed each knuckle. Tawny eyes met hers. Desire battled with fatigue.

"Go to sleep." She turned onto her side to face him and touched his hair. The brown strands felt like silk. "I'll stay for a while. It's all right."

His lids drifted closed and his breathing slowed. Twenty minutes later, she softly spoke. "Logan?"

There was no answer.

She slid off the bed and walked to the lamp. With a turn of the switch, the room was plunged into darkness. Finding her way out more by memory than sight, she paused by the bed.

"I love you, Logan Phillips."

Two nights later, Melissa walked to the kitchen and glanced out the big window. No car, no Wendi, nothing. She let the curtain fall back in place and resumed her pacing.

The length of the house was a nice feature, she thought as she stalked the halls. It took her two minutes to travel from the end of Logan's bedroom to the far corner of his daughter's. She'd made the round trip ten times. Wendi was now—she glanced at her watch—fifty minutes late.

She'd already called Sally's house. The girl's mother had informed her that a teenage boy had taken them to get ice cream. Mrs. Johnson had questioned the arrangement, but Wendi and Sally had told her it had been cleared . . . by Melissa.

"I'll kill her," Melissa said as she passed the foyer. "And I don't care if I go to prison."

She heard the sound of a car engine and the slamming of a door. Finally! Taking a deep breath to calm herself, she sat on the corner of the sofa.

Wendi flew in the front door and slid to a stop. "Hi. Is my dad home yet?"

"No, he's still at work."

"Oh. Okay. I think I'll go to my room. Night." With a quick smile, the preteen turned toward her bedroom.

"Just one minute, young lady. Do you know what time it is?"

Wendi paused. "No." She looked up at the clock over the mantel. "Gosh, it's late. I had no idea, Melissa. Sorry. Night." She started walking away.

"Get back here." Melissa's voice was low and controlled, but she felt the rage bubbling under the surface. This wasn't the time to lose her cool, she reminded herself.

"What?" Wendi moved slowly through the living room and sat on the rose-colored wing chair. Her eyes were wide and the lids fluttered in what Melissa supposed was an expression of innocence.

"The first problem is that you are exactly one hour late. You said you'd be home at eight-thirty. Tomorrow is the last day of camp and you have to be up early. Where were you and why didn't you call?"

"I was at Sally's, like I said."

"Did her mother bring you home?"

Wendi shifted uncomfortably. "Of course."

"And why didn't you call?"

"I forgot."

Even if she hadn't already known the truth, the girl's fidgeting would have given her away. The twisting fingers and uneasy swallowing highlighted the fact that she was a poor liar. The only consolation was that it wasn't something she tried very often.

The cowardly part of Melissa wanted to simply send the girl to her room and tell Logan when he got home. He was Wendi's father, let him deal with it. The logical part of her said that she'd been hired to look after his daughter. And that meant all the time and not just when things were going well.

"When you didn't come home on time, I called Sally's house."

Wendi sprang to her feet. "You what? How dare you check up on me?"

"How dare you lie?"

"I didn't—"

Melissa cut her off with a look. "Mrs. Johnson told me about the boy. *You* said I knew about it and thought it was fine. You lied to her about that and you lied to me about where you were going and who you were going to be with."

"I didn't do it on purpose." Wendi folded her arms over her chest and walked to the French doors leading out to the pool. "When I got to Sally's, I found out that Alan might come by. He wanted to take us out. How could we say no?"

Your lips form the word and it just comes out, Melissa thought as she struggled with her temper. "Who is this Alan person?"

"Mark's older brother."

Mark? Oh yes, the one Wendi liked at her camp. "Did Mark go for ice cream as well?"

"Yes."

At least Wendi wasn't hanging out with sixteen-year-olds. That was something to be grateful for.

She drew in a deep breath and pressed her hands into the sofa cushion. "The first mistake was not calling and saying you'd be late. The second was lying to Mrs. Johnson about Alan. The third was getting in a car with someone I haven't met or okayed. Did I forget anything?"

"No." Wendi stared at the ground. Despite her height and trendy shorts with matching shirt, she looked like a guilty toddler caught with her hand in the cookie jar.

"The rules exist for a reason. Not to make your life miserable."

"Right," Wendi muttered.

Melissa ignored her. "The rules are to keep you safe. How long has Alan been driving? Does he know how to handle a car? What if he'd decided that he wanted something you didn't want to give?"

Wendi whirled to face her. "This is none of your business. I can do what I want. You're not my mother."

"Just because I'm not a relative doesn't mean I don't care. I was worried about you, Wendi."

"Sure. That's why you're yelling at me." She turned to stand with her back to the room, but the quiver in her voice indicated she'd started to cry. "Go on and tell my dad. I don't care. You're leaving anyway."

Melissa slowly rose to her feet. At last they'd reached the heart of the matter. The whole evening had been staged to find out just how much anyone cared about her. No, not anyone... Melissa. "You're right, I am leaving. But that doesn't change the fact that I was worried. You're important to me, Wendi. Don't you know that by now?"

"Then why are you going away?"

"Because I was only hired for the summer."

"But I'll talk to Dad." She turned around and wiped the tears from her face. "Mrs. Dupuis is okay, but she doesn't do stuff like you do. She won't bake or go shopping with me. And she's old."

Melissa bit back a smile. According to Logan, the housekeeper was just over forty. "Wendi, I can't stay. I have my own life to live and it's not here."

"But..." The tears pooling in her eyes added sparkle to the emerald depths.

"You're a beautiful girl and you're going to be a beautiful woman. In a couple of years, you'll be so busy with school and your friends, you wouldn't have time for me anyway." She stepped next to her and wiped her face. "We'll stay in touch."

"P-promise?"

"Of course."

"I'm going to go to my room now." She sniffed.

"Not just yet. There's the small matter of your punishment."

"Oh." Wendi bit her lip. "I'm ready."

"When you get home from camp tomorrow, there'll be no phone calls all evening and Friday as well. When you get back from your mother's on Sunday, you'll stay home until school starts Tuesday morning."

"Is this being grounded?"

"Yup."

Wendi smiled. "I've never been grounded before. It's not so bad."

"It beats a close encounter with a paddle."

"Are you going to tell my dad?"

"No."

The girl visibly brightened. "Really? Great. I know he'd completely—"

"*You* are."

"What?"

Melissa patted her arm. "Tomorrow. At dinner. Better think about what you're going to say."

Saturday morning dawned warm and clear. The day promised to be hot and sunny, perfect weather for the last three-day weekend of summer.

After her shower, Melissa dressed quickly and headed for the kitchen. She'd told Wendi she'd prepare a special breakfast before the girl left to spend the night with her mother. While Fiona lavished gifts on her daughter, apparently she didn't have a clue as to what twelve-year-olds liked to eat.

She turned into the room and stopped short at the sight of Logan sitting at the table and reading the morning paper. "You're up early," she said, pouring herself a cup of coffee.

"I've got a ton of work to get through. I thought I'd get a head start. And I wanted to talk to you."

The white T-shirt clinging to his chest brought out the bronze in his tanned skin. Long legs stretched out and rested on the seat of the chair opposite him. One lock of dark hair fell carelessly across his forehead. The admonition to be strong rang especially hollow this morning, she thought as her stomach flip-flopped.

She pulled a bowl of strawberries out of the refrigerator and set it on the counter. "Talk away."

"You did good with Wendi."

The quiet praise filled her with satisfaction. "Thanks."

"You handled the situation well. I liked the punishment and that you made her tell me herself. I really think she learned a lesson."

Melissa grinned. "You left out the best part."

"And what's that?"

"You liked the fact that you weren't here to deal with it."

"I admit that was appealing, as well. You're a good woman, Melissa VanFleet."

His bare feet had made no noise, for suddenly he was standing behind her. His breath fanned the back of her neck. She could feel the puffs of air, the way her hair lifted slightly, then fell into place.

Her fingers slowed their task of shucking the strawberries, then stilled altogether. Would he touch her now? Would he take her and make the ache inside go away?

"You've changed us," he murmured. "It will never be the same. You have a gift for affecting those around you."

It wasn't a gift, she wanted to scream. It was caring. She'd changed them because she loved them . . . him. Everything, the nurturing, the cooking, the waiting, had all been done because he meant everything to her. To walk away with only memories of what might have been...no, what should have been, was going to be the hardest thing she'd ever done.

"Logan, I..." She turned until she could meet his eyes. The gold flecks blinded her to everything but her desire. She wanted him. Opening her mouth to tell him, she saw a flash of movement in the hall.

"Wendi" she said, sliding away.

"Morning, kitten." Logan gave his daughter a hug. "Ready for your busy day?"

"Yes. A shopping marathon." The girl sighed. "It's the only good part of going back to school." Stealing a strawberry from the bowl, she plopped down in a chair. "When do we eat?"

"After someone sets the table," Melissa said.

Logan made a timely retreat to his office.

"You couldn't possibly mean me," the twelve-year-old said.

"Oh, couldn't I?"

"Tyrant."

"Brat."

Wendi stuck out her tongue. Melissa did the same back.

"Hand me four eggs and then get to work."

After combining the ingredients for pancakes, Melissa beat the batter, then adjusted the temperature on the electric griddle.

"Can I cook some?" Wendi asked.

She glanced down at the girl's outfit. "You'd better not. What if you spill on your clothes?"

The white romper was all ruffles and tucks. The cuffed shorts exposed long, tanned legs and new leather sandals. Melissa knew there wasn't a speck of makeup on Wendi's face, but her lashes were disgustingly long and her cheeks naturally pink.

There is no justice, she thought as she turned over the first batch of pancakes. Logan's daughter would probably get through high school without a single blemish.

"I'll do the juice." Wendi opened the bag of oranges and began cutting them in half. Her long hair brushed against the counter.

Melissa pulled it away from the food. "Go on, get out," she ordered. "Go talk to your father. I'll call you when everything's done."

Wendi laughed, then scampered away.

"I can't eat another bite," Wendi said as she leaned back in the chair and patted her stomach. "Did you see how many pancakes I ate? Six."

"Seven." Melissa offered Logan the last piece of bacon. When he shook his head, she popped it into her mouth. "Not that anyone is counting."

"Good thing I'm going to be walking all day. Otherwise I'd blow up like a blimp."

Melissa eyed the girl's slender frame. "*Fat* chance."

Logan groaned and pretended to clip her chin. The three of them laughed together. These were the times, Melissa thought to herself. Moments caught between the bright light of reality, when she could pretend this was hers. That the smile on Logan's lips meant more than gratitude, that the love shining from Wendi's face would last forever. That they were a family with happiness and sorrow, harmony and discord.

What would she give to hold on to this second forever? Had she done enough good to deserve the chance?

Wendi slipped out of her seat and started clearing the table. While the girl's back was turned, Logan smiled at Melissa and winked.

Maybe, she thought. Just maybe all this could be hers. If only Logan would allow himself to trust her, to care about her. She didn't need him to love her, not right now. That would come in time. She only needed the chance to prove that she would never leave him, would never betray what was between them.

Wendi leaned down and wrapped her arms around Melissa's neck. "Thanks for the yummy breakfast."

"You're welcome, kitten."

Melissa reached up and patted the girl's cheek.

"How terribly cozy."

Melissa froze. She knew that voice. She had listened to it, yelled at it, pleaded with it. For years she had seen slow motion in the movies, but she'd never expected to experience it in real life. Her heart stilled and the air rushed from her lungs.

"Good morning, Fiona." Logan stood up and tossed his napkin onto the table. "We didn't hear you come in."

The tall, black-haired beauty set her purse on the counter and held her arms open to her daughter. "So I see. How are you, Wendi?"

"Good, Mom."

The preteen clung a little too tightly and Fiona stepped back. Her white jumpsuit was the long-pant version of her daughter's outfit. The sleeveless bodice exposed trim arms and a small but perky bosom. Narrow hips supported endless legs.

Melissa tried to stand up, but her muscles refused to cooperate. "Hi," she said weakly.

"Well." Fiona smiled. White teeth gleamed in an expression that was more challenging than friendly. Raven hair cascaded down her back like a river of onyx. Wide-set emerald eyes flickered from the top of Melissa's head down to her bare feet. "You must be Melissa. I've heard—" her gaze drifted to Logan, then back "—so much about you. Oh, all good of course. I've always...admired domestic women. All that energy over cooking and cleaning. I just can't find the time.''

Logan felt the anger begin to uncoil. Moving away from the table, he stepped between Melissa and his ex-wife. ''I believe Wendi's bag is by the door.''

''Is that a hint?'' Fiona chuckled. The low throaty sound had once enticed him, but now it reminded him of a cartoon villain.

He shrugged. ''You can take it as one.''

''Oh, Logan. Haven't you learned any manners yet? Melissa and I haven't had a chance to become properly acquainted. I'm sure she has a lot of questions for me and there are one or two things I'd like answered. Tell me, does she take care of *all* your needs?''

He heard Melissa's audible gasp. ''I know you and Wendi have a busy day planned. You should go ahead and get an early start.''

His ex-wife laughed, then reached out and plucked a strawberry from the bowl. ''Your favorite, Logan. How well you keep them trained.'' Before he could wrap his hands around her neck, she stepped back and picked up her purse. ''It was such a pleasure seeing you again. We should do this more often. Maybe dinner?''

''I'm busy,'' he growled.

She laughed again. ''Temper, temper. Come on, Wendi. We've got some shopping to do. So nice to have met you, Melissa. Be sure to keep in touch.''

In a few seconds, she was gone. Only the overpowering scent of her expensive perfume lingered behind like an unwanted guest.

''I'm sorry about that,'' he said as his hands formed tight fists. ''I guess I left the front door open when I went out to get the paper.''

Melissa stood up and tossed the remaining berries into the sink. ''I thought she had a key.''

"No. I changed the locks the day she moved out."

She didn't respond to his comment. Logan started to leave for his office, then paused, drawn back by the stiff set of her shoulders.

"Is something wrong?" he asked.

"Yes." She slammed the dishwasher shut and turned to face him. Rage and anguish flared out from her eyes. Two bright spots of color stained her cheeks. "How could you? After all I've done for you and your daughter? I know I'm not like Fiona. I'm not one of the beautiful women who waltz in and out of your bed. But I'm a person with real feelings. Don't you ever talk about me with her again."

The hurt was a tangible creature drawing the life from her body. The battle for control was won, but he wondered at what price. Somehow she'd been hurt. And *he'd* been the one to hurt her. "Melissa, I don't understand."

He stepped forward to comfort her, but she shrank from his touch. "Don't!"

"What did I do? Tell me."

"You made fun of me behind my back."

"I'd never do that."

She folded her arms over her chest as though holding the pain inside. "Terribly domestic? Keeping me well trained? I'm not some woman you just picked up. I deserve better treatment than this. At the very least, you owe me a little respect."

"Melissa, you've got to believe me. She's shooting in the dark. Fiona and I never even talk on the phone. She leaves a message with my secretary telling me when she'll pick up Wendi. She hates the idea of anyone being happy. It's her nature to make trouble. Trust me, I know."

Doubt and distrust mingled in Melissa's eyes. He couldn't bear the condemnation.

"I wouldn't hurt you for the world," he said.

"Please. I know my place. I'm just the hired help, Logan."

Her lower lip trembled, and he wanted to pull her close and offer comfort. "You know you're more than that."

"Oh? Exactly what am I to you?" She brushed away his attempt to speak. "Don't bother. I know the answer. If it hadn't been for Wendi, I would have left months ago."

He took a step toward her. She didn't move back, but she didn't move forward, either. "I'm glad you stayed."

"Why?"

The pain continued. He could feel it but didn't understand the source. All this suffering wasn't about a careless comment by his ex-wife; it went deeper than that. What was she to him? Not a lover, although he wanted her with a hunger that could never die. Not just an employee.

"Because you're a good friend."

She looked away. "Gee, thanks. I'm overwhelmed with emotion."

What the hell was wrong? What did she want him to say? Frantically he tried to recall every word since Fiona had left. Only one stood out. Beautiful.

For the first time, he looked at her. Not as someone who enjoyed her quirky humor and gentle smile, but as a stranger. She was...nothing like Fiona. Six months ago, he would have passed her on the street without a single glance. But since the accident, all that had changed.

"I didn't realize," he said quietly. "The accident was the best thing to ever happen to me."

Her gaze jumped back to him. "What?"

His hand cupped her face. "Do you remember that morning we went swimming?"

Her skin flushed. "Yes."

"I promised I wouldn't try anything again."

She tried to pull away, but he held her fast. "So?"

He leaned forward until their lips were inches apart. She smelled of magnolias and strawberries, warm days and hotter nights. "I want you. I've wanted you from the moment you half carried me into this house. Let me show you how beautiful and special I think you are. Release me from my word."

Chapter Twelve

"I don't want your pity," Melissa said.

"And I don't want yours."

"Why would I . . ." It didn't make sense. Logan had everything going for him.

"Because of what happened with Fiona." Vulnerability took the edge off the desire in his eyes. "Tell me you want this as much as I do. Say yes."

She could deny him nothing. Why should she? She loved him. "Yes."

In a single fluid motion, he picked her up in his arms. Her arm went around his neck as she clung tightly. Did he mean to carry her to the bedroom? It was *so* romantic. She sighed and was lost.

Bending over, he nudged the refrigerator open with his foot. "Champagne. Back shelf."

She leaned forward and grabbed the bottle. "Logan, it's nine in the morning."

He looked down at her, hunger etching harsh lines from his nose to his lips. Gold eyes darkened. "We'll only have a first time together once."

"Oh." His voice licked along her skin, feeding the need and want just below the surface. Clutching the bottle, she leaned her head against his shoulder.

This was a side of him she'd never seen before. The thin veneer of civilization had crumbled, leaving behind a passionate and possibly dangerous man.

They collected a single fluted glass, then he walked out of the kitchen. After making sure the front door was locked, he began the journey toward his bedroom. His arms made her feel secure, as though he would hold her forever. Did he know how much more than her body she was willing to share?

Melissa could feel his heart pounding against hers. The rapid beat promised the world . . . and made her a little nervous. The scent of soap and clean skin mingled with the unmistakable fragrance of desire. Anticipation made her mouth go dry, her palms damp. What if she couldn't please him? What if he realized that, compared with the other women in his life, she was just . . . ordinary?

The doubts and fears that had haunted her all her life crashed in on her. When Logan reached his room and let her slip slowly to the ground, she found herself unable to look up at him.

He took the champagne from her hand and quickly opened the bottle. The bubbly liquid foamed in the glass. He offered her a sip, but she shook her head and stepped back.

The room was still. She could hear their breathing and the foaming of the bubbles. Her eyes still lowered, she could only see his bare legs and feet, but she could *feel* his confusion.

He set the glass on the nightstand. "Melissa, what's wrong?"

"I don't think this is a good idea."

He touched her chin and forced her to look at him. "Why?"

Because I'm scared, she thought with a flash of temper. *Because I need you to promise you won't turn away again.* "I'm not sure why. It just isn't."

"I want you," he said quietly, his face harsh with passion. Each word was crisp and distinct, as if to make sure she couldn't misunderstand. "But I'll respect your decision."

She watched him battle for control, the tendons in his neck tightening with tension, and yet his fingers barely grazed her cheek. The combination of desire and restraint was her undoing. She could deny him nothing—she loved him. Wasn't this moment the culmination of her hopes? The heat from his body surrounded her in a protective cocoon, drawing her ever closer.

Bending her head, she kissed the hand that cupped her jaw. "I want you, too."

The drapes were still drawn, leaving the room dim and mysterious. Logan stepped to the window and pulled the cord. The heavy fabric was swept aside and the area was flooded with morning sun. The shadows were chased to the far corners; the bed was illuminated by soft light.

"I've thought about this for so long," he said. "I need to see everything." His husky voice vibrated with need.

Slowly she raised her eyes to his. The gold was blinding, as though desire had set fire to the tawny depths. The slightly parted lips, the rapid rise and fall of his broad chest all indicated that he wanted...her. Not just a convenient body but her.

"Oh, Logan." She flung her arms around his neck and pressed her face against him. His T-shirt was soft against her skin, contrasting with the hard muscles beneath. Warm, strong hands soothed her head and back.

At his urging, she moved slightly. Lean fingers slipped under her shirt and caressed her sensitive skin, then moved to the front and began unfastening the buttons. Haste made him clumsy.

"I know," he said, glancing down at her. "But I've been fantasizing about your breasts since...well, you know. And now, I can't wait a minute longer. Is that all right?"

"Yes." She shrugged, letting the shirt fall from her shoulders.

He swallowed and held himself perfectly still. "Take off your bra...please."

Now it was her turn to be unsteady. She fumbled with the catch, still fighting shyness. Never taking her eyes from his face, she removed the lacy garment and let it drift to the floor. The sound of his quick intake of breath brought a pleased smile to her lips. So this is the power of which they spoke. She was strong now.

He bent down and pulled her close. Their lips met, brushing once, twice, fleeting contact that gave her courage. His arms wrapped tightly around her, as if he'd never let her go. His head tilted slightly and the kiss deepened.

At the moment their mouths opened, rediscovering tastes and textures, his hands began to caress her back. Slow strokes became faster, broader, then slipped around to trace her sides and up higher...closer.

Her breasts swelled in anticipation, straining for his touch. They ached for the release. It was like slamming into a wall of pleasure, she thought as she clung to him. Her body trembled, her legs barely able to stay straight. Wave after wave of sensation crashed.

As his tongue met and danced with hers, he reached the full curves. He took them in his palms, his fingers finding the turgid peaks of her nipples. Fingertips flickered across the nubs, sending fire racing to all parts of her body. It heated, aroused, then moved to the core where it burned in uncomfortable impatience.

Her hands moved from his shoulders to the hem of his T-shirt. When he made no move to release her, she was forced to find her way across his chest from under the cotton. Fingers lost themselves in the rough texture of his hair and traced patterns around male nipples, as hard and sensitive as her own. When frustration became unbearable, she pulled her head back.

"Take this off now," she whispered.

He chuckled, pulled the shirt off and tossed it on top of her clothes. "Better?"

"Much," she said as she reached for him.

"Not so fast. I want to see everything."

In a flash, she recalled those thousand extra sit-ups she'd been promising herself. Inadequacy reared its ugly head. But when he reached for the snap on her shorts and she felt the unsteadiness in his hands, the fears fell away as easily as the rest of her clothes.

They stood naked before each other. She'd never realized a man could be beautiful. He was all long, hard lines of flowing muscle dipped in bronze. The deep tan was even, except for the light patch highlighting his arousal.

His arms hung loosely at his sides and he dared her with his smile. She reached out to touch the erect length of him. He allowed her one slow stroke, satin slipped over steel, then covered her hand with his. "Easy, my love, or we will have finished before we've begun."

"I would have thought a big, strong man like you would have more self-control, Logan."

He swept her up in his arms and set her on the unmade bed. "I do, but there's been a certain lady leading me on a merry chase for the last three months. It's enough to try any man's patience." He nibbled on her neck. "Or control."

She arched against his touch and gasped. "It's been three months?"

His eyes met hers. Honesty and desire flared in equal measures. "Longer. Much longer."

Opening her arms, she drew him to her. Tongues and fingers traced, discovered, tasted. Each breast was given thorough attention. The underside was nibbled, the hollow between licked. She could only lie back and give in to his intense attention.

"How does it feel?" he asked, then ran his tongue across her right nipple.

Her breath caught in her throat. "Wonderful."

"Tell me more."

"I feel like..."

He moved up to her neck and trailed moist kisses to her ear. "Say it."

It was difficult to concentrate with his hands dancing along her ribs. They slid lower, teasingly close to the apex of her thighs. "Wh-what?"

"Are you on fire?"

Flames raced through her body. "Oh, yes."

"Good." His lips touched hers. "I imagined us...together...many times, but I never knew it would be..."

The kiss was brief...too brief. "Would be?" she prompted, running her hands across his back.

"Perfect. That you'd be so perfect."

He plunged his tongue inside her mouth as his fingers found her moist heat. Instinctively she raised her hips slightly to meet his touch. She could feel him seeking her core. Their legs brushed. Then one finger found the magic. It moved slowly, filling her with pleasure.

He raised his head and smiled; like a conquering warrior, he savored his victory. Her hands clutched at his shoulders as she began the journey to release. Her breathing came faster, her hips shifted slightly.

"Not yet," he whispered, rolling to his side and pulling her next to him. "I want to play some more."

Play? If this was a game, she didn't think she'd survive the real thing.

After settling on his back, he urged her to slide on top of him. "I couldn't," she mumbled, avoiding his eyes.

"Of course you could." His gold-brown eyes flared. "I want to see as well as touch. I need you. Only you."

"Logan, I . . ."

He kissed her softly, gently, explaining his desire in the oldest of languages.

Her fingers lost themselves in the curly hair on his chest. Slowly she rose over him, shifting one leg until she rested upon the ridge of his desire. The hardness pressed exquisitely against her dampness. By rocking her hips gently, she kept them both somewhere between pleasure and madness. His hands lifted and massaged her breasts.

"You are obsessed," she teased, then groaned when he gently pinched the nipples.

"And you're beautiful. I've been dreaming about your breasts for ages."

She leaned down and nipped his side. "That's for telling stories."

"It's true." He grinned. "The first time you helped me into the house, I almost fell. When you leaned on me, I felt them pressing against me and I've been fascinated ever since."

His compliment brought a blush to her face. In the past, she would have turned away to hide the embarrassment, but now, naked with their most private parts ready to be joined, she was able to expose the secrets within her soul.

He pulled her down so their lips could touch. His tongue outlined her mouth with a continuous wet line, then dove inside to mate with her own. It was time.

He rolled them until she was on her back and he knelt above her. Reaching for the nightstand drawer, he smiled. "I assume you aren't protected."

"You're right."

"I'm glad."

"Why?"

"Male ego."

She quivered in anticipation. "You're forgiven."

Her legs spread to welcome him. When she felt the tip of his desire press against her, she raised up slightly. Inch by inch, he slipped inside . . . filling her.

There was no space left he didn't touch. Unused muscles stretched to accommodate him. Breath fanned her cheeks as he rained gentle kisses on her face and neck. Around her, she inhaled his scent from the pillow. The knowledge that her head rested in the same place his did each night was as much an intimacy as the joining of their bodies. Her hands moved down to cup and squeeze his buttocks. She felt an answering reflex deep inside.

When he moved, it wasn't with the fierceness she had expected. A man who had been without for so long could be forgiven a quick completion. But Logan withdrew and reentered with slow, lingering strokes. If he sought to drive her crazy, he was successful. If he yearned to make her whimper, he was a master.

The pulsating want grew. Their breathing increased, the tandem rush of air fueling the flames that licked along her skin. She felt him tense.

Raising himself up, he touched his fingers to the secret spot between her legs. A half-dozen strokes brought her to the edge of release.

"Open your eyes," he growled.

She looked at him. Passion hardened the planes of his face, drawing his mouth into a straight line and deepening the hollows in his cheeks. He drew closer to the peak. Muscles tightened in his neck and his head rolled back.

And then there was nothing left to do but fall into the vortex. Concentric circles of pleasure and heat rippled through her body. She rose with him to a summit, then slipped lower and lower until she was once again able to draw in air and refocus on the world.

He withdrew and moved beside her, then pulled her closer until they touched from shoulders to toes. His fingers pushed the wispy bangs away from her face, leaving her bare to his searing gaze.

"What are you looking for?" she asked quietly.

"The place where you keep your passion hidden. I want you to show me that door and promise you'll never lock me out." He pressed a quick kiss to her forehead, then a longer one to her lips.

Their legs entwined. The rough hair grated deliciously against her calves and thighs. She could lie with him forever.

Logan leaned over and picked up the glass of champagne. He held it steady while she sipped.

"Five minutes after ten in the morning isn't any less decadent than nine," she said as she reached up to wipe away a drop clinging to the corner of her mouth.

"Allow me." His tongue flicked away the moisture. "And when was the last time you were decadent? Let go. Reach for the stars."

The only thing she wanted to reach for was him . . . again. The hunger was satisfied, but only for the moment. She knew, with a certainty that couldn't be ignored, she would always want him. That Logan should be the one to claim her heart didn't seem fair. While she wanted to believe he loved her, the issue of trust had yet to be resolved. There would be no other man for her, but how did Logan feel?

"I'm not tall enough to reach the sky," she said finally, hoping the joke would break the serious tone.

"Then reach for me."

With a swiftness that startled as much as it excited, he claimed her again. This time the coupling was quick and hot. Like a firecracker in the summer sky, their lovemaking flared brightly and exploded.

He rested his weight on his elbows, his chest pressing lightly on hers. "You make me feel like I'm seventeen," he whispered into her ear.

"I could tell." She smiled. "I think I'm going to walk funny for a while."

He smirked. Lazy satisfaction stole into his eyes. She pushed at his shoulder and wriggled out from under him. "Don't you dare laugh."

He bent toward her thighs. "I could kiss it better."

"No." She swatted at him. "I'm going to take a bath in that oversize tub of yours and you're going to get some work done."

He stood up, six feet of sleek, contented male. "Can I watch?"

"Watch what?"

"You. In the bath."

"No!" She pulled the sheet around her body. "It's perverted."

"It's exciting and you're gorgeous. I'll wash the front."

She made her way to the bathroom door and glanced at him over her shoulder. "You're supposed to offer to wash the back."

He looked down at her bottom and smiled. "I like that part, too, but the front..." He shrugged. "What can I say? It's my favorite."

"Leave me alone." She shut the door with a bang.

But when he crept in and lathered the soap in his hands, then showed her how carefully he could minister to her sensitive flesh, she didn't do anything but lean back and let him have his way.

Logan finally sat down to work. They ate lunch together, then he resumed his study of the blueprints. Melissa made the beds, her fingers lingering as she inhaled the scent of their passion. Yes, she walked funny. Yes, it had been worth it. She'd walk funny for the rest of her life if it meant loving and being loved by Logan Phillips.

The afternoon was spent reading her textbooks, with occasional side trips into his office. The tender look on his face when he saw her standing in the doorway never failed to send a shiver of joy down her spine. By five, her aches had subsided and her wants were growing.

They only had tonight. Wendi would be home sometime tomorrow and they'd be forced to return to their frustrating, platonic existence. She walked toward the office door. Maybe they could sneak around at night. She grinned, imagining herself tiptoeing down the hall to join Logan in his big bed. There were worse fates.

"Hi," she said softly as she stepped into the room.

"I was wondering where you'd run off to." He tossed his pencil down onto the desk and leaned back in his chair. "How about a kiss?"

"In a minute." She was careful to stay back from the desk and keep her arms folded over her chest. "What would you like for dinner."

"In addition to you?"

The leer made her blush . . . and smile. "Yes."

"How about dining out?"

"At a restaurant? With you?" He wanted to take her out! It would be like a date! She sighed.

"Yes, with me. I was thinking, we've never been out alone."

She raised one hand and tucked her hair behind her ear. "Sounds fun."

"Tell me about your clothes."

"What?"

He chuckled. "I've made reservations at a nice restaurant near here, but I just realized you may not have brought anything dressy to the house."

She thought about her recent shopping trip with Wendi. "Would a silk jumpsuit be okay?"

"Perfect. The reservations are for seven. Is that enough time?"

It was almost two hours. Who took that long to get ready? "No problem," she said as she backed toward the door. "Oh, and Logan?"

"Yes?"

She dropped her hands to the bottom of the shirt and pulled open the sides, exposing her bare breasts. After their lovemaking she hadn't wanted to put on a bra. His eyes feasted on her chest. He sprang to his feet and made a dash for her.

"No," she squealed as she took off down the hall. "I was just giving you a little look. You can't possibly do it again. You're too old."

By the end of the living room, she could feel him behind her. He caught hold of her waist in the dining room. With a single lift, she was perched on the table with his crotch nestling between her legs.

"What was that about being old?" he asked before taking a nipple in his mouth.

The gentle sucking awakened nerves all the way to her toes. "That wasn't me," she gasped, leaning her head back and offering herself more fully. "I was momentarily possessed."

"Uh-huh." He raised his head and began fastening the buttons on her shirt.

"What are you doing?"

"Making you decent."

"Why?"

"Because I have about an hour more of work. If you let me finish, I'll be available all night and tomorrow."

She thought for a moment. "Okay. It's a deal."

He kissed her nose. "Good looks and brains. I've got quite a lady here."

Melissa borrowed earrings from Wendi. Her own jewelry assortment was sadly limited, and she told herself the girl wouldn't mind. With the last stroke of the hairbrush, she was done.

Stepping back from the full-length mirror, she tried to view herself objectively. But all she could see was the look on Logan's face when he had first entered her. The need and hunger and want had been scored onto her soul. If only...

No, she told herself. No if-onlys, no almosts. Tonight was magic. Cinderella and her prince. If the morning turned her back into just a housekeeper, then so be it. She would have her memories and her love for Logan. That would have to be enough.

She glanced at the reflection. Her eyes seemed to sparkle. It was either the new eye shadow or the sex. Maybe both. The jumpsuit was all Wendi had claimed, clinging in the right places, skimming forgivingly over the others. The high heels made her legs look long...sort of. She looked like what she was . . . a woman in love.

There was a knock on her door. "Are you ready?" Logan asked.

"Yes. You can come in."

Had he always been so handsome? The jet-black dinner jacket accentuated the width of his shoulders and chest. The white shirt set off his tanned face and the gleam in his eyes. Dark trousers and a perfectly executed bow tie completed the formal look.

She reached up and touched the knot. "Let me guess. You did that yourself."

"Of course. Doesn't everybody?"

She laughed. "No."

"You look lovely."

"And you look hot."

"Hot?" He raised an eyebrow. "I like that. Come on. We've got some hell to raise."

The restaurant was small and elegant—one of those Beverly Hills establishments with a sign so discreet you had to be a detective to find it . . . or a regular.

Melissa knew she was in trouble when the maître d' greeted Logan by name. Their table was tucked in a corner, isolated from the noisy groups in the center of the room. A band played softly. A few couples swayed on the eight-by-eight square of parquet flooring. Her palms were sweaty and she had the irresistible urge to make a break for the outside.

When Logan sat with his back to the room, her first thought was that he was ashamed of being seen with her. Get real, she told herself as she drew in a deep breath. Glancing around, she saw all the other couples were seated with the man facing in. Must be etiquette for the rich, she thought, and felt herself begin to relax.

"Would madam like something from the bar?" their tuxedo-clad waiter asked.

Double scotch on the rocks and just leave the bottle? "Uh, white wine, please."

Logan ordered the same.

"Are you nervous?" he asked when they were alone.

"No. I always get the urge to throw up in restaurants."

He laughed, then reached across the table and took her hand. "You'll be fine. Maybe we should start by dancing."

She swallowed. "I've never had lessons."

"Are you saying you can't dance?"

"No, but I didn't come out or go to a cotillion or anything so don't expect dips or twirls."

He threw back his head and laughed. The other diners looked at them and she saw the envy flash in the women's eyes.

"Come on." He rose and offered her his arm. "Nothing fancy. Just a little swaying and a chance to have you touching me."

"Lech."

He leaned down and pulled her close. "Admit it. You love me this way."

Dear God, she loved him any way. Hadn't he figured that out yet?

She survived the dance and the first course, which consisted of unidentifiable green leafy things topped with white chunks of . . . stuff.

"Tell me about when you were growing up," she said.

He leaned back in his chair. "What do you want to know?"

"Were you smart?"

"I did okay. When I was younger, I was more interested in sports than schooling."

She sipped her wine. "What did you play?"

"Football, basketball. Baseball was my favorite. I played first base on my Little League team." A faraway look stole into his eyes. "I remember one year, I think I was Wendi's age, I wanted a new mitt. There wasn't anything wrong with mine, but I begged and pleaded. Finally my dad told me if I improved my report card, I'd get a new glove." He grinned. "We had a big project in science. Even then I liked to build things. I made a volcano. You know, the kind that erupts steam and everything?"

She nodded.

Their food arrived, but he ignored his plate. "While the teacher was grading the projects, something went wrong. The top blew off mine. Foam sprayed all over the walls and ceiling and the teacher. No one was hurt, but..." He shrugged. "Needless to say, I didn't get a good grade in science, or the glove."

Melissa felt her heart melting. Even now, the disappointment echoed in his words. "But you had worked really hard," she said.

"My family wasn't as concerned with effort so much as results."

"You must have felt they'd let you down."

He shrugged. "Maybe. It was a long time ago. I gave up baseball when I decided I wanted to be an architect. I needed the hours to study."

"Is that why you barely looked at Wendi's report card from camp?"

"I don't really care what her grades are, as long as she's passing. The important thing to me is that she tries. If she works hard, she's a success in my eyes." He laughed. "Enough about me. Our very expensive dinners are getting cold."

Melissa cut into her steak. She'd thought Fiona had been the first person to hurt Logan and let him down, but now she saw the wound went much deeper. His ex-wife hadn't taught him not to trust, she'd simply reenforced something he'd always suspected was true.

The stars hung low in the sky. Logan led Melissa out of the living room and onto the patio.

"What are we...?"

"Shh." He covered her mouth with his fingers. "No talking. I want to finish what we started a few weeks ago."

"Out here?"

Her outrage made him smile. "You weren't protesting before," he reminded her. "And that was broad daylight. It's almost eleven. No one will see."

After dinner, they'd seen a recently released movie. The film had been a lighthearted romantic adventure romp. All Logan had cared about was that enough time had elapsed to allow them to have digested their dinner.

"I couldn't," she said.

"Nonsense."

A full moon turned the red silk of her jumpsuit to liquid fire. His fingers made quick work of the bodice and slipped the garment from her shoulders. Light brown eyes met his. Want and uncertainty in the smoky depths made him reassure her.

"I'll stop if you'd like." His hands rested on her waist.

"No. Don't stop."

Her skin was satin—warm, soft and alive as he traced every line. Her reaction—quickened breathing, dilated pupils—caused a matching response in him. When her clothes lay in a tangled puddle at her feet, he began to undo his tie. She leaned forward and assisted with the shirt. In a matter of moments, they stood naked.

He led her to the pool. The warm water lapped invitingly. It caressed as they stepped deeper and deeper into the waiting darkness. When they'd reached chest level on her, he boosted her to the side.

"This isn't where we were before," she said softly.

"I know, but it works for what I have in mind."

Lifting one of her feet out of the pool, he started at her ankles. Nipping, licking, sucking, he made his way up one leg and then the other. Then his tongue found her sacred place and lavished it with patient attention. Half-muted cries, the sudden tension in her legs, the way her torso arched kept him connected to her response. As the waves of pleasure washed over her, he felt his own need tighten and ache. Soon, he thought. This was for her.

When she had regained her composure, she looked down at him. Emotions chased across her face. One made him smile, another satisfied, the last...concerned. He tried to prevent her from speaking by pulling her into his arms and kissing her lips. It was no use. She touched the side of his mouth and drew back.

The moonlight outlined her face and exposed the faint tremble in her smile. "I love you, Logan."

The pain was as swift as it was unexpected. He should have been more prepared, he thought. He should have prevented this from happening. She was his responsibility, and he'd allowed her to do the one thing guaranteed to break her heart.

In a corner of his soul, apart from the darkness that marked his existence, was a place that warmed to her words. For the time it would take him to once more claim her, he would allow himself to believe in happy endings.

"Melissa," he murmured as he plunged inside of her. Later, when she lay next to him and he tasted the tears upon her cheeks, he wondered if she cried for him...or for herself.

Chapter Thirteen

"Melissa! Where *are* you? Jeez, this is important."

Melissa walked into the living room. "What's all the screaming about? Did you get in trouble on your first day back to school?"

Wendi dropped her books on the sofa and twirled in a circle. Her short ruffled skirt flared out, revealing matching panties below. Trust Logan's little girl to be perfectly dressed, she thought with a grin.

"It's Mark," Wendi said dramatically. "He asked me if I'd like a ride with him to the dance on Friday. Yes. Yes. Yes." She punctuated each word with a jump. "There's going to be a group of us, so it's not like a date or anything, but still. I'm going to the dance. I'm going to the dance. Okay." She stopped and grinned. "I need a new dress. A green one to match my eyes. And shoes. And a purse. And..."

"Slow down, young lady. No one has said you could go."

Wendi's jaw dropped. "Y-you're kidding?"

"Yes."

She pretended to punch Melissa in the arm. "You scared me. Don't do that with important stuff."

"Sorry. I'll remember for next time." She walked into her bedroom and picked up her purse, then returned to the foyer. "Do you have homework?"

"On the first day of school?" The preteen looked outraged.

"Yes or no?"

"Yes." She sighed heavily. "In algebra. Don't you just hate that?"

"What grade did you get in math last year?"

"An A. Why?"

"Do you promise to do your homework right after dinner, with no phone calls to interrupt?"

"Sure, but..."

Melissa opened the front door and grinned. "We have a dress to buy. What was it? Green to match your eyes?"

"Really?" Wendi danced out the door. "Melissa, you're the greatest. Wow. A new dress. We'd better get something, you know, conservative, so Dad won't have a cow this time." Linking her arm with Melissa's she skipped along the walkway. "You've sure been nice these last couple of days. Are you happy about something? Did you get some good news or..."

"These have been the longest three nights of my life," Logan said as he slipped into bed beside her.

Melissa rested her head on his shoulder and rubbed her hand across his chest. "You shouldn't even be here now. What if Wendi comes looking for one of us?"

"It's almost midnight. Besides, I checked on her and she's sound asleep. I've set my watch to beep in two hours, at which time I'll sneak back into my own bed. Unless of course you don't want me here."

He lifted the covers as if to leave. She grabbed his arm. "You've made your point."

He laughed. "I knew you'd see things my way. It's the charm. Gets 'em every time."

"Oh, does it? How very convenient for you."

"Isn't it though." He slid between her thighs. His gaze lingered on her face before dropping to study her bare body.

"Tell me about this charm," she said. "I certainly haven't seen it. Do you keep it in the closet and bring it out for company?"

"Very funny." Leaning down so their lips could touch, he drew his brows together. "I've missed you."

The tender embrace that followed the words allowed her to once again pretend their time together was real. As his hands and tongue took her to the edge of pleasure and back, while her body accepted and caressed his, the space beyond the four walls of her room ceased to exist. They were a man and a woman engaged in a ritual as old as time.

It was only when their breathing had returned to normal that she was forced to deal with the truth. Logan had never said he loved her.

There were countless explanations, but only one she believed. He wasn't ready to trust her. She'd given him everything she had and it wasn't enough. Now what? she wondered. Her time left was pitifully short.

They rested side by side, their hands locked together, their legs touching.

"Mrs. Dupuis will be back soon," she said quietly.

"I know." Logan turned on his side and raised himself up on one elbow. "It will be easier when you have a place of your own. I think Wendi's too young to deal with her father sleeping with the housekeeper." He grinned.

Melissa took a deep breath, not allowing herself to hope. "Are you saying you want to continue to see me?"

"Of course. What did you think? That I'm some sleaze taking advantage of the hired help?" Reaching down, he kissed her. "In all the years Mrs. Dupuis has worked here, I've never once been tempted to have my way with her."

It wasn't going to end. The tight band around her heart began to ease. If he wanted to continue the relationship, then he must have plans for them . . . for the future.

She wanted to tell him she loved him but held back. She'd said the words once and he'd been unable to respond in kind. Until he could admit that he cared for her, she'd remain silent. When Jeff had wanted to leave her, she'd begged him to stay. The pleading had only made his departure more difficult. That was a lesson she'd learned well. She would offer her heart once, and if it wasn't accepted, she would go on with a small amount of pride intact.

"How many more nights?" Logan asked as he traced a pattern on her ribs.

"Eleven."

"Isn't Wendi going out on Friday?"

"Yes. From about seven thirty until . . . eleven." Her voice became breathless as he continued the game with his tongue.

"Friday, huh? We'll have to do something memorable to keep us going until then."

And so they did.

"Daddy, can I talk to you?"

Logan looked up from his work. "Sure, Wendi. What's up?"

His daughter walked into the office and perched on the corner of his desk. Her chestnut hair was pulled back in a thick braid. Her eyes came from her mother, but the grin was his. She was a pretty girl who would grow into a stunning woman. What he wouldn't give to keep her grounded in the real world.

Melissa had been a great help this summer, he thought with a slight smile. Her down-to-earth approach had shown Wendi how the other half lived. It had been good for the girl.

"I'm confused." Wendi toyed with the hem of her skirt. "It's about Mom. I know she's busy and all, but she's not like a regular mother. I still love her and I know she loves me, but..."

Logan pulled Wendi onto his lap. Anger at his ex-wife was overpowered by compassion for his daughter. "Fiona loves you very much, kitten."

"Daddy, is it wrong to want her to do other things?"

"Like?"

She shrugged. "I wish she'd cook dinner for me and we'd just sit and talk about school and boys and stuff. We never do that. Usually, she leaves me with the maid and goes out with one of her boyfriends."

Her words painted a bleak, lonely picture. He'd suspected Fiona's activities but had never wanted to have them confirmed.

"Would you rather not go see her anymore?"

"No. I like going there. Daddy...are you..." She looked up at him, her green eyes filled with tears. "Are you and Mommy ever going to get back together again?"

He would do anything to make her happy...anything but lie. "No, sweetheart, we're not."

"Because you don't love each other anymore?"

"Yes."

She leaned her head against his shoulder. Her body might be reaching toward womanhood, but her heart was still that of a girl. Closing his eyes, he wondered what he could have done differently to have saved his baby this pain. If he hadn't married Fiona, she would never have had his daughter. If he'd stayed in the marriage...

He sighed. Staying hadn't been an option. Living with someone who enjoyed breaking her vows had been hell. Women couldn't be trusted. They didn't believe in commitment. When things got tough, they were gone.

Wendi shifted on his lap and rubbed her stomach.

"You feeling okay?" he asked.

"I think so. My tummy's kind of upset. Must be all the excitement about the dance."

"It couldn't possibly be the extra serving of ice cream at dinner, could it?"

"No." She laughed, then grew thoughtful. "Do you love Melissa, Daddy?"

"What?"

"I worry about that."

His back stiffened. "You worry about my loving Melissa?"

She giggled. "No, silly. I worry that I love her. Is it wrong? Because of Mom, I mean."

His pulse returned to normal. That had been a close one. For a moment he'd thought Wendi had found out that he and Melissa were...involved.

His daughter's question lingered. Did he love Melissa? Of course not. He'd sworn never to love a woman again. She was more caring than Fiona had ever been. He even trusted her with his child. But there was a part of him that doubted. There was a cold empty space in his soul that expected one day she too would leave.

"Wendi, it's not wrong for you to care about Melissa. She's been very good to you. Your friend, Sally—does she have any brothers or sisters?"

"One of each."

"Do her parents love only one of the children?"

"No. They argue about who's the favorite, but I think her mom and dad love them the same."

He patted his daughter's back. "The human heart is an amazing thing. The more people you love, the more love you have to give. It's perfectly all right to care about Melissa and your mother. You don't have to pick one over the other."

Melissa leaned against the hall wall and smiled. She'd finished ironing the girl's dress for the dance tomorrow night and wanted to show her how it came out. The conversation she stumbled upon made her insides swell with gratitude. How like Logan to reassure his daughter. He was a wonderful man.

As she turned to tiptoe away, Wendi spoke again.

"Daddy, are you going to marry Melissa?"

She froze in place. Her heart stopped to wait for the answer. She heard him clear his throat.

"No, kitten, I'm not. I guess I'm not the marrying kind."

Somehow Melissa made it back to Wendi's room. She hung the party dress in the front of the closet, then made sure the shoes were tucked away in their box.

It didn't hurt, she told herself firmly, ignoring the way her lungs burned with each breath. He hadn't said anything she didn't already know. Over and over he had told her how he felt about commitments. He didn't want a long-term relationship, certainly not marriage. The desire to see her again was just that—desire. An affair to keep him satisfied for a few weeks. And then it would be over.

All her hopes and dreams had been foolish plans made by a lonely heart. Even if Logan loved her, he wasn't willing to trust her. And without trust, there was nothing.

A shell formed around her heart. The painful case locked in all the love she had offered...the love he had rejected. If she didn't think about what could have been, she'd get through the next moment, and the next. Soon a day would have passed, and another, then she'd be free to leave. Only when this was a faded memory would she dare examine what had happened.

Maybe she should cry, she thought as she made her way back to her room. Although the tears formed hot pressure behind her eyes, they refused to flow. The wound was too deep. It would be like trying to fill a chasm with a single grain of sand.

The door to Logan's office was still partially closed. She heard his low voice, then the sound of Wendi's laughter. For the first time since she'd arrived in the house three months before, she was an outsider—the third wheel that didn't belong in the family's inner circle.

Sometime during the night, Melissa rose from her empty bed and stole down the hall to Logan's room. In the dim shadows, she could make out the shape of his body, the way the sheets tangled in his legs and left his chest bare to her gaze.

The love trapped inside her heart swelled against the confining shell and threatened to crush her soul. If only...if only she hadn't cared; if only Fiona hadn't hurt him; if only she'd never taken the job in the first place.

Why? she asked silently. Why won't you trust me?

But she knew the answer.

The sun was creeping over the eastern horizon before she finally found rest. Even then, her dreams were tormented by what should have been.

"What do you think?" Wendi spun in a slow circle, then stopped and smoothed her hands over her ruffled skirt.

The green dress was the exact shade of her eyes. It brought out the color in her face and the shine in her curly hair. The matching pumps made her slender legs appear long and curvy. She looked like a model for springtime.

"You're perfect," Melissa said, then smiled. "Mark is a very lucky boy."

"Thanks. I'm going to go show Dad." She grabbed her purse and took a long, running step. The high heels made her lose her balance and she reached for the wall. "I guess this growing up thing is harder than I thought."

"You'll catch on. Have a good time, Wendi. And..."

She held up her hand. "Don't say it, I know. Eleven o'clock, not a minute later. Jeez."

Her complaints about the curfew drifted back as she walked into the living room. Melissa stayed behind and began picking up the girl's room. The piles of clothing and makeup made the quarters look like a tornado had blown through.

After hanging and folding the garments, she made the bed and picked up the bathroom. Anything to keep from returning to the main part of the house and facing Logan. By pretending to sleep late this morning and helping Wendi get ready this evening, she had managed to avoid being alone with him. But the time was drawing closer. He expected them to make love tonight and she didn't have a clue as to what she would do.

Part of her wanted to give in to his embrace, to hold fast one more time. To gather memories to last through the winter of her life. Her pride, on the other hand, reminded her that she knew he had no intention of anything more than an affair. And she wasn't the type of woman who dallied in affairs.

Finally the room was clean. Taking a deep breath for courage, she walked into the kitchen.

"There you are," Logan said as he opened a bottle of wine. "I wondered where you were hiding. We only have three and a half hours. We'd best take advantage of our time."

When he smiled like that, all warm and full of desire, she wanted to pretend that she'd never overheard his conversation with Wendi . . . but that wasn't possible.

"Logan, I don't think we should . . ."

He looked up at her, his eyes filled with concern. "What's wrong?"

"Nothing. I just can't—" she stared at the floor and spoke softly "—make love with you."

"What?" He moved next to her, the bottle of wine abandoned on the counter.

"There's no point in continuing. The relationship would have ended anyway. Why prolong the inevitable?"

He put a hand under her chin and forced her to look at him. "What the hell are you talking about?"

She read anger and confusion and something that might have been hurt. Give in, her heart pleaded. Take what he has and be satisfied. It's better than being alone.

But if she let him take her to his bed, she might weaken enough to confess what she'd overheard. He'd pity her then, and the pity would be more than she could bear.

"Logan, how do you feel about me?" she asked. "Do you care for me at all?"

Logan dropped his hand from her face and stuffed it into the front pocket of his jeans. Although her voice was gentler and the words slightly different, the purpose was the same. "How much do you love me?" Fiona had taunted. "Enough to take me when I've been with another man? Enough to have me and wonder if you're better?"

His mind replayed the angry scenes until the past and present blurred together.

"If you expect me to beg and say I love you, you can forget it. No woman is worth that."

Melissa stepped back and jerked her head as though he'd slapped her. All the color drained from her face, leaving behind the pale cast of someone robbed of life.

"I never mattered to you at all." She wasn't asking a question. Her eyes grew dark, with pain this time, not passion. "I see that now."

He wanted to deny her words. Of course, she'd mattered. His anger began to fade. Maybe if he explained what her question had made him remember . . .

"I suppose, under the circumstances, I'd better leave."

He glanced at her. Her shoulders were stiff, her spine unyielding. Naturally, he thought. All women left in the end. Melissa was no different. Oh, she hadn't been unfaithful, he'd give her that, but maybe she simply hadn't had the chance.

He waited for the rage to burn again, but there was only emptiness. A hollow space Melissa had once filled.

Don't go. The thought came from nowhere. It grew in his mind and pressed against his tongue. Say you won't go.

No! He wouldn't beg . . . no matter what it cost.

Ask me, Melissa pleaded silently. *Ask me to stay and I will. Tell me there's a chance that we can make this work.*

He said nothing. His tawny eyes faded until the gold existed only in her memory. Hard pride scored his features.

She spoke first. "I'll call an agency in the morning and get someone in until Mrs. Dupuis returns."

"Leave your address on my desk and I'll mail your last check."

That was it? she thought. A discussion of money, as though she were some whore he'd picked up on Sunset Boulevard? Tears threatened. She knew she wouldn't cry, not today, not for several weeks to come, but she used the burning as an excuse to turn away.

"I need to start packing."

"Fine."

He walked past her and into his office. The door closed with a quiet click.

"Logan, please . . . I love you. Nothing can change that. I want to stay."

But he wasn't there to hear her plea.

Melissa heard the key in the front door about nine-thirty. She'd been trying to read in the living room, but the words had danced unintelligibly before her eyes. Last night she hadn't thought it was possible to hurt any more, but now she knew the disillusionment she'd felt yesterday was only the beginning.

Tossing the book onto the sofa, she walked into the foyer. The door opened and Wendi looked up at her. Mark stood on one side; an older man who looked like his father stood on the other.

"Hi," Wendi said. "I'm home early."

Dark half circles shaded the area under her eyes, and her mouth was pulled into a straight line.

"What's wrong?"

The preteen shrugged. "I didn't feel very good, so I asked Mark's dad to bring me home early." Wendi turned to Mark and gave him a wan smile. "I had a really good time. Sorry I made you miss all the fun."

"No problem." The tall, lanky blonde leaned forward and kissed her cheek. "See ya at school on Monday. Hope you feel better."

"Thanks." She stepped inside and closed the door. "I think I'll just go to bed."

Melissa touched her forehead. "You don't have a fever. What hurts?"

"My stomach. It feels heavy and achy, but I don't think I'm going to throw up."

"You didn't eat anything for dinner. It's probably hunger. Go put on your pajamas. I'll fix some toast and weak tea and bring it in."

"Thanks." Wendi stepped out of her shoes, then bent down and picked them up.

While Melissa boiled the water, she debated whether or not to tell Logan. He was the girl's father; he had a right to know she wasn't feeling well.

However, two hours before, the man had broken her heart. Walking in to face him in his study seemed to be a clear case of emotional suicide.

He solved the dilemma by finding her first.

"Did I hear Wendi come in?" he asked as he entered the kitchen.

"Yes." She was careful to only look at the toast she was lightly buttering. "Her stomach hurts. I think it's because she hasn't eaten all day."

"It was bothering her yesterday, as well. You don't think there's something wrong?"

The worry in his voice broke through her reserve and she risked glancing up. "I don't think she has a fever, but I'll take her temperature to be sure. Don't worry, Logan. If this doesn't clear up in the next day or so, I'll get her to the doctor first thing Monday."

"You won't be here Monday."

He sounded so bitter, she thought angrily. Her leaving was all *his* fault. Spinning to face him, she folded her arms across her chest. "I can't call the agency until then, so I will be here. Any other complaints?"

Was it her imagination or did his eyes seem empty? Was he waiting for her to say something? She shook her head. There was nothing for her *to* say. He was the one who couldn't make a commitment. It was his problem, he'd have to solve it himself. The kettle began to whistle and she turned off the stove.

Cheap talk, she thought as she poured the boiling water into the cup. She'd be in his arms in a second, if he'd just admit he loved her.

He reached out to touch her arm. She held her breath, a silent prayer forming in her head. Then his hand fell back to his side and he turned away.

"No more complaints."

He's a fool, she told herself. A certified card-carrying fool. But if calling him names was supposed to make her feel better, it didn't even come close.

She picked up the tray and carried it to Wendi's room. Pausing outside the door, she took a moment to collect herself. If the girl wasn't feeling well, the last thing she needed to know was that the people around her were having problems.

"Hi, kiddo. How are you doing?"

Wendi sat up in bed. "I don't know. I'm a little better."

Melissa set the tray on her lap. "Get started on that tea and toast. I want to take your temperature, then poke around at your tummy."

The thermometer showed no fever, and the area around the girl's appendix wasn't tender.

"Seems fine to me," Melissa said as she pulled the pajama top down. "Probably a bug or nerves. If you aren't back to your cheerful self by Monday, I'll take you to the doctor."

"Swell." Wendi nibbled on her toast. "Aren't you going to ask?"

"Of course." Melissa sat on the edge of the bed. "I want to hear all the details, from the moment he knocked on the door until you threw up on the dance floor."

"Ple-ease. I did *not* throw up. You'd have been very proud of me. I felt fine until about an hour ago. I went in the bathroom and splashed water on my face. When that didn't help, I asked Mark to bring me home."

Melissa leaned forward and kissed her temple. "Very smart. It's better to be safe than sorry. I am proud of you. Now tell me the good stuff. Did you dance?"

"Yes." Wendi leaned back and smiled. "It was wonderful. The gym was decorated with crepe paper and balloons. The band wasn't great, but they were loud."

"That is important."

"I'm ignoring you," Wendi said. "At first they just played fast songs, but then they played something slow." She sighed. "Mark took me in his arms and . . ."

As she recounted her story, Melissa wondered how she would tell Wendi goodbye. Logan wasn't the only one who had stolen a piece of her heart. His minx of a daughter had a good chunk of it in her possession, as well. Maybe she could talk to Logan about visiting Wendi from time to time.

Get a life, she told herself. Wendi would be thirteen next month. In a year or so, she wouldn't have time for someone who used to be her housekeeper.

This must be a little of what it's like to get a divorce, she thought as she watched Wendi speak. Leaving behind bits of her identity until she wondered if there was enough left to make up a whole person.

". . . and then, while we were waiting outside for his dad to come and pick us up . . . he kissed me. On the lips."

"How was it?"

"Not as gross as I thought. That after-shave was a little overpowering, but guys are like that."

"Oh, they are, are they?" Melissa smiled. "When did you get so worldly?"

"I read magazines. I know what goes on between a man and a woman."

The knife turned in her back. "I bet you do. Now, come on. Lie down and try to rest. I'll check on you during the night." She put the tray on the nightstand, then smoothed Wendi's bangs off her face. "If you start to feel worse, come get me."

"I will." Melissa leaned down and Wendi kissed her cheek. "Thanks, Melissa. Good night."

"Night, kitten."

* * *

She looked in on the girl at midnight and again at two. Both times Wendi was sleeping soundly. Her skin was cool, her color good.

Must have been nerves, she thought as she stumbled back to her bed. Despite the late hour, she still hadn't slept at all. The conversation she'd had with Logan kept playing over and over in her mind.

Was there something else she could have said? Words that would have made a difference, maybe changed his mind and the course of their relationship? Or had it been destined to failure from the beginning? Had her dreams been just that . . . dreams?

Once again the sun had already crept into her room before she was able to find some sort of rest.

By ten, Wendi still hadn't come out of her room. Melissa glanced at the clock, then the closed door. If she was sleeping, she didn't want to disturb her. But Wendi wasn't normally a late sleeper.

Knocking softly, she entered the room. The bed was unmade but empty.

"Wendi? Are you hungry? Do you want some breakfast?"

The girl wasn't there. Walking into the bathroom, she saw it was empty, as well. The usual piles of junk littered the marbled counter, but a familiar booklet caught her eye. It was the one from the clinic.

The open pamphlet rested under a jar of moisturizer, the pages exposed included the section on menstruation. The first line made her stop breathing.

This is the day you change from a girl to a woman.

"Oh, Wendi." Melissa picked up the booklet and saw the torn pink box. No wonder her stomach had been hurting, she'd been having cramps.

Why now? she thought as she raced from the room. Wendi hadn't been reconciled to growing up. She was still fighting the changes in her body. More than anything, she wanted to please her father, and her father wanted to keep her his little girl.

"Logan! Logan!" Melissa quickly checked the kitchen and living room.

He met her in the hall. "What's the problem?"

"Have you seen Wendi this morning?"

"No. Why?"

She showed him the brochure. "I think she got her period last night. She's not in her room and I can't find her in the house."

She turned to run outside, but he grabbed her arm and held her fast. "What are you going on about? Maybe she's with a friend."

"Wendi wouldn't leave without saying something. Besides, I've been in the kitchen all morning and would have seen a car pull up. You know your daughter wouldn't walk to someone's house. It's not the cool thing to do."

A careful search of the house and yard showed that Wendi was gone.

"I'm phoning the police," Logan said, walking toward the kitchen.

"Wait. Maybe you were right and she's with one of her friends. Why don't we try calling them first?"

His hair was untidy, the result of his fingers being dragged through it. Worry deepened the furrow between his brows and the lines from nose to mouth. "That's a good idea."

They found her address book. The loose-leaf binding allowed them to split the pages. "I'll call the first half of the alphabet," she said.

"Use this phone. I'll use the one in the kitchen." He walked out without looking back.

Please let her be okay, Melissa prayed as she dialed the first number.

"Hello. This is Melissa VanFleet. I'm calling for Logan Phillips. Is his daughter Wendi there?"

The phone calls took a half hour. She joined him in the kitchen.

"Anything?"

He shook his head. "Nobody's seen her or talked with her since yesterday."

Melissa drew in a deep breath. "Then I'm afraid she's run away."

"What? Why would she do that?"

"Because, you pigheaded fool, you've spent the last three months telling her not to grow up."

Chapter Fourteen

Bracing his arms on the counter, Logan hung his head. "I never saw it that way. But I was so damned afraid she'd turn out like Fiona."

"The important thing now is to find Wendi," Melissa said as she poured them each a cup of coffee. "I wonder if she's gone off to think things through. Maybe she'll come back on her own."

"Do you believe that?" His tawny eyes were haunted. "I'm calling the police." His hand reached for the phone, then paused as if he were waiting for her to tell him it wasn't necessary.

"I think that's a good idea." She picked up her purse and headed for the front door. "I'm going to drive down to the mall and see if she's there. I'll call every half hour to give you a report, or find out if she's back."

He nodded.

"Logan?"

"What?"

"It'll be all right."

Logan clenched his jaw. "You don't know that."

She paused as if she were going to say something more, then walked out of the house. He wanted to call her back and tell her he wasn't being a jerk on purpose, that he'd never been so worried in his life, but the police department answered the line.

"My daughter's missing," he told the officer.

He answered the questions as best he could. No, he didn't know what Wendi had been wearing or the approximate time of her disappearance. Yes, they'd called all her friends.

After finishing with the police, he made a quick call to Fiona.

"What?" she squawked when he'd told her what had happened. "No, she's not here. My God, Logan, what the hell is going on over there?"

"Nothing," he said, glaring at the phone. "Melissa thinks she got her period and is confused about growing up."

"Oh, that. If she's anything like me, she's just pissed at the inconvenience."

With any luck, his daughter was nothing like Fiona. "Let me know if she shows up there."

He heard the sounds of rustling sheets. She must still be in bed. At one time, the thought of Fiona warm and naked would have been intriguing, but not anymore. All he could think of was how he'd blown the two most important relationships in his life. Wendi had run away and Melissa wasn't that far behind. How the hell had everything gotten so out of hand?

"Logan? Are you listening to me?" Fiona sounded irritated.

He dragged himself back to the conversation. "What were you saying?"

"I want to come over and wait with you. The maid can call the house if she comes here, but I don't think she will." Fiona drew in a breath. "I'm not the maternal type. Wendi thinks of me as a playmate rather than a parent." Regret stained her tone. Before Logan could wonder if he'd misjudged her, she gave a little laugh. "Besides, if we make a television appeal, I think it should be done from the house. The natural light is so good there."

He hung up without saying a word.

Melissa checked the boutiques, then the food court at the mall. No Wendi. She went from store to store, showing her picture to clerks, but no one had seen the pretty young woman.

At eleven-thirty, she stopped to call the house. She should have checked in twenty minutes ago, but she had hoped to phone with good news.

Logan answered on the first ring. "Melissa?"

"Yes?"

"She called. Wendi's down at the park I used to take her to. I don't know how she got there, but I'm on my way to pick her up."

"Oh, Logan. That's wonderful. I'll be right there."

She stood in the phone booth for several minutes, trying to stop the tears. Thank you, she prayed. Thank you.

She found her car and quickly drove to the house. An unfamiliar vehicle was parked in front. Must belong to one of Logan's friends, she thought as she let herself in the front door.

"Wendi?" she called.

"In here."

Melissa stepped into the living room and stopped.

Standing in the center, next to the coffee table, were Logan, Wendi and Fiona. Their arms were wrapped tightly around one another. She gasped.

Wendi turned at the sound and smiled sheepishly. "I'm sorry I took off without telling you. Dad said you figured out what happened. Pretty dumb, huh?"

Her throat was closing as though a giant fist were crushing her entire body. "Of course not," she forced out. "I—I'm glad you're safe."

"You'll probably want to ground me for a year."

Melissa forced herself to laugh. "Something like that."

The girl stood between her parents. It was so easy to pick out the features. Her eyes and skin from her mother, her hair and smile from Logan. Three special people... the "perfect" family at home. Someone should get out the camera and take a picture.

"I'm so grateful you took the time to look for my little girl," Fiona purred as she patted Wendi's arm. "Logan and I were so concerned."

"I—I'll be in my room. Excuse me."

Melissa fled from them all, trying to ignore the knowing look in Fiona's emerald eyes. Once alone, she locked the door behind her. Fiery ribbons of pain coursed through her body. The last of her hopes turned to ashes in the onslaught like a dried leaf in a forest fire.

Fiona had returned. If not at this moment, then soon. She wanted Logan and Wendi, and Fiona was the kind of woman who always got what she went after. How could that strong, lonely, virile man resist the opportunity to regain his first love?

The thought of them together was so awful her stomach clenched in protest. She went into the bathroom and pressed a cold washcloth on her cheeks and neck.

The face staring back in the mirror belonged to a stranger. Wan skin, frightened eyes, trembling lips. She had to get out of here... now.

* * *

"Ready to talk, kitten?" Logan asked as he closed the door behind Fiona.

"Do I have to?" She bent down and made an elaborate show of retying her shoelaces.

"Yes." He waited until she'd completed the task, then tugged her to the sofa and sat next to her. "I want you to know that it was wrong of me to make you feel bad about growing up. That's what kids are supposed to do. I guess I want to keep you young enough to need me."

"Oh, Dad. I'll always need you." She snuggled closer. "It was scary when I woke up this morning. At first I was afraid I was really sick, but then I remembered what Melissa had told me. I thought you might be mad or something. I don't know why I went to the park. It's been a long time since we were there."

"Maybe too long." He rested his chin on her head. "You and I haven't been doing a lot of family stuff together lately."

"We could go shopping."

"Ah, how about dinner and a movie?"

"Okay."

Wendi tilted her head until she could look up at him. "Daddy, can you make Melissa stay?"

As always, the answer he gave was as honest as he could make it. "I don't think so. She...people have different needs in their lives."

"But we need her and she needs us."

"When did you get to be so smart?"

"Yesterday." She grinned. "So why can't she stay?"

"Needing isn't enough."

"Why?"

He ruffled her bangs. "It just isn't. There has to be more."

"Do you love Melissa, Daddy?"

"The truth?"

She nodded.

Did he love her? He needed her and he wanted her. Was that love? Had he loved Fiona? He'd lusted after her and had been blinded by the light of her beauty. Was that love? "I don't know."

"Does she love you?"

"Not anymore." He knew it had to be the truth. He'd seen the look on her face when she'd walked in on the family reunion. Then why did he hope he'd just told Wendi the first lie?

"I don't want you to go." Wendi folded her arms over her chest and turned from the bed.

"I'm sorry. I don't want to leave you, either, but I can't stay." Melissa folded her bathing suit. Her hands lingered over the shiny Lycra as she recalled the way Logan had peeled the straps from her shoulders.

"You promised to take me to the doctor if I didn't feel better. Right now my stomach hurts awful."

"It's called cramps."

"It's not." Wendi spun to face her. Tears ran down her cheeks. "It hurts because you're leaving me. Don't go."

Each sob battered at Melissa's self-imposed control until all that was left was a thin layer of pride.

"Hush." She held the young girl next to her, feeling the fragile bones of youth. Who would tell Wendi about boys and kissing and how to know when she fell in love? Would Fiona take the time? Would Mrs. Dupuis? Would there be a string of beautiful women who played with Wendi's emotions in an attempt to curry favor with her father?

"I'm not leaving you," she said finally. "I promise I'll call every week and we can do something together."

"It won't be the same." Wendi sniffed.

"I know. But it's the best I can offer right now."

Wendi stepped back. "I'll be in my room. Tell me good-bye before you leave."

"I will."

She pulled open the bedroom door and ran past her father. Melissa bit back a groan. Was the entire Phillips family lined up to speak with her? Would Fiona be next?

"I heard," he said, jerking his head in the direction of Wendi's room.

"And?"

"How can you do that to a little girl? I thought you said you'd stay until I found a replacement." His eyes accused her.

"I did, but things have changed."

"What things?"

Did he have to stand so damn close? The scent of his cologne brought back memories best left forgotten.

"Do I have to spell it out?" She began folding a sweat-shirt.

"Yes." He tore the garment from her hands and tossed it onto the floor. "Dammit, Melissa, doesn't Wendi mean anything to you? She needs you."

"*She* needs me? No, that's not what this is about." She tried to step away, but he grabbed her hands and held her in place. "What about what I need? And what about you, Logan? Are you willing to admit *you* need me?"

She was close enough to see the faint scars crisscrossing his left cheek and the dark hair curling through the vee in his short-sleeved shirt. Close enough to feel the desire spreading through her body. Before she could weaken and give in, she wrenched her hands free and moved back.

"We had something very special," she said. "I gave you everything I had, including my heart. I cared for you, encouraged you, loved your daughter and loved you. But it wasn't enough."

He made a move to speak. She shook her head. "I'm not finished. Even now, when I'm ready to walk out of your life, you keep talking about Wendi. 'Wendi needs you, Melissa. Stay for my little girl.'" She mocked his deep voice. "You'd rather live alone for the rest of your life than admit you care about me."

"I care."

"Ah, Logan." She leaned forward and touched his chest with her palm. "I feel it beating and I know it exists, but you've hidden it under so much pain, I don't think it can be found again. You say you care. All right. I'll buy that."

She picked up the sweatshirt and folded it, then placed it in the suitcase. After glancing around the room, she pushed down the top and flipped the latch.

"There was a time when caring would have been enough. I would have accepted less than the best. But you—" she smiled sadly "—you've taught me that I'm worth more. I deserve the best. Unfortunately, that means you."

"Then stay."

"No. I need more."

"Melissa . . ." He moved closer.

"I need you to love me. I need you to trust." She held up her hands. "Do you trust me?"

His eyes met hers, then looked away. It was all the answer she needed. "I believe I've packed everything. If you find something I've forgotten—" she paused "—throw it in the trash."

For several minutes, Logan continued to stand in the center of the room. He listened to Melissa say her farewells to his daughter, then the front door closed and he heard the sound of her car engine. Finally there was silence.

He sat on the bed and rested his forearms on his knees. The house seemed so empty, but not as vacant as the dark place inside himself. She'd left. He'd known she was going to, but the leaving was still a shock. What about her presumed love and commitment? In the end, they had all been meaningless words.

Glancing up, he saw a small glass bottle resting on the dresser. Liquid filled the bottom quarter inch. Her perfume—she'd accidentally left it behind.

He rose and picked up the container, then clutched it in his hand. Wendi stood in the hall. She looked at him.

"What will you do now, Daddy?"

He stepped out of the room and shut the door behind him. "Not a damn thing."

It took Melissa less than a day to get everything settled in her apartment. A top-to-bottom cleaning took another two, and still the rest of her life loomed ahead.

College would be starting soon; that would help to fill the time. And she had her challenge exams next month. She'd be busy. Surely the memories of Logan would begin to fade, if not this year, then soon after.

At the end of the first week, Wendi called. Her sweet voice, laced with tears, made Melissa feel like the villain in a slasher movie.

"But why won't you come back?" the girl asked.

"Wendi, please. Can't we talk about you? How was school today? Have you talked to Mark since the dance?"

"Yes. He called last night. A bunch of us are going to the movies on Friday. Mrs. Dupuis came back earlier, so that was kinda nice. My mom's been over here a lot."

Melissa closed her eyes at the mention of Fiona. It was already starting. By the end of the month, the raven-haired beauty would have moved back into the house. She'd left just in time.

"I'm glad you're doing well," she said, gripping the receiver.

"Dad's not. He's grouchy all the time and isn't eating. Mrs. Dupuis has been fixing all his favorites, but he says he's not hungry."

Oh, Logan, what are you doing? she asked silently. Was this his way of making her feel guilty for leaving? It wouldn't work. She'd done the only thing she could. The next move was his. He had to admit he loved her...and trusted her. She had a feeling it was going to be a long, cold winter.

"I have to go, Wendi. I'll call you in a couple of days."

"Okay. Should I tell my dad you said hi?"

"If you'd like. Goodbye."

Logan walked up to the front of his house and went to insert the key. The door was partially open. Stepping inside, he set his briefcase in the corner and slipped out of his suit jacket.

"I'm home, Wendi," he called.

"I'm afraid she's out with Mrs. Dupuis," Fiona said as she stood in the entrance to the kitchen. "You'll have to make do with me." She smiled and winked.

Logan froze in the act of undoing his tie. "Why the hell are *you* here?"

"Logan." Her red-stained lips pursed in an exaggerated pout. "That's no way to talk to your wife."

"Ex-wife. And every day I thank God for that fact."

She flipped her dark hair over her shoulders. A bright pink T-shirt clung to her chest, clearly outlining her lack of an undergarment. Tiny shorts, more suited to Wendi than a thirty-something TV star outlined her trim hips. Bare feet, complete with red toenails, finished the star-at-home photo opportunity.

"You're such a kidder," she said as she sashayed back into the kitchen. "If I didn't know you'd had a terrible day, I'd be very hurt."

He walked over to the liquor cabinet in the living room and poured a tumbler half full of Scotch. "You still haven't answered my question. Why are you here?"

"To see you, of course. Come in and have some dinner."

"With you? I'd rather starve."

She stuck her head around the entrance. "You're worse than Wendi. Come on."

"Did you cook?" He moved forward and glanced at the cartons of Chinese takeout. "Oh, you should have said you'd gone to all the trouble of preparing your speciality."

Fiona walked over and touched his arm. "Logan, I know you're pleased to see me."

"Hardly."

"You still want me," she whispered as she reached up to kiss his neck.

The sensation of her hot breath against his skin made his stomach clench. He stepped away. "Stop it, Fiona. If you're between men, call an escort service."

Her emerald eyes flashed fire. "Admit it. I'm quite a temptation."

He stared down at her. There was nothing except a longing for another woman and a vague sense of disgust with himself. How could he have ever thought he loved Fiona?

"You're making a fool of yourself," he said quietly. "I'm still not interested."

She looked him in the face. "My God, what's wrong with you? How dare you turn me away! Damn you to hell, Logan Phillips. It's that Melissa person, isn't it?"

"If you're that hard up for a guy, I understand the personal columns can be very successful." He sipped his drink.

"Bastard." She grabbed her purse and shoes in one hand. "Don't think you can come crawling back to me ever again."

"I never crawled to you in the first place, Fiona. You're the one with the dirty belly."

She glanced around the room. "If things are so wonderful, why isn't she here?"

Her question hung in the air, but he didn't have an answer. Long after Fiona had left, he stood staring out the window. The night grew dark and still the truth eluded him.

The first day of the third week dawned clear and warm. Logan drove north on the freeway, then east across the valley. When he reached the church, he parked his car and walked around to the back.

Only the sounds of the children playing in a nearby schoolyard indicated that summer had slipped into fall. In the garden, the flowers still bloomed, although the vegetable garden had been harvested. A few pale pumpkins sat like fat kings awaiting their festival.

The olive tree stood in the center and beneath it was the stone bench. He sat down in the spot where he'd rested before and remembered the pleasure of Melissa's company. It was here he had confessed his darkest secret. It was here her tears had washed away the last traces of his anger and bitterness. It was here she'd begun to make a place for herself in his heart.

For three weeks, he'd struggled to forget her. Every room in the house contained fragments of her essence. There were still frozen meals in the freezer. A couple of his shirts had been ironed by her hands. Mrs. Dupuis continued Melissa's practice of leaving fresh flowers in the rooms.

Sometimes, when he was tired, he'd turn suddenly and expect to see her standing beside him. He missed her most when she wasn't there waiting for him after a long day. The attempts to forget were wearing him down physically, and he was no closer to eliminating her from his mind than he had been the day she'd left. This visit to the church garden was a last-ditch effort to find some peace.

The silence was broken by conversations from the past. "I was meant for more than just one man," Fiona's voice taunted.

"I gave you everything . . . including my heart," Melissa echoed.

Staring at the ground, he pictured his ex-wife. From a purely aesthetic standpoint, she was perfect. But her attractiveness formed a thin layer over a core of selfish ugliness. Melissa's beauty ran true and clear all the way to her soul. He'd understood that when he'd first met her, long before the bandages had been removed from his eyes.

He picked up an olive from the bench. The green fruit was smooth as he rolled it in his hand. In Greece, the tree was considered a gift from the gods. No part was wasted. It provided oil and food. When it was too old to bear a life-giving crop, the branches and trunk offered warmth and shelter. It asked for nothing in return, except water and sunshine.

When the original church had burned, many on the building committee had wanted to tear the tree down. It was old, they said. Ugly. It dropped olives, attracted too many birds. At the time, Logan hadn't cared about the argument. He'd been more interested in the structure than the surroundings. But the monsignor had insisted it be spared. The giving of life, he had said, was more important than physical appearance.

Logan stood up and turned to stare at the gnarled trunk and thick, twisted branches. He'd never really looked at the tree before today. But then there were many things he'd been blind to.

It was all Melissa, he thought with dawning understanding. She had taught him to see past the surface flaws to the perfection hidden below—that beauty indeed came from within. She'd made him search for the truth in the world and inside himself.

There were two kinds of people: those who gave and received in a complex dance of caring and trust, and those who took without ever giving back. He'd always thought of himself as one of the former, but now—as he reviewed the details of the past summer—he realized the enormity of his deception. He'd instinctively recognized the giving nature of Melissa's heart, and he'd taken all that she'd offered without a thought for her feelings. He'd allowed her to hope for a future he had no intention of sharing . . . he'd used her. In his effort to turn away from the horror of his ex-wife, he'd allowed himself to become as greedy and grasping as the one person he despised.

He'd been such a fool. Melissa hadn't left . . . he'd pushed her away. He'd drawn everything from her, then cast her aside, empty and broken.

Oh, he'd cared, but caring wasn't enough. It hadn't filled the hole left behind when she'd given him her heart. It would take trust and love to do that. He wasn't sure he had enough of either.

She deserved so much. If riches were measured in gifts of the heart, then she was Midas and he was a pauper.

He removed the small cut-glass bottle from his jeans pocket. For three weeks, he'd kept it on his dresser as a symbol of all he'd lost. After pulling out the stopper, he inhaled her scent. Sweet, spicy magnolia drifted up to greet him. The fragrance gave him hope, the pain in his gut from missing her, determination.

He loved her. He loved the changes she'd made in Wendi and in himself. She provided the purpose and beauty in his life. He only hoped it wasn't too late to convince her to come back.

Melissa pulled the books out of the front seat of her car. Whoever wrote these lengthy psychology texts should seriously consider how much they weighed, she thought as she balanced them on her hip and tried to find the right key.

Her notepad slipped out of the pile and fell. She turned to reach for it and bumped into a warm male body.

"Logan?" Her books and purse tumbled to the ground.

"Melissa." He took her hands in his.

Her gaze hungrily searched his face, noting the deep lines around his eyes and lips and the weary shadows marring his perfect features.

"Is e-everything all right?" she asked. Her heart began to flutter foolishly against her ribs. Was this visit about Wendi or . . . did she dare allow herself to hope?

"You'll have to tell me." His husky voice rubbed against her skin. The flecks of gold glowed with an unearthly light, almost blinding her with brilliance. "You have no reason to believe me, but I love you with my heart and soul. I know I've been a fool to throw away the most precious part of my life. I can only hope you have enough love left to give me another chance."

She swallowed against the lump in her throat. "Do you trust me?"

His eyes met and held hers. One by one, the shutters fell away and she could see into his heart. The need there made her catch her breath.

"With my soul," he said. He leaned forward and kissed her lips. The contact was painfully familiar. "Melissa VanFleet, will you marry me?"

She wrapped her arms around his neck and grinned. "Convince me."

He looked around the driveway. "Right here, in front of God and the neighbors?"

"You have a point there. Yes, I'll marry you, Logan Phillips. Now carry me inside and show me I made the right decision."

Epilogue

Two years later

"I'm still in shock," Logan said as he sat on the edge of his wife's hospital bed.

Melissa adjusted the blanket-wrapped baby in her arms. "The doctor did warn us."

"I know, but I thought he was kidding."

She giggled. "You'd better get a good night's rest because it'll be the last one for a long, long time."

"What I need is a stiff drink." Logan touched his index finger to the newborn baby's cheek.

"Jeez, Dad, twins isn't so bad." Wendi carried the other infant over to the bed. "I think it's great."

"And you got a son," Melissa reminded him.

"I would have been as happy with all girls."

"Just think." Wendi grinned down at her half sister. "Two of everything. Two cribs, two playpens."

Melissa took up the list. "Two birthdays, two teethings."

"Two college educations." Logan shook his head. "Good thing I received a raise when I made senior partner."

"Speaking of college, I have an announcement." Wendi walked closer to the window. "The twins will barely be three years old when it's time for me to go to college."

Melissa shared a tender look with her husband. Wendi's announcements were legendary. What would this one be?

"And?" she prompted.

"I'm not going away. I want to go to the local school and watch my new brother and sister grow up."

"That'll last until the first diaper change," Logan said.

"Oh, Dad. I'm very mature for my age."

Melissa started to laugh, then groaned as she shifted on the bed.

Logan took her free hand. "Can I get you anything."

"No. I need some rest, too. Between graduating with my master's last week and the twelve hours of labor today, I feel like I went ten rounds with the heavyweight champion of the world."

"I'm proud of you for both accomplishments." He kissed her gently on the mouth. "You're always gorgeous to me."

"I know. That's one of the reasons I love you."

"And what are some of the others?"

She glanced over at Wendi, then whispered. "I'll tell you when we're alone."

"I'll count the hours." His eyes held hers, the love there flickering in the tawny depths.

Even now, it was difficult to believe she'd won her handsome prince. But the proof of his love lay in the two sleeping bundles only a few precious hours old. It was true what they said, she thought contentedly. Beauty was in the eye of the beholder.

* * * * *

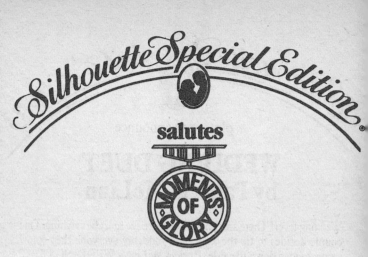

Silhouette Special Edition

salutes

MOMENTS OF GLORY

from Lindsay McKenna

In a country torn with conflict, in a time of bitter passions, these brave men and women wage a war against all odds... and a timeless battle for honor, for fleeting moments of glory, for the promise of enduring love.

February: RIDE THE TIGER (#721) Survivor Dany Villard is wise to the love-'em-and-leave-'em ways of war, but wounded hero Gib Ramsey swears she's captured his heart... forever.

March: ONE MAN'S WAR (#727) The war raging inside brash and bold Captain Pete Mallory threatens to destroy him, until Tess Ramsey's tender love guides him toward peace.

April: OFF LIMITS (#733) Soft-spoken Marine Jim McKenzie saved Alexandra Vance's life in Vietnam; now he needs her love to save his honor....

SEMG-1